Tess wasn't
Holt Chan
company so that he did

No doubt he would have issued the same invitation to any woman he struck up a conversation with at the bar.

But the fact was that he'd sat down beside *her*. He'd struck up a conversation with *her*. And Tess was enough of a romantic—or maybe enough of a fool—to still harbor a bit of a crush on the boy he'd been in high school. The one who'd stopped to help a flustered freshman when his friends had stood back and snickered.

Even then she'd known who he was, of course. No one could grow up in Whispering Canyon and not know who the Chandlers were. They weren't just popular because they had the biggest cattle ranch in Wyoming, but also because they were every bit as handsome and charming as they were rich.

Though she admired him from afar, Tess knew Holt would never be interested in her. Not only because he was four years older, but because he was a Chandler and she was a Leonard and that story had already been written—and it did not have a happy ending.

As if she needed any more proof that her crush was entirely one-sided, throughout the rest of her freshman year, Holt had never spoken to her again. While she'd spent the next ten months crushing on him from afar, he'd been living his life. Cowboying at his family's ranch, prepping for college, hanging with his friends and dating all the prettiest girls in school.

But he was here with her now...

Dear Reader,

Welcome to Whispering Canyon, Wyoming! I'm thrilled to be starting a new series for Harlequin Special Edition, excited to show you around this new Western town and eager to introduce you to a new cast of characters—including some very hunky cowboys!

According to local legend, Whispering Canyon got its name from the late-night murmurings of ghostly guardians—believed to be the restless souls of those killed during a nineteenth-century stagecoach robbery—who inhabit the valley between twin mountain peaks known as the Two Sisters.

But that's ancient history...until past and present collide when wealthy patriarch Raylan Chandler is wounded in a hunting accident that might not have been an accident at all.

Physiotherapist Tess Barrett has mixed feelings when she's assigned to help the cattle rancher rehabilitate his injuries. Aside from the complicated history between their families, she also has to contend with her secret crush on her patient's grandson—and the consequences of the one night they spent together.

When Holt Chandler learns of Tess's pregnancy, he immediately steps up. But Tess would rather be a single mom than settle for a marriage of convenience, and Holt soon realizes that his growing feelings for her aren't the least bit convenient. Is it possible the rancher has finally met a woman who can lasso his heart?

I hope you enjoy this introduction to Whispering Canyon and Tess and Holt's story!

xo *Brenda*

THE RANCHER'S TEMPTATION

BRENDA HARLEN

If you purchased this book without a cover you should be aware that this book is stolen property. It was reported as "unsold and destroyed" to the publisher, and neither the author nor the publisher has received any payment for this "stripped book."

Recycling programs for this product may not exist in your area.

ISBN-13: 978-1-335-40236-3

The Rancher's Temptation

Copyright © 2025 by Brenda Harlen

All rights reserved. No part of this book may be used or reproduced in any manner whatsoever without written permission.

Without limiting the author's and publisher's exclusive rights, any unauthorized use of this publication to train generative artificial intelligence (AI) technologies is expressly prohibited.

This is a work of fiction. Names, characters, places and incidents are either the product of the author's imagination or are used fictitiously. Any resemblance to actual persons, living or dead, businesses, companies, events or locales is entirely coincidental.

For questions and comments about the quality of this book, please contact us at CustomerService@Harlequin.com.

TM and ® are trademarks of Harlequin Enterprises ULC.

Harlequin Enterprises ULC
22 Adelaide St. West, 41st Floor
Toronto, Ontario M5H 4E3, Canada
www.Harlequin.com

Printed in Lithuania

Brenda Harlen is a former attorney who once had the privilege of appearing before the Supreme Court of Canada. The practice of law taught her a lot about the world and reinforced her determination to become a writer—because in fiction, she could promise a happy ending! Now she is an award-winning, RITA® Award–nominated, nationally bestselling author of more than sixty titles for Harlequin. You can keep up-to-date with Brenda on Facebook and X, or through her website, brendaharlen.com.

Books by Brenda Harlen

Montana Mavericks: The Trail to Tenacity

The Maverick's Resolution

Harlequin Special Edition

The Cowboys of Whispering Canyon

The Rancher's Temptation

Match Made in Haven

A Chance for the Rancher
The Marine's Road Home
Meet Me Under the Mistletoe
The Rancher's Promise
The Chef's Surprise Baby
Captivated by the Cowgirl
Countdown to Christmas
Her Not-So-Little Secret
The Rancher's Christmas Reunion
Snowed In with a Stranger
Her Favorite Mistake
A Rancher of His Own

Visit the Author Profile page
at Harlequin.com for more titles.

For Steph & Dan Gorman, with much love—and a solemn promise to never talk about Flight Club. xo

Prologue

When Raylan Chandler was a boy, he felt certain he wouldn't ever love anything more than he loved traversing the hills and valleys of West River Ranch on horseback with his dad and his granddad. He surely couldn't have imagined anything more beautiful than the vast expanse of land that the Chandler family had been ranching for more than a hundred years. But now that he was a grandfather himself—and a great-grandfather, too—he could acknowledge that traversing those same hills and valleys with the next generations might be the one experience that could top his childhood memory. Because being out here with two of his sons, RJ and Wyatt, and four of his grandsons, Austin, Colby, Greyson and Holt, on a clear, sunny day in late April was pretty close to perfection.

Colby, leading their riding party today, held up a hand, halting the group's progress.

"What is it?" RJ asked.

"I saw something—someone—in the trees."

"A person?" Greyson sounded dubious. "Are you sure?"

They were deep in the hills of West River Ranch, far away from their nearest neighbors and even farther from the Bureau of Land Management territory upon which members of the public were allowed to hunt, so long as they had a state-issued license permitting them to do so.

Though fences marked the perimeter around West River Ranch, it wasn't unusual for sections to come down during the winter months, allowing easy access to trespassers—accidental or intentional. There had been more than a few occasions when hunters had found their way onto their private land in pursuit of their prey. It was less common, though still not unheard of, for hikers to wander off the trail, which could result in an unexpected tumble down a hill or an unplanned dip in West River.

"I'm sure," Colby said, but he nudged his horse, continuing on, anyway.

Raylan heard the shot almost at the same moment he felt a burning sensation in his left biceps.

Glancing down at his arm, he saw blood and a tear in the fabric of his sleeve where the bullet passed through.

Well, hell, he fretted. *Eleanor's going to be pissed that I've ruined my new shirt.*

That was his last thought before the reins slipped through his hands, the ground rushed up to meet him and everything went black.

Chapter One

"You're doing great," Tess Barrett said encouragingly to her patient. "Just one more and then you're done for the day."

"I've already done ten," Patricia Reeves grumbled.

"You've done nine," Tess corrected her gently. "One more will be ten."

Her seventy-four-year-old patient sighed wearily but gritted her teeth and lifted her leg off the table.

"Five…four…three…"

The woman's leg dropped.

"Two, one," Tess completed the count.

Patricia looked at her.

"Close enough," she said.

"So when can I go home?" her patient wanted to know.

"When you can navigate the stairs." Tess gestured to a set of adjustable risers on the opposite side of the room. There were three steps up to a landing and three steps down again, with handrails on both sides. "Are you ready to give them a go?"

"I might have been, if you hadn't tired me out with squats and leg lifts."

Tess glanced at the clock on the wall and did some quick mental calculations. "I could swing back this way around three o'clock, if you want to try later."

Now her patient beamed. "That would be wonderful."

"When you can do the stairs, I'll talk to the doctor about releasing you."

"By the weekend?" Patricia asked hopefully.

"*If* you're steady," Tess said. "Up *and* down."

"I will be."

"Positive thinking—I like that." She glanced up when a broad-shouldered man with dark hair and eyes stepped into view and offered a smile.

Her elderly patient followed the direction of her gaze, taking a moment to study the handsome bearded man wearing a gray T-shirt, black track pants and running shoes.

"Boyfriend?" Patricia asked curiously.

Tess shook her head. "My next patient."

"Do you have a boyfriend?"

"Not at the moment." And not that it was any of her business, but Tess had long ago realized that sharing personal insights and stories helped develop rapport with her patients, leading to their feeling more invested in their treatment and often resulting in more favorable outcomes.

"Then this is your lucky day," her patient said. "Because my grandson Jordan is stopping by for a visit this afternoon."

"Sounds like it's *your* lucky day," Tess countered. "Visitors help alleviate the monotony of a hospital stay."

"He's very handsome," Patricia said. "Of course, my opinion is likely biased. But whenever Doreen—she's my closest friend and also my neighbor of more than forty years—sees him, she says, 'That boy sure is a handsome one.'"

Tess smiled. "Well, if Doreen says so, it must be true."

"And he has his own business—a very successful one," her patient said, continuing to extoll her grandson's virtues.

"Good to know." Tess signaled for an aide to assist Patricia back to her room.

"He's single right now, too," the elderly woman added.

"I appreciate your efforts, Mrs. Reeves. But if you're trying to play matchmaker, you should know that I'm not interested in dating right now."

"Why not?"

"Because I'm taking some time to focus on my career."

"That sounds to me like someone who's nursing a broken heart," Patricia mused.

Not broken, just a little bruised.

The truth was that Tess's heart had never really been broken, because she'd never managed to fall all the way in love. Not because she was afraid or even reluctant to commit. In fact, the opposite was true. She wanted to know how it felt to give her heart one hundred percent to another person and to trust that they would treat it with care, even if she was proven wrong and had it smashed into a thousand pieces. But while she'd had a few relationships with decent men she'd been attracted to and genuinely cared about, she never managed to move past *caring* to *loving*. It was as if there was some indescribable, inexplicable thing holding her back. Something that made her incapable of falling in love. Even with the man she'd once planned to marry.

She'd grown up in a fairly traditional family, with an older sister and a mother and father who were not only married to one another but evidently still in love. So what was wrong with her, Tess wondered?

Megan Wheeler, her best friend (also her cousin and roommate), insisted that there was nothing wrong with Tess—that she just hadn't yet met the right person. And maybe it was true. Or maybe she was too much like her grandmother, the infamous Tallulah Leonard.

In her youth, "Lula" had reputedly enjoyed the company of various and numerous men, though never any one exclusively or for very long. She'd never married, insisting that the purpose of the institution was to force women into indentured servitude to their husbands, but she had given birth to three children—by three different fathers.

Tess had dated a few different guys when she was away at college and had even been engaged for a short while, but since her return to Whispering Canyon five years earlier, she'd had only a handful of casual relationships. The fact that none of those guys had been "the one" made her suspect the concept was nothing more than an elaborate fabrication of poets and songwriters.

Not that Tess intended to share any of that with her patient. Casual conversations were one thing; baring her deepest insecurities was another.

"I'll see you later this afternoon," she reminded the other woman. "Get some rest between now and then so that you're ready to tackle the stairs."

"I'll be ready," Patricia promised.

Holt Chandler was usually an easygoing guy who subscribed to the philosophy of live and let live. But there was nothing usual about his grandfather taking a bullet while out on a leisurely ride and, in the aftermath, Holt was both furious and terrified.

After the shot, in the few seconds it had taken everyone to realize what had happened, chaos erupted. Wyatt and Colby had taken off in pursuit of the hunter who'd carelessly fired the bullet, and Holt pulled out his phone to call 911 while his dad dropped to the ground beside his father, fashioning a makeshift tourniquet to staunch the flow of blood.

Less than an hour later—forty-eight minutes that felt like days!—Holt was striding through the emergency room doors of Whispering Canyon Medical Center.

"Raylan Chandler?" he said to the clerk at the desk.

She glanced up from her computer screen. "I don't suppose there's any point in telling you that ER patients are limited to one companion?"

"He's my grandfather," Holt said. "I was there when he got shot."

"Exam room three," she said, pressing the button on her desk to release the doors.

"Thank you," he said, already rushing through them.

The exam room wasn't very big.

Or maybe it was just crowded.

Eleanor Chandler was seated on a hard plastic chair beside the bed, holding her husband's hand. Raylan's eyes were open and glassy with pain, his jaw clenched. Or maybe it was the indignation of wearing a hospital gown that had him gritting his teeth.

Glancing around, Holt saw his parents and his brother Flynn, Uncle Clayton and Aunt Laura and two of their sons, Austin and Greyson. Also crammed into the room were his cousins Colby and Jackson. What he didn't see, anywhere in the crowd around his grandfather's bed, was anyone wearing a white coat and a hospital badge.

"Where's the doctor?" Holt demanded. "Why isn't there a doctor in here?"

"The triage nurse promised that a doctor would be in shortly," his grandmother said, her tone measured and calm.

"The doctor should be here now," Austin chimed in, obviously as impatient as Holt.

"Maybe this isn't the best place for Gramps," Holt said.

"It's a hospital," Eleanor pointed out reasonably.

It was that, but the name—Whispering Canyon Medical Center—made it sound like a bigger deal than it was. In reality, it was the local clinic where cowboys went when they dislocated their shoulders after being bucked off the backs of broncs or broke their collarbones when they were tossed aside by ornery bulls. He suspected that gunshot wounds were much less common.

"He should be at a trauma center," Holt said now. "We should have called an air ambulance to take him to Billings."

"I don't need a trauma center," Raylan said tersely. "The bullet went right through. All I need is a doctor competent enough to stitch up my arm and put my shoulder back in its socket."

"With all due respect, Gramps, as you didn't go to medical school, I'm not sure you're in the best position to assess your needs."

"Far as I know, you didn't go to medical school, either," Raylan pointed out.

"Lucky for both of you, I did," a female voice said from behind them.

The family members crowded around Raylan's bed parted to make way for the doctor.

"I'm Lindsay Tierney," she said, introducing herself to the group before zeroing in on the patient. "How are you feeling, Mr. Chandler?"

There were more than a few people in attendance who could—and did—answer to that name, but as it was apparent the doctor was speaking to Raylan Senior, the others remained silent.

"Foolish," Holt's grandfather responded.

"I don't think you can blame yourself for getting hit by a stray bullet," the doctor said.

"Maybe not," he allowed. "But I can and do blame myself for letting it knock me off my horse."

She smiled at that as she peeled back the dressing the paramedics had applied to get a closer look at the wound.

"You're going to have a scar," she told him.

"That's the least of my worries," he said.

"Anything hurt other than your pride?"

"I think I dislocated the other shoulder when I fell."

"Did you hit your head?"

"Not that I can recall," he told her.

"Any loss of consciousness?"

"Yes," his morning riding partners chorused before the patient could hedge again.

"Apparently," Raylan said dryly.

The doctor glanced at the others who'd spoken. "How long was he out?"

"Only a few minutes," RJ said. "Two, maybe three, at the most."

She shone a penlight into Raylan's eyes.

"Do you know what day it is, Mr. Chandler?"

"Wednesday."

"Date?" the doctor prompted.

"April thirtieth."

"Your birthdate?"

"November fifth."

"And how old are you?"

"Too old to flirt with a pretty doctor in front of my wife of almost sixty-five years," he said.

She looked up from her clipboard. "But young enough to be prepped for surgery?"

"Surgery?" He scowled. "Can't you just stitch me up?"

She shook her head. "I need to take a closer look at the tissue damage and make sure there aren't any bullet fragments left that might cause problems in the future."

"I'm almost eighty-seven years old," he grumbled. "I'm more worried about right now than the future."

"And finally the right answer to my question," she noted.

"I'm sure I don't need surgery," he said.

"You might be sure, but I'm the one who went to medical school," she reminded him.

He sighed. "I guess I'll see you in surgery, then."

Holt followed Dr. Tierney out. "Could I have a minute?"

The doctor pivoted to face him. "I'm on hour sixteen of a twelve-hour shift and on my way to prep for another surgery, so whatever questions you have about my qualifications, I hope you can ask them in a minute," she said wearily. "Better yet, the hospital offers free Wi-Fi, so you could go to the WCMC website and read my bio."

"Does your bio attest to any experience with gunshot wounds?" Holt asked.

"It mentions my emergency medicine rotation in Baltimore," she told him. "Trust me. I've seen more than my share."

He nodded. "Thank you."

Dr. Tierney's expression softened then, just a little. "I promise Mr. Chandler will get the best possible care we can give him. Not because your family's name is at the top of the donor tree in the main foyer, but because we give every patient that comes through our doors the best possible care, irrespective of their status in the community."

"I guess that put me in my place," Holt muttered under his breath, as the doctor walked away.

"I don't think that was her intention," a voice said from behind him.

Startled, he turned around and found himself face-to-face with a stunningly beautiful woman dressed in purple hospital scrubs.

"If Dr. Tierney seems abrupt at times—and I know she does—it's because she's got a hundred things waiting for her attention and twice that many on her mind," she told him.

"I had to ask," he said, aware that he sounded defensive. "I needed to know that my grandfather's in good hands."

"Dr. Tierney's are the best," she promised.

He nodded, feeling unaccustomedly awkward and tongue-tied.

He'd dated his share of attractive women—some of his friends might argue more than his share—so it usually took more than a pretty face to capture his interest. But there was something about this one that immediately snagged his attention and stirred his blood.

She stood about five feet seven inches, he guessed, with a slender build, though the shapeless uniform made it hard to tell. She had a flawless peaches-and-cream complexion, high cheekbones, a slightly pointed chin, gorgeous moss-green eyes framed by long, dark lashes, and temptingly full lips. Her pale blond hair was pulled away from her face in a bouncy ponytail and her fingers—long and slender with neatly trimmed, unpainted nails—were devoid of rings.

"How's your grandfather holding up?" she asked now. "And your grandmother? This must be traumatic for her, too."

Her questions yanked him back to the present. "You know my grandparents?"

She smiled. "Everyone in Whispering Canyon knows your grandparents—or at least who they are."

"Do they know you?" he asked.

"They do," she confirmed, as the door to exam room three opened behind him and various family members spilled out.

Tess stepped back and silently berated herself for being unable to stay away. Usually, she took advantage of any free time she had between patients to catch up on her charting, but when she heard that Raylan Chandler had been brought into the ER, she'd found herself heading in that direction. Even if there wasn't anything she could do, she felt compelled to check in on the family—especially the rancher's wife, who had always been kind to her.

Raylan and Eleanor had three sons, each of whom had gone on to have three sons, and every one of them was ridiculously good-looking. Tess might not have been able to pick Austin out of a crowd, and Colby and Jackson looked similar enough that she might have mixed them up, but she'd always known Holt—the object of her adolescent fantasies.

Running into him now had been…unexpected. But she was pleased that she'd managed to hold her own during their brief conversation. Unlike in high school, when passing him in the hall or even seeing him from a distance made her heart pound and her knees weak.

Several of his family members walked by now without even glancing in her direction, but Eleanor wasn't one of them.

"Tess." The Chandler matriarch smiled warmly as she reached for her hands. "I didn't expect to see you here. Are you working at the hospital now?"

"I spend a few hours in the IRU—the inpatient rehabilitation unit—three days a week," she said, aware that Holt continued to hover nearby. "That's where I was when I heard Mr. Chandler had been shot."

The old woman exhaled a weary sigh. "A hunter's stray bullet."

But Tess knew an accidental shooting could be every bit as deadly as a targeted one.

"I know I can't stop men with guns from being careless," Eleanor continued, "but I wish they'd stay away from West River Ranch."

"I guess that's a greater risk to ranchers whose property abuts BLM lands," Tess noted.

"Of course, Raylan seems more perturbed by the fact that he fell off his horse afterward than by the shooting itself."

"He was conscious, then, when they brought him in?"

"Conscious and cantankerous," the rancher's wife confirmed.

"And how are you holding up?" Tess asked her. "Is there anything you need? Anything I can get for you?"

"I'm doing okay." As Eleanor spoke, another—younger—woman came to stand by her side.

One of the daughters-in-law, Tess guessed. Average height with a slender build, perfectly styled hair, immaculately applied makeup, dressed in dark trousers and a matching jacket over a snowy white shell.

"And she's got family here if she needs anything," the daughter-in-law chimed in.

It was the woman's dismissive tone even more so than the designer labels she wore that told Tess she didn't belong. That she wasn't one of them.

As if she needed any kind of reminder that the Chandlers were akin to royalty in town while the Barretts were mostly unknown—which was at least preferable to being known as a Leonard.

Tess's watch vibrated against her wrist, a welcome distraction and a reminder that she had a session in fifteen minutes.

"You have somewhere you need to be," Eleanor realized.

"I do," she agreed. "But if there's anything any of us on staff can do to help, you only need to ask."

"Thank you, dear." The old woman managed to smile again. "It was nice to see you, despite the circumstances."

"And you," Tess replied, as the daughter-in-law took Eleanor's arm and steered her toward the waiting room.

She turned to make her way back to the rehab unit when Holt spoke again.

"Hey! Wait a sec."

She paused and he breached the distance between them in a few quick strides. There was something about being near him that affected her in a visceral way, even if she hadn't been this close to him since her first day at Aspen Ridge High School, nearly a dozen years earlier. And just like that day, her heart was suddenly pounding so fast and hard against her ribs, she was certain he must be able to hear it.

His gaze dropped to her chest, seeming to confirm her suspicion. "Tess, right?"

He wasn't looking at her chest, she realized with a combination of embarrassment and relief, but the ID badge hanging around her neck.

"Yes." The response was barely audible.

Being near to him now made her feel like a hormonal teenager again—all flushed and giddy just because a cute boy was talking to her. Except that Holt was definitely not a boy any longer, and the heat that flooded her system was unlike anything she'd ever experienced as a girl. She cleared her throat and tried again.

"Yes," she said, and added a nod for emphasis.

He held her gaze for a long minute.

Or maybe it was only a few seconds, but it felt like a long minute. Certainly long enough for the fire rushing through her veins to liquefy her bones.

And yet, she somehow managed to untangle her tongue enough to ask, "Is there something you need?"

He shook his head. "No. I just wanted to say thanks."

She appreciated the sentiment but was admittedly a little confused. "I didn't do anything."

"You came out of your way to check on my family," he noted. "And we appreciate it—even if we don't all show it."

"Any time a loved one is in the hospital is stressful," she said sympathetically.

Now he nodded. "My grandparents have been the anchor of our family for even longer than I've been alive. And my grandfather always seems so strong and capable, I sometimes forget that he's almost eighty-seven years old and not going to live forever.

"But he's got a lot of life in him yet, and it pisses me off—excuse my language—to think that a stray bullet fired by a careless hunter could have cut it short."

A surge of sympathy had her reaching instinctively for his hand. But what was meant as an innocent gesture of comfort turned into something else entirely when a current of electricity raced up her arm. She started to pull her hand away, but he tightened his fingers around hers.

Their gazes locked, held.

Tess swallowed. "He's going to be okay."

Holt nodded. "I know," he said. "Because I can't imagine any other outcome."

"Dr. Tierney wouldn't have hesitated to send him to Billings if she didn't believe we were able to give him the care he needs."

"Have you worked with her a long time?" he asked.

"I don't work with her," Tess felt compelled to clarify. "We just happen to work in the same hospital. But three years ago, my dad went into sudden cardiac arrest at the auto repair shop where he works when Dr. Tierney was there to pick up her vehicle. She immediately recognized what was happening, took action and saved his life."

"It would be hard to get a stronger endorsement than that," Holt mused.

"Your grandfather is in the very best hands," she said again. "But now I really have to run or I'll be late for my next appointment."

Holt watched Tess walk away, sorry to see her go.

Because for the few moments that he'd been looking into her moss-green eyes, everything else had faded into the background.

His grandmother had greeted the young woman warmly—suggesting that Eleanor Chandler knew more about her than the name printed on her badge. More surprising to Holt was the chill in his mother's voice when she spoke to Tess. Obviously Miranda hadn't been pleased to see her there and had tried to nudge her along. Meanwhile, his dad hadn't shown any outward reaction at all, as if RJ was oblivious to her presence. Their disparate responses suggested some kind of history of which Holt was unaware.

Unaware of and unbothered by, because for the few minutes that he'd been standing beside her, he'd been able to pretend that he wasn't in a hospital corridor and that his grandfather hadn't been shot.

"Holt?"

He started at the sound of his mother's voice, then turned slowly to face her. "Yeah?"

"Come and sit with your grandmother," she urged.

"I don't think I can sit right now."

"She could use your support."

"It looks like she has plenty of support," he said, noting that Uncle Wyatt and Aunt Kristin had arrived and were taking turns embracing Eleanor.

"So maybe *I* would appreciate your support," Miranda said, tucking her arm through his.

"What's the story?" he asked.

"I'm not sure I know what you're asking," she said evasively.

"I'm asking why you were so eager to send Tess away."

Her lips thinned, a telltale sign of disapproval. "That girl had no business coming around here, feigning worry for Raylan, faking sympathy for Eleanor."

"Her concern seemed genuine to me," he noted.

"No doubt she was working some kind of angle," his mother remarked. "Trying to worm her way in where she doesn't belong."

Holt frowned at her response. "Why would you say that?"

Miranda shifted to give him her full attention now. "You don't know who she is," she realized.

"Should I?"

"Her last name might be Barrett, but her mother was a Leonard."

Although *that* name sounded familiar, apparently Holt didn't put the pieces together quickly enough because his mom huffed out an impatient breath before she clarified, "Tess's grandmother is Tallulah Leonard."

And suddenly, the pieces snapped into place, making him realize that the hottest woman he'd crossed paths with in a very long time was completely off-limits to him.

Chapter Two

"There she is," Patricia Reeves said brightly, when Tess stepped into her room. "I told you she'd be back."

"I'm back," Tess confirmed, managing a smile for her patient, while her mind remained in the ER with Holt Chandler. "Are you ready to tackle those stairs now?"

"Young people these days are always in such a hurry," Patricia lamented.

"I've got a schedule to keep," Tess reminded her.

"Well, before we head to the PT room, there's someone I want you to meet," the other woman said. "Tess, this is my grandson, Jordan."

It required considerable effort for Tess to keep the smile on her face when she recognized him. His brows lifted in surprise, confirming that he recognized her, too.

"Tess Barrett," he said.

"Jordan Denninger," she replied.

"You two know each other?" Patricia sounded both surprised and pleased by this revelation.

"We were at Aspen Ridge High at the same time," Tess explained.

"I was a senior when Tess was a junior," Jordan clarified, his gaze skimming over her now with interest.

"I should have guessed that you'd likely gone to high school together," his grandmother noted.

"There's only one in Whispering Canyon," Tess pointed out.

And Jordan had been popular at Aspen Ridge. A first-string running back on the football team—tall, blond, good-looking—and all too aware of it. (Though, in Tess's estimation, not nearly as hot as Holt Chandler.)

Despite his popularity, Jordan had also been a bit of a jerk. One of those guys who'd reach past a girl for something and "accidentally" brush against her breast. Or who'd drop something on the floor so that he could peek up a classmate's skirt when he bent to pick it up.

"We lost touch after high school," Jordan said. "A fact that I'm sincerely regretting right now."

"We were never really in touch," she pointed out.

Except inappropriately.

"Well, perhaps this is the perfect time for you to get reacquainted," Patricia suggested.

"I'm up for that," Jordan said.

Tess would be lying if she said she wasn't flattered by his obvious interest. Because he was even better-looking now than he'd been in high school, his adolescent frame having filled out nicely. Unfortunately, she suspected that once a creep always a creep, and she wasn't eager to have that suspicion proven correct.

"Actually, this is the perfect time for you to tackle the stairs," Tess reminded her patient.

"I'm ready," Patricia promised.

"Are you up for the walk or do you want me to get a transport chair?"

"I can walk." Patricia glanced at her grandson. "If Jordan will walk with me."

"It would be my pleasure," he said sincerely.

Which made Tess consider that maybe he wasn't the same creep she remembered from high school. Because Patricia truly was a lovely woman—albeit one without any understanding of boundaries—and there was obviously a genuine shared affection between her and her grandson.

Jordan walked at a measured pace, cognizant of the old woman's limitations, her hand tucked into the crook of his arm. And when they got to the rehab center, he lowered his head to kiss her cheek.

"I'll see you tomorrow," he said to his grandmother. Then he looked at Tess. "Maybe I'll be lucky and see you tomorrow, too."

"Maybe," she said, deliberately noncommittal.

"Oh, he likes you," Patricia said, when her grandson had disappeared from sight.

Tess took her arm to guide her to the stairs. "I think he'd like you to focus on your rehab rather than matchmaking so that you can go home soon."

"I can multitask," Patricia assured her.

Tess had to laugh at that. "Let's see if one of those tasks is the stairs."

Eleanor Chandler wasn't overly fond of hospitals.

Though she appreciated the doctors and nurses and all the other staff who cared for the patients that came through the doors, she had too many memories of too many hours spent in rooms just like this one to be able to relax here now.

She didn't like the bright lights, the antiseptic smells or the constant beeping and whooshing of various machines. But it was the distant sound of quiet sobbing—because it seemed as if there was always somebody sobbing—that made her heart ache.

She'd been here when Clayton needed seven stitches to close up the gash in his knee, the result of jumping out of a tree; when RJ broke his collarbone after tumbling from the hayloft; and when an ornery stallion cracked three of Wyatt's ribs. She'd been at her mother's side, too, in this very hospital, when Lorraine released her last breath, taken by cancer far too soon.

Of course, hospitals could also be places of celebration. There was joy in the ring of the bell when a patient finished chemotherapy. In the exhale of giddy relief when a coding patient was brought back from the edge. And especially in the first cry of a newborn baby.

Eleanor had been here when Boone's wife, Nadine, brought their beautiful twin boys into the world—and again, less than two years later, when a previously undiagnosed bladder infection led to septic shock that took the young mother's life.

But she was here for Raylan now. And though Dr. Tierney had assured her that the surgery was routine, he was closing in on his eighty-seventh birthday, and she couldn't help worrying that something might go wrong.

"How long is this going to take?" Wyatt's question drew her back to the present.

"As long as it needs to," Eleanor told him.

Her husband's youngest son scowled. "How can you be so calm about this?"

"Because we've been through a lot in nearly sixty-five years of marriage, and I don't believe for a minute that a stray bullet will take him down."

"Is there anything you need, Grams?"

She offered Holt a weary smile. "A time-travel machine to take us all back to this morning?"

"If I had one, it would be yours," he told her.

"I know."

She appreciated that everyone had abandoned what they were doing to be here. Even Boone was on his way, having cajoled Willow—Raylan and Eleanor's longtime housekeeper—into babysitting the twins. But at the same time, she wished they hadn't abandoned everything, because it made the shooting seem like A Very Big Deal. And she didn't want it to be A Very Big Deal.

"You don't all need to hang around here," she said now. "Your presence isn't going to make the surgery finish any sooner."

"Where else should we be?" RJ asked her.

"At the ranch, doing whatever it is you do every other day," she said.

Of course, she knew very well the numerous and various tasks that they performed on a daily basis. She'd been a rancher's wife for more than six decades and a rancher's daughter for two more before that. There had been a time that she could ride and rope with the best hired hands. She'd pulled countless calves and later helped vaccinate and brand them. She'd dug postholes and fixed broken fences and fired her rifle to warn off coyotes that were sniffing around the herd.

Her responsibilities hadn't lessened so much as they'd changed when she became a mother, and she'd turned her attention to bandaging skinned knees and wiping unhappy tears. As the boys grew up and became more independent, her responsibilities changed yet again. Then each of her sons had married and the cycle started again as she'd helped care for her grandchildren.

She was pleased to know that they'd found suitable partners and built loving families. Of course, she wasn't naive enough to think that their marriages were without trials and tribulations, but what mattered, in her opinion, was that the love between husband and wife had proven strong enough to hold them together against whatever forces might have tried to tear them apart.

The sound of knuckles rapping on the open door of the waiting room interrupted her musing.

"Sheriff," she said, acknowledging his presence.

The lawman lifted his hat off his head and held it in his hands—an outward sign of respect that she suspected was more for show than anything else. She'd known Billy Garvey since he was in kindergarten with Wyatt, and she knew that he'd always resented everything the Chandlers had—just like his father before him.

Billy stepped into the room. "How's Raylan doing?"

"He's in surgery right now," she said. "Though he didn't seem too much the worse for wear when he was brought in."

"That's good to hear," he said.

"What can we do for you, Sheriff? Deputy?" she added, acknowledging the second man in uniform, standing behind his boss.

She'd always liked Sawyer Wells better than the sheriff—and had greater trust in him. He'd been a classmate of both Ellis's and Flynn's in school and had aspired to wear the badge for all the right reasons.

"I was hoping to speak with everyone who was with Raylan when he was shot," Billy said now.

She understood that there were questions to be asked and answered—and she did want the shooter to be held responsible for his carelessness. But her attention was on Raylan right now, as she knew was true of everyone else in the waiting room.

"Can't this wait?"

It was Wyatt who asked the question that was on the tip of her tongue before she had a chance.

"The longer we wait, the less likely it is that we find whoever shot your father," the sheriff told him.

RJ frowned. "That sounds like you think he was targeted, when this was obviously a hunting accident."

"Nothing is obvious at this point," Billy said.

"You think someone shot him *on purpose*?" Austin asked.

"Maybe the shooter was aiming for Raylan. Or maybe he was after someone else in your riding party."

"An equally ridiculous suggestion," Clayton said dismissively.

"Is it?" the sheriff challenged. "West River Ranch is the biggest spread in Wyoming—and about to get bigger, from what I understand. You don't get to be that big without making some enemies."

"Dale Bellows came to us and asked if we'd be interested in acquiring his property," RJ informed him.

"Doesn't mean his other neighbors were happy with the deal you made," Billy pointed out.

"It's quite a leap from unhappy to homicidal," Wyatt noted.

The sheriff puffed out his chest, and Eleanor was suddenly reminded that the lawman and her youngest son had frequently been in competition with one another over the years—from their earliest days in junior rodeo through to their graduation from high school. They'd fought over Kristin, too, she remembered now, and was certain it had stuck in Billy's craw that the girl he'd always wanted had chosen Wyatt instead.

"Or maybe, like I said, Raylan Senior wasn't the intended target at all," Billy noted.

"There was no target," Austin said.

The sheriff turned to Greyson. "You're the defense attorney—what do you think?"

"You're asking if I have any enemies?"

"Of course you have enemies," Billy said. "The question is, can you think of anyone who might hate you enough to want to put a bullet in you?"

"Certainly no one on my current client list," Greyson assured him.

"There have also been rumors circulating around town that a local handyman has been spending time with a married lady for whom he did some household repairs."

"A complete fabrication," Colby immediately asserted in defense of his younger brother.

"I'm sure you're aware, being a crackerjack investigator, that the married lady in question has been separated from her husband for more than six months," Jackson said. "But the rumors are still nothing more than that."

"Instead of rumors or suppositions, you might want to look for some actual evidence to determine what happened," Eleanor suggested now.

"In the absence of physical evidence, figuring out the motive can be the key to putting the pieces together. I'll give you some time now," he said, as if he was doing them a big favor. "But I'm going to need statements from the witnesses sooner rather than later. The longer we wait, the less likely it is that we'll ever find who shot Raylan."

As Billy and Sawyer exited the room, Eleanor couldn't shake the feeling that not finding the gunman wouldn't bother the sheriff even a little bit.

Chapter Three

After her shift was finished, Tess went to the locker room to change out of her scrubs and into a pair of slim-fitting jeans with a V-neck sweater and low-heeled boots to meet Meg at The Bootlegger for dinner. A quick glance at her watch confirmed that she was running behind schedule, but she took another minute to brush out her hair and swipe gloss over her lips, anyway.

Unsurprisingly, Meg was already seated at the bar when Tess walked in, five minutes after six.

"I'm late," she acknowledged, settling onto the vacant stool beside her friend.

"No worries," Meg said. "I've just been sitting here pretending I didn't work a ten-hour shift today, fueled only by a Kit-Kat, an apple and half a dozen cups of coffee."

"I only worked six hours," Tess confided. "But during that time, I ran into Jordan Denninger."

"The 'sorry-I-accidentally-on-purpose-touched-your-boob' guy from high school?" Meg guessed.

"The same," she confirmed, smiling her thanks to Owen, the bartender, when he set a glass of Diet Coke with a wedge of lime in front of her.

"Hopefully you ran into him hard enough to hurt him," Meg said, making Tess laugh.

"It was a figurative rather than a literal run-in," she told her friend.

"Too bad." Meg took a sip of the single glass of wine she allowed herself to enjoy when she was out.

Like Tess, Meg had never been much of a drinker. Of course, she had a three-year-old daughter at home, and parenting was a 24/7 job. Not to mention that, by her own admission, the last time she'd overindulged was the night Emma was conceived. And while Tess knew that Meg truly believed her daughter was the best thing that ever happened to her, she also knew that her volatile relationship with Emma's father was the worst.

"So how did Jordan Denninger happen to cross your path today?" Meg asked now.

"You know Patricia Reeves?"

"Our former middle school teacher who just had a knee replacement?"

Tess nodded. "Jordan's her grandson."

"I never would have guessed."

"Me, neither."

"Do you ladies want food tonight or just drinks?" Owen asked, as he measured and mixed some kind of fancy cocktail.

A lot of bartenders couldn't be bothered with patrons who didn't drink alcohol, as that was how the bar made most of its money, but Owen always gave Tess and Meg the same attention as all his other customers. It was only one of the reasons The Bootlegger was their favorite place to grab a bite and a drink after work.

"Food," Meg immediately replied.

"Definitely food," Tess confirmed.

He finished with the cocktail first, straining it into a champagne coupe then floating a dehydrated lemon wheel on top and adding a sprig of...lavender?

"That looks interesting," Tess noted.

"A Lavender French 75," Owen said. "Want to try one?"

"You know I'm a loyal Diet Coke girl," she reminded him.

"I do know, but I keep hoping you'll let me tempt you," he said with a wink.

"If anyone could tempt me, it would be you," Tess said.

She enjoyed flirting with the bartender, because—after two dates and one disappointing kiss a few years earlier—they both knew it wasn't ever going to lead to anything more than that.

"Did you work through lunch today, too?" Meg asked, when Owen went to punch their orders into the computer.

"Not on purpose," Tess said. "I was heading to the cafeteria when I heard the buzz, so I detoured to the ER to see what was going on."

Meg nodded, acknowledging that she knew which patient had generated the buzz. "I assisted with the surgery," she said. "It was a simple, straightforward procedure, and his vitals remained stable throughout, so he should make a quick and complete recovery. From the gunshot wound, anyway. The dislocated shoulder's going to require some rehab."

"That's good news," Tess said. "About the gunshot wound, I mean, not the shoulder."

"There was one weird thing, though," Meg noted.

"What's that?" Tess asked, sipping her soda.

"Dr. Tierney picked several bullet fragments out of his arm."

"Is that unusual?"

"No, but the whitish powder on the fragments was unusual, suggesting that the bullet was made of lead. Oxidized lead, to be more precise."

"Which means…it was an old bullet?" Tess guessed.

"That was her conclusion," Meg confirmed. "Though she cautioned that she's only a bit of a civil war buff, not a weapons expert, and sent them to the lab for analysis."

The phone Meg had set beside her drink vibrated on the bar. She turned it over to glance at the screen and sighed. "I have to go."

There had been both weariness and worry in her sigh, prompting Tess to ask, "Emma?"

Meg nodded.

"Do you want me to come with you?"

Now her friend shook her head. "No point in both of us missing dinner."

"I can get Owen to box up our food."

"No," Meg said again, taking some money out of her wallet. "Stay and enjoy your burger."

"Put that away," Tess said, declining the bills her friend offered. "I'm not letting you pay for food you're not even going to eat."

"Well, you shouldn't have to pay for two burgers when you're only going to eat one."

"Maybe I'm hungry enough to eat two."

"Unlikely."

"Or maybe I'll bring the second one home."

Meg kissed her cheek. "Just don't rush home. Stay and flirt with a handsome rancher—or two or three."

Tess had to admit there didn't seem to be any shortage of those in the bar tonight. Denim & Diamonds, the honky-tonk on the edge of town, was known for its live music, cheap beer and willing women—all of which added up to frequent bar fights. The Alchemist was at the opposite end of the spectrum—a more upscale setting with fancier drinks (and matching prices!) that was a common date night destination. The Bootlegger hit the sweet spot right in the middle, at least in Tess's opinion. A casual atmosphere with good food and friendly service.

Obviously she wasn't the only one who thought so, because she recognized several colleagues, including Richard Holland, her immediate boss. Of course, the restaurant's close proximity to WCMC and happy-hour specials also contributed to its popularity with the hospital staff.

She watched as her friend headed toward the exit. The door had barely closed at Meg's back when it opened again and another customer entered.

Holt Chandler.

Tess's heart stuttered.

The cowboy glanced around the bar, as if looking for someone.

Or maybe he was just looking for an empty seat, as those were in short supply tonight.

His eyes lit with recognition when his gaze locked with hers, then his lips curved, as if he was happy to see her.

Or maybe he was just happy to see a familiar face. Though considering that he was a Chandler, if he didn't know everyone in the restaurant, she suspected they likely knew him.

He weaved through the tables, making his way to the bar, and paused behind the stool Meg had vacated.

"Is this seat taken?" he asked.

"Not anymore," she told him.

"Do you mind?"

"Of course not."

He settled onto the stool and took a moment to survey the liquor bottles on the shelves behind the bar.

"I heard your grandfather's surgery went well."

He nodded. "I got to see him for two minutes before I left."

"Only two minutes?"

"By the time he was in recovery, almost the whole family was there," he noted. "Which meant that there were fourteen of us waiting and why we were each allowed two minutes."

"How was he doing when you saw him?"

"A little groggy. A lot grumpy."

Tess smiled at that. "And your grandmother?"

"Strong and steady."

Owen made his way over and Holt ordered a whiskey, neat.

The bartender poured the drink, and Holt lifted the glass to his lips, swallowing the entire contents in one gulp.

The bartender held up the bottle and Holt answered the silent question with a nod, then emptied the glass again.

Tess put a hand on his arm, intending to urge caution. But

when she felt an immediate tingle in her fingertips, she quickly yanked her hand back again.

"Don't you think you should slow down a little?" she suggested cautiously. "Or at least put some food in your stomach to soak up the alcohol?"

"I had breakfast," he said, turning his wrist to glance at his watch.

A Tissot, she noted.

"Fourteen hours ago?" she guessed.

"Or thereabouts," he agreed.

Lucy, one of the servers, appeared then with two platters of food. She looked questioningly at Tess.

Tess gestured to herself and then Holt.

The server set the food down and left.

Holt frowned at the plate in front of him. "You didn't order this for me?"

"No," she admitted. "A friend of mine was sitting there before you came in, but she had to leave."

"I can't eat her burger," he protested.

"You can and you should," Tess told him. "Because she's not coming back and, if you don't eat it, it will go to waste."

"You're sure?"

"I'm sure," she confirmed.

"In that case—" he waved Lucy over again "—can I get ketchup for the fries?"

Tess chuckled as she lifted her own burger from her plate. The brioche bun was lightly toasted, the juicy patty topped with two slices of cheese—pepperjack and cheddar, crispy onions, tomato, lettuce and pickles. She bit into the sandwich and nearly moaned with pleasure.

Or maybe she did moan, because Holt's lips twitched, as if he was fighting a smile. "That good?"

"Better."

He sampled his own, nodded.

Halfway through the meal, Owen put another glass in front of Tess, and Holt asked for a Coke.

He tilted his head to study her as he dragged a fry through the ketchup on his plate. “I feel like I know you from somewhere.”

“Possibly the emergency room from a few hours ago?”

He flashed a quick grin. “No, I mean like before that. Although a man could be forgiven for not immediately recognizing you as the woman he met at the hospital,” he said. “You look a lot different dressed in street clothes and with your hair down.”

“Like Clark Kent without his glasses?” she teased.

“Something like that.”

She sipped her soda. “We did cross paths once before,” she told him. “Several years ago.”

“Did we…?” His brows lifted as the question trailed off suggestively.

She felt her cheeks heat.

Only in my dreams.

“No,” she said quickly. “It was twelve years ago. The first day of the new school year. I was a freshman at Aspen Ridge High. You were a senior. I tripped on the steps leading up to the main doors and my books and papers went flying.”

He looked apprehensive. “Did I laugh?”

She immediately shook her head, smiling a little. “Actually, you stopped and helped me gather my things.”

And while he was picking up her papers, her heart had fallen out of her chest and gone *splat* at his feet.

“Our paths never crossed again after that?” he asked.

“Not that you noticed,” she said lightly.

“I guess I did live in my own world in high school.”

“Why wouldn’t you, when you were king of that world?”

He laughed, a little self-consciously. “Hardly.”

“Anyway, I was too tongue-tied that day to even stammer out a thank-you, so thank you.”

"I'm sure it was my pleasure."

Tess ate as much as she could, then pushed her plate aside.

Holt, having already devoured Meg's burger and fries, finished—with her permission—the onion rings that Tess had left on her plate, too.

"I guess I was hungry," he acknowledged, when both empty platters had been cleared away.

"Feel better now?" she asked.

"Yeah." He finished his Coke and pushed the glass aside, then ordered another whiskey.

Tess sipped her soda and told herself to bite her tongue, but didn't manage to follow her own advice. "Being at the hospital three days a week, I've made plenty of friends in the ER and heard too many horror stories about the consequences of people drinking and driving."

"This is only my third whiskey. And I'd never get behind the wheel if I believed my ability to drive was impaired," he assured her.

"Well, do me a favor and give me a twenty-minute head start so that I can get home before you're on the roads?"

"It's sweet that you're worried about me," he said.

"I'm more worried about the other drivers who didn't choose to get behind the wheel after a few drinks," she said bluntly.

"Touché," he said.

"I'm sorry if I sounded harsh," she said. "Drinking and driving is one of my buttons."

"No need to apologize. And I'm really not in the habit of getting behind the wheel after a few drinks. Two beers is usually my limit."

"Is there someone you can call to pick you up?"

"Not necessary," he said. "I planned to come back to the hospital in the morning to see my grandfather again, anyway, so I might as well stay in town and skip the drive back and forth."

"You don't have to do stuff with the cows and horses in the morning?"

Another smile tugged at the corners of his mouth. "There are plenty of hands to do stuff with the cows and horses if I'm not there for one day."

"What kind of stuff do you do?" she asked curiously.

"With the cows and horses, you mean?"

"Yeah."

"The day-to-day chores on a ranch can't be summarized in a quick conversation," he said. "If you really want to know, you should come out to the ranch sometime to see for yourself."

"Thanks, but I'm not sure your mother would approve of me accepting that invitation."

"Do you really care what my mother thinks?"

"No, but you probably should."

He swiveled his stool, so that he was facing her and their knees were touching. The casual, incidental contact sent a jolt of electricity through her veins that threatened to melt her bones for a second time that day. And that was before he settled his hands on her knees.

"Right now my mother is the last person on my mind," he assured her.

"You're thinking about your grandfather," she guessed.

"No." He shook his head for emphasis, his thumbs lightly brushing over the denim, an almost imperceptible—but also intimate—caress. "I'm thinking that spending the night at the inn would be much more pleasant if you were there with me."

Tess choked on her soda.

Holt's thumbs paused their rhythmic movements, but he didn't lift his hands away.

"Did I misread the chemistry between us?" he asked, when she'd stopped coughing and sputtering.

"Chemistry?" she echoed, wondering if that was the reason she was suddenly feeling hot and tingly all over.

"Perhaps the whiskies have impaired my ability to assess the situation," he acknowledged, and now he did remove his hands. "I apologize if I offended you."

She set her glass on the bar. "So…you're withdrawing your invitation?"

He tilted his head. "I can't quite decipher your tone," he confided. "Are you relieved? Disappointed? Indifferent?"

"I'm…confused."

"Does that mean you're considering my not very smooth proposition?"

"I shouldn't be," she told him. *Admonished herself.*

"And yet?" he prompted, leaning forward with a hopeful smile.

"I'm tempted," she admitted.

His smile widened and the intensity in his gaze obliterated the last vestiges of her resistance.

"That sounds like a *yes* to me," he said.

Tess wasn't under any illusion that Holt Chandler wanted *her*. He just wanted company so that he didn't have to be alone. No doubt he would have issued the same invitation to any woman he struck up a conversation with at the bar.

But the fact was that he'd sat down beside her. He'd struck up a conversation with her. And Tess was enough of a romantic—or maybe enough of a fool—to still harbor a bit of a crush on the boy he'd been in high school. The one who'd stopped to help a flustered freshman while his friends stood back and snickered. The one who'd smiled and winked and made her naive heart pound hard and fast inside her (sadly undeveloped) chest.

Even then she'd known who he was, of course. No one could grow up in Whispering Canyon and not know who the Chandlers were. It wasn't enough that they operated the biggest cattle ranch in Wyoming, they were also every bit as handsome and charming as they were rich. All the boys wanted to be their friends; all the girls wanted to be with them.

Tess had never harbored any such illusions.

Though she admired him from afar, she knew Holt would never be interested in her.

Not only because he was three years older, but also because

he was a Chandler and she was a Leonard and that story had already been written—and it did not have a happy ending.

As if she needed any more proof that her crush was entirely one-sided, throughout the rest of her freshman year, Holt had never spoken to her again. And when he'd initiated conversation with her at the hospital earlier, it had been readily apparent that he didn't remember her from that day nearly a dozen years earlier.

And why would he?

While she'd spent the next ten months crushing on him from afar, he'd been living his life. Cowboying at his family's ranch, prepping for college, hanging with his friends and dating all the prettiest girls in school.

But he was here with her now, and still waiting for an answer to his question.

"Yes," she agreed.

Chapter Four

Holt gestured for the bill.

While Tess was digging her wallet out of her purse, he was already offering his credit card.

"I'm not letting you pay for my dinner," she said.

He took his receipt from the bartender. "Too late."

She huffed out a breath as he stood up, offering his hand to help her off her stool. He continued to hold onto her as they made their way to the door, and Tess knew that their synchronized exit had not gone unnoticed.

People would talk, as they always did. But in that moment, she didn't care. In that moment, nothing mattered except that her wildest dreams were about to come true.

But when they stepped outside and Holt immediately turned toward the adjacent Outlaw Inn, she balked.

"I can't walk in there with you," she told him.

"Do you want me to carry you?" he asked, obviously teasing.

She blushed. "My uncle owns the hotel, and I know most of the people who work there. If someone sees me with you…"

"Are you saying that you've changed your mind?"

"No," she said. "I'm saying that I don't want the front desk clerk telling everyone she knows that I went up to your room."

He considered the situation for a minute. "What if I check in alone and then text you my room number?"

"That would work," she agreed, ridiculously relieved that he hadn't been put off by her hesitation.

Another woman might not have been fazed by the prospect of being named Holt Chandler's latest conquest, but Tess wasn't another woman. Abby Barrett had impressed upon her daughters the importance of ensuring they didn't become the subject of gossip or scandal, and not even the promise of being with Holt Chandler could compel her to ignore those deeply ingrained lessons.

"Then I'm going to need your number," he said, opening his contacts list and offering her his phone.

She punched in her details.

He tucked his phone away again, then drew her into his arms so that they were aligned from chest to thigh, and everything inside her quivered.

She tipped her head back to meet his gaze. "What…um… what are you doing?"

"It occurred to me, obviously belatedly, that I should have at least kissed you before inviting you back to my room."

"That's the more usual order of things," Tess acknowledged.

"This hasn't been a usual day," he pointed out. "But I'd like to kiss you now, if you have no objections."

"No." She swallowed. "No objections."

"Good," he said.

There was nothing tentative about his kiss. It was the kiss of a man who knew how to both tempt and please a woman, and she felt certain that when they parted ways in the morning, she wouldn't be disappointed. But for now, he seemed content to simply kiss her, and she was content to let him.

She'd never known a kiss could generate so much heat, but it pumped through her system like molten lava, making her burn for him. Somehow, without her being aware, his hands had found their way beneath the hem of the T-shirt under her sweater to her breasts. Through the silky lace barrier of her bra, his thumbs rubbed back and forth over the already peaked nipples as his tongue danced and dallied with hers.

He kissed her until her knees were weak and her mind was

blank, and when he finally eased his mouth from hers, it was to trail kisses along her jaw, down her throat, raising goose bumps on her flesh and making her shiver. "I want you, Tess."

She knew he did—she could feel the press of his erection at the juncture of her thighs. And she wanted him, too. More than she could remember ever wanting another man. So much so that her panties were already damp, her body aching.

"Now might be a good time to get that room," she suggested, when she managed to catch her breath.

"Good call," he agreed.

But first, he kissed her again, slowly and deeply.

"Promise me you aren't going anywhere," he said, finally ending the kiss to whisper the words against her lips.

"The only place I'm going is to the room number you text to me," she assured him.

"Five minutes," he said, then kissed her one more time—a brief, hard press of his lips—before he stepped back and turned away.

Of course, as soon as Holt was gone and Tess's head cleared enough to allow her to form a coherent thought, she started to second-guess her impulsive acceptance of his invitation.

Was she really going to go to his hotel room knowing full well that she'd be naked and in his bed within minutes of crossing the threshold?

She'd never had a one-night stand, and she wasn't proud of the fact that she was on the verge of one now. Winona, her college roommate, had brought home a different random guy—and occasionally a random girl—every weekend. Tess had never judged her choices; she'd simply made different ones for herself. And she'd only ever shared her body with men with whom she'd been in an exclusive relationship—which was probably why she could count the number of intimate relationships she'd had on two fingers.

She didn't know much more than Holt's name—and the few additional details she had were common knowledge. He was a Chandler. His family were ranchers. Wealthy. He had two brothers and several cousins, most of whom resided at West River Ranch. Three generations living on the land and raising cattle together.

Actually, four generations, since Holt's oldest brother had become the father of twins. Boys, of course, because it seemed as if the Chandler men only ever fathered boys.

Aside from that general information, she knew that Holt kissed like a dream. She knew that when he looked at her, he made her heart pound and her knees weak. She knew that he made her want like she'd never wanted before. And maybe she'd have regrets in the morning, but she suspected she'd regret it more if she didn't seize this once-in-a-lifetime opportunity.

Her phone vibrated in her hand, startling her so much she nearly dropped it.

3C

That was the extent of his message, but what had she expected? A heart-eyed emoji? Hugs and kisses?

This wasn't going to be a romantic seduction, and if she expected one, she was going to be disappointed.

A second message immediately followed.

Keycard required for entry. I'll prop open the back door on my way up.

She stayed in the shadows as she made her way around the building. She entered through the open door, then secured it behind her. A long hallway stretched ahead, and she knew if she followed it, she'd find herself in the reception area. Immediately to her left was a door marked Basement, and just beyond that access was a staircase leading to the upper floors.

She paused with her foot on the bottom step, taking a moment to attempt to calm her racing heart. Breathing in deeply, she caught the faint scent of lemons, no doubt from the oil that had been used to polish the wood trim to a high gleam. The carpeted stairs muffled her footsteps—or maybe it was only that she couldn't hear anything over the beating of her own heart.

There were pictures in heavy wood frames on the walls of the staircase—and more as she made her way down the hall on the third floor, looking for the door marked 3C. Sepia-tinted cowboys with bushy eyebrows and heavy mustaches, beaten up hats on their heads and neckerchiefs knotted around their throats. Some had rifles tucked in the crooks of their arms while others were on horseback with mountains in the background. There was a rodeo competitor on the back of a bucking bronco; a lonely heart strumming a guitar; a weary traveler with a shot glass in hand and a bottle of whiskey at the ready; a gambler staring at the cards fanned out in his hand; a trio of saloon girls in fancy dresses with low-cut bodices and ruffled skirts.

According to family lore, Tess's great-great-grandmother had been a saloon girl. Not a prostitute, though many assumed the painted ladies supplemented their income by also working in the rooms above the bar. The truth was, saloon girls made good money selling drinks to the patrons and didn't need to sell their bodies, but the genteel ladies of town liked to believe they did, no doubt so that they could feel superior.

Tess came from a long line of women who were accustomed to being made to feel inferior. As Miranda Chandler had attempted to do in their brief interaction at the hospital.

But tonight Holt Chandler had invited her to come back to his room. Tonight she'd been chosen. And if that didn't make her feel superior, it at least made her feel special. And maybe, a tiny part of Tess acknowledged, accepting his invitation and sharing his bed was akin to giving a metaphorical middle finger to the woman who'd made it clear she didn't think Tess was good enough to be in the same room with her son.

Holt must have been watching through the peephole for her

arrival, because he opened the door before she had a chance to knock.

"I was starting to worry that you'd gotten lost," he said, stepping back so that she could enter. "Or changed your mind."

"I'm here now. And I haven't changed my mind." But her heart was pounding with a combination of anticipation and trepidation as she crossed the threshold.

"I'm glad," he said, with a warm smile that somehow succeeded in both amping up her anticipation and quieting her trepidation.

She managed to smile back as she glanced around the room.

Of course, the centerpiece was the king-size four-poster bed covered by a thick duvet decorated with a dark blue brocade bed scarf and coordinating throw pillows. On either side of the bed were antique tables with bronze lamps. On the adjacent wall, between two windows, was a mahogany piecrust table holding a porcelain vase filled with yellow lilies, green roses and white carnations. Twin wingchairs upholstered in the same fabric as the bed scarf flanked the table. On the wall facing the bed was a long antique dresser above which was mounted a flat-screen television, and beside the dresser was a glass-front minifridge, the two appliances being the only evidence that the room existed in the twenty-first century rather than the nineteenth.

Holt watched Tess survey the room, her gaze quickly skittering away from the enormous bed that served as its centerpiece, making him think that—despite her assertion to the contrary—she *was* having second thoughts about being here with him. It was understandable if she was. They were practically strangers who'd met only a handful of hours earlier—because he didn't think one brief interaction almost a dozen years earlier in high school miraculously changed their status from new acquaintances to old friends.

"Can I get you something to drink?" Holt asked, hoping to put her at ease. "There's a fully stocked minibar."

She shook her head. "I'm fine. But you go ahead, if you want."

"I don't want another drink," he admitted. "But I also didn't want to jump your bones as soon as you walked through the door."

"Oh."

"Of course, I could hardly blame you for thinking that I have absolutely no finesse," he acknowledged. "My proposition to you was rather…direct."

"Less chance for misinterpretation that way," she noted.

"Still, I feel like I need to clarify something."

"What's that?"

"I didn't know who you were when our paths crossed at the hospital earlier," he said. "But I knew who you were when I sat down beside you at the bar."

"You mean you know who my grandmother is," she concluded, her cheeks burning.

He nodded.

"That's why you invited me to come up here," she surmised. "Because you figured Tallulah Leonard's granddaughter would be an easy lay."

"No," he immediately denied, shaking his head. "I invited you to come up here because I haven't wanted another woman as much as I wanted you—the first minute I saw you—in a very long time. And finding out who you are didn't change that at all."

"Thank you?" she said dubiously.

"And never have I fumbled so horribly with a woman as I'm fumbling right now," he confided.

"Well, I haven't walked out the door," she pointed out.

"Not yet," he agreed.

Her lips curved, just a little. "Maybe I will have a drink," she decided. "If there's a Diet Coke in the minibar."

"There is." He opened the fridge and pulled out a small can. "What can I mix it with for you?"

"Straight up works for me."

His brows lifted as he popped the tab to open the can. "You said you were a freshman when I was a senior, so unless you skipped a lot of grades, I'm guessing that you are old enough to drink?"

"I'm twenty-six," she told him. "Just not much of a drinker."

She wasn't the only person he knew who chose not to imbibe, though he found himself wondering if her grandmother's reputed alcoholism was the reason for her choice. Not that he was going to make the mistake of mentioning Tallulah Leonard again.

"Fair enough," he said instead, offering her the soda that he'd poured into a glass.

"Thanks." She lifted it to her lips and sipped.

"Is that what you were drinking at the bar?" he asked now.

"It's my evening drink of choice," she confirmed.

"So what do you drink in the morning?"

She set the glass aside and lifted her arms to link them behind his head, drawing his mouth down to hers. "Why don't you ask me in the morning?"

Tess woke up early, aware that she'd made a very big mistake. She didn't regret spending the night with Holt—because how could she regret what had been, without a shadow of a doubt, the most incredible night of her life? Not just *a* fantasy but *all* her fantasies come true. But the fact that she didn't regret making love with Holt didn't mean it was any less of a mistake.

He might have lamented a few fumbles and missteps on the road to getting naked, but once their bodies were entwined in his bed, it was clear that the man did not need any kind of playbook. Truth be told, he had some serious skills in the lovemaking department, touching her in ways that made her wonder if she'd ever been touched before and making her feel things she was sure she'd never felt before.

Looking at him now, stretched out on the opposite side of

the bed, facedown on the mattress, she realized that she didn't know the protocol for the morning after a one-night stand.

Should she stay or should she go?

If she stayed, there was the potential for awkward morning-after conversation.

If she went, she might never see him again.

Okay, that was certainly an exaggeration considering that they both lived in the same town. However, he spent most of his time at West River Ranch while she lived and worked in town, so the opportunities for their paths to cross were limited.

In the end, she decided to avoid the awkward morning-after conversation and slipped out of bed to collect her discarded clothing. She took inventory as she gathered up the items: sweater, T-shirt, socks, underwear, jeans.

Where was her bra?

She caught a glimpse of pink satin peeking out from beneath his pillow and acknowledged that she now faced another dilemma.

The bra was from Victoria's Secret—fairly new and not inexpensive. And as she wasn't a woman who could comfortably walk around braless, she tiptoed closer to the bed again and hooked a finger around the strap, giving it a gentle tug.

The garment didn't move—but Holt did.

He shifted on the mattress and she took an instinctive step back, exhaling a quiet sigh when he remained asleep.

Apparently, she was leaving without her bra.

She quickly donned the rest of her clothing, trying not to let herself be distracted by the naked man still sprawled in bed. Not an easy task as the sheet was now shoved down to his waist, leaving his broad shoulders and muscled back exposed.

The man was impressively built—all taut muscle and bronzed skin. She'd studied anatomy extensively to attain her DPT degree, but nothing she'd read in any of the textbooks had prepared her for the sheer masculine muscular perfection of Holt Chandler. And he knew just how to use that body—and his hands and his lips—to take a woman to heights of pleasure she might previously only have imagined.

With sincere regret that their time together was at an end, she tucked her feet into her boots, picked up her purse and slipped out the door with fingers crossed that her departure would be as unobtrusive as her arrival.

Holt needed to get back to the ranch.

Now that he'd seen his grandfather and been reassured that Raylan was on his way to recovery, there was no reason to hang around the hospital any longer.

No reason except that he was hoping to see Tess again.

He'd been looking for comfort and companionship when he invited her to join him at the hotel the night before. He'd had an awful day that he wanted to forget, at least for a few hours, in the pleasure of mindless sex. It was possible that any woman might have fit the bill, though the truth was he hadn't been with a woman in…months, he realized with some surprise now.

It used to be that he was out at a bar or a club every weekend, if not with a woman then looking for one. But somewhere along the line—perhaps as he'd marched further away from twenty and closer to thirty—he'd grown bored with casual relationships and meaningless hookups.

Not that he was in any hurry to settle down. While he'd always assumed that marriage and kids would figure somewhere in his future, that future was still somewhere far in the distance. But for now, he might be ready for a steady relationship with someone with whom he could enjoy the occasional quiet night at home instead of every night out.

He'd experienced a brief pang of disappointment when he woke up in the morning to find that Tess was already gone. Though, like Cinderella, she'd left something behind in her haste to escape. Something a lot more tantalizing than a glass slipper.

As he'd examined the satin-and-lace garment he'd discovered beneath his pillow, he couldn't help but remember the way she'd sighed and arched in pleasure as he suckled her breasts through the cups. Which, of course, led to recalling her throaty moans when he unhooked the closure and dispensed with the fabric barrier to put his mouth on her bare flesh. Those moans had coursed through his system like a drug, making his blood race and his heart pound, and just the echo of those sounds in his mind was enough to make him hard again.

If she'd been there with him when he'd woken up, he might have had the pleasure of making love with her again—hence his disappointment. Even if they'd already used the condom from his wallet and the one from her purse, a man and a woman could have a lot of fun without needing to insert Tab A into Slot B.

Even as that thought formed, something niggled at the back of his mind… But whatever that *something* was, it remained elusive, so he pushed it aside and continued toward the rehab wing of the hospital.

Holt wasn't in the habit of chasing after a woman, and he wouldn't be here now except that it didn't feel right to go back to West River Ranch without at least saying goodbye to the woman who'd shared his bed. And sure, he had her number, but sending a text message to say "thanks for last night" seemed a bit crass.

The doors automatically parted as he approached, and he spotted Tess farther down the hall. Even with her back to him, he recognized her bouncy ponytail. And though the boxy scrubs she wore—teal today—disguised her feminine curves, he couldn't help but smile as he recalled the pleasure he'd found in examining every inch of her delectable body.

It wasn't surprising that he didn't remember her from high school—especially if the brief encounter she'd described had been their only interaction. He'd been part of a fairly large social group that didn't require him to look outside of it for company or companionship. Even when he dated, it was almost exclusively from within that group, though he was careful to never date any one girl for long enough that she might start thinking of a future for them together.

He knew his parents had met—and started dating—in high school, and while he was glad it had worked out for them, Holt hadn't been anywhere near ready to settle down then. He still wasn't ready, but he was more open to considering the possibility of an exclusive relationship with the right woman.

But even though the chemistry with Tess had been off the charts, the history between their families precluded any possibility of a future with her. Which raised the question—why was he seeking her out now? What was the point of pretending they could ever share anything more than the one night they'd already spent together?

It was that disappointing but nevertheless undeniable fact that made him resolve to walk past her, as if he didn't see her and hadn't taken this specific route through the hospital in hope of running into her.

A plan that fell apart when she caught sight of him. Her eyes widened and her lips started to curve, suggesting that she was surprised but also pleased to see him. Her smile made his heart knock hard against his ribs and made him wish—if only for a minute—that he might be wrong to dismiss the prospect of seeing her again.

Then someone else stepped into view, approaching Tess from the opposite direction. He frowned as he recognized Jordan Denninger. The other man had been a couple years behind Holt in high school, so he didn't know him well, but Jordan's brother, Jarrod, had been in some of his classes—and once put the moves on a girl that Holt was dating.

Déjà vu, he thought, as Jordan intercepted Tess.

Except that it wasn't, because he and Tess weren't dating.

They were simply two people who'd spent one night together.

So Holt kept walking, not meeting her gaze and not saying a word as he moved past her to the exit.

Chapter Five

Tess knew better than to let her emotions make decisions for her. And while she never thought she'd be happy to see Jordan Denninger, when Holt walked by—pretending he didn't even see her!—she'd gratefully turned to the other man, eager for even a brief moment of distraction from the unexpectedly painful rejection. Which was how she'd found herself impulsively accepting his invitation to dinner.

Definitely an emotional decision.

And a regrettable one.

But if she hadn't enjoyed the evening, it wasn't his fault. He'd been attentive and charming and the meal at The Hideaway had lived up to the restaurant's exceptional reputation. Unfortunately, the whole while she'd been with Jordan, she couldn't stop thinking about Holt.

Thinking that once again she'd let herself be fooled by a man who'd feigned interest only long enough to get her into bed and then completely forgotten about her.

Not that Holt was entirely to blame. When she'd agreed to go to his hotel room, they'd both known it was a one-night thing. But she'd thought there was a real connection between them, and it had hurt to discover that she'd not only been wrong about that, she'd been dismissed.

When Jordan dropped her off at the house she shared with Meg and Emma on Walnut Street, he'd offered to walk her to the door—tried to insist on it, in fact. But Tess leaned across the center console to give him a quick kiss on the cheek before letting herself out of his vehicle.

"I hope you weren't waiting up for me," Tess said, when she found her roommate snuggled deep in one of the matching Adirondack chairs on the front porch with a knitted blanket on her lap.

"I'm not in the habit of going to bed before nine o'clock," Meg said dryly.

"You're also not in the habit of sitting outside in the dark."

"It's a nice night."

"It is," Tess agreed, settling into the vacant chair beside her friend. "It's too bad Buddy can't be out here with you, but obviously you don't want him barking at some random passerby and waking up Emma."

Meg lifted a brow. "Buddy?"

"Our dog."

"I figured that from the barking part," Meg acknowledged. "But when did we get a dog?"

"I wasn't clear on that detail," Tess admitted.

"Okay—*why* did we get a dog?"

"Because two women living alone with a young child felt that a dog would provide companionship and security."

"That's reasonable," her friend agreed. "And why did we name him Buddy?"

Tess shrugged. "It seemed an appropriate name for a loyal companion."

"Not very creative, though," Meg remarked.

"I was under pressure."

"So what kind of dog is Buddy?"

"A mixed breed. From the local rescue, of course."

"Of course." Her friend sounded equally baffled and amused. "Now I'm going to have to go to the rescue tomorrow to look at dogs."

"Emma would love to have a dog, but she wouldn't be the one taking care of him."

"I'll take care of him," Tess promised.

Meg rolled her eyes. "Sometimes I feel like I have two kids."

"I'll feed him and walk him and—"

"We're not getting a dog," Meg said firmly. "And we're definitely not getting a dog just because you lied about having a dog to a guy you're never going to go out with again, anyway."

"What makes you so sure I won't go out with Jordan again?"

"The fact that you lied about having a dog so he wouldn't walk you to the door and kiss you good-night."

"It's scary how well you know me," Tess said.

"What I don't know is why you agreed to go out with him tonight," Meg said.

Tess sighed. "It was Holt Chandler's fault."

"How is he responsible for you having dinner with another man?"

"I'm kind of curious to hear the answer to that question myself."

Tess and Meg gasped simultaneously in response to the male voice coming from somewhere in the darkness.

Holt stepped forward then, climbing the four steps leading to the porch so that he was standing in the soft light that spilled out through the living room window, his hands in the air in the universal gesture of surrender.

"My apologies, ladies," he said. "I didn't mean to scare you."

"Then you shouldn't have snuck up on us," Meg admonished sternly.

"I didn't sneak," he denied. "I walked from my car, parked across the street, directly up the flagstone path."

Meg narrowed her gaze at their visitor. "I told you that I'd have Tess call you when she got home."

"Wait—what?" Tess said, confused.

"He stopped by earlier, looking for you," her friend explained.

"Why?" Tess asked, directing her question to Holt this time.

"I wanted to talk to you," he said.

"I got the impression earlier today that you had nothing to say to me," she noted.

"There was a lot I wanted to say, but I didn't know how to say it."

"But you've figured it out now?" she asked dubiously.

"Not really," he admitted. "But the one thing I know is that I want to see you again."

"Again?" Meg pounced on that word like a hungry cat on a fat mouse. "When did… *Oh.*" Her eyes shifted from Tess to Holt and back again. "Last night?"

"Can we talk about this later?" Tess asked her friend.

"You texted to say you weren't coming home, but you didn't say *why,*" Meg noted, apparently not willing to wait until later to continue the conversation. "And in all the time that we've lived together, you've never not come home."

"*Later,*" Tess said again. "Please."

"Fine," Meg agreed. "It's just that I was worried." Her gaze shifted to Holt again. "I was worried."

"Because she never doesn't come home?" he guessed.

Meg nodded. "And she doesn't ever bring guys back here, either. She says it's because she wants to set a good example for Emma—my daughter. But the truth is, she hasn't even had a date in…at least six months."

"I was on a date tonight," Tess felt compelled to remind them both.

"And home before nine o'clock."

"I have to work tomorrow."

"You don't work on Fridays," Meg pointed out.

"I have a meeting with my boss tomorrow," Tess clarified.

And if the meeting wasn't until the afternoon, that wasn't anyone's business but her own.

"You had to work today, too," her friend noted. "But you still stayed out last night."

"But she was in bed before ten," Holt said with a wink.

Meg grinned and settled deeper into her chair. "Now the story's getting interesting."

"Shouldn't you go check on Emma?" Tess said pointedly.

Her friend gestured to the baby monitor on the windowsill. "She hasn't made a peep since she went down tonight."

"Maybe you should check on her, anyway."

"She's trying to get rid of me," Meg said to Holt. "As if I'm not her best friend and she won't recount every word of your conversation to me later."

Holt chuckled. "No secrets between you two, huh?"

"None," she confirmed.

"Excuse me while I go put an ad on Craigslist for a new best friend," Tess interjected.

"Okay, I'm going." Meg scooped up her blanket and the baby monitor, then paused with her hand on the doorknob to look at Holt again. "It was nice to meet you, Holt Chandler."

"Though no official introductions were made, I have to say—the pleasure was mine, Meg…"

"Wheeler," she supplied.

"I look forward to seeing you again," he added.

"I really hope you do."

Tess waited until the door closed behind her friend before turning to Holt.

"You had something you wanted to say?" she prompted.

"I did," he confirmed. "But first, I want to know how I bear any responsibility for your decision to go out with Jordan Denninger tonight."

"He caught me at a weak moment," she admitted. "When I was feeling foolish and rejected because the man I'd spent the night with walked by as if he didn't see me."

"Did you spend the night?" he challenged. "Because when I woke up, you were gone."

"I spent the night," she assured him. "But I had to leave early so that I could shower and change before going back to work."

"You probably needed new undergarments, too, because you

left this—" he pulled a pink satin bra out of his pocket, dangling the strap from a fingertip "—in my bed."

She snatched it from his hand and shoved it into her purse, hopefully before Ramona Martin—whose nose was pressed to the glass of the window facing her neighbors' porch—could figure out what it was. Thankfully, the retired librarian's eyesight wasn't what it used to be, when she could spot a contraband candy bar hidden behind a textbook from the resource desk twenty feet away.

"I walked through the rehab wing on purpose, on my way out of the hospital, because I was hoping to see you," Holt confided now.

Her gaze narrowed suspiciously. "So why did you pretend that you didn't?"

"Because by the time I got there, I was starting to have doubts about the wisdom of seeking you out."

"And yet, you're here now," she noted.

"Because I haven't stopped thinking about you all day," he confessed.

"I'd say that's a *you* problem, because I have no desire to be with someone who makes me question my own worth."

"Is that why you went out with Jordan?"

She shrugged. "He was pretty clear about what he wanted."

His gaze skimmed over her, slowly, provocatively. "I thought I was pretty clear about what I wanted last night."

"Then you got what you wanted last night and did a one-eighty today."

"I acted like an ass," he acknowledged.

"Yes, you did," she agreed.

"And I'm sorry."

"I appreciate and accept the apology," she said. "But now I really do need to call it a night."

"How about tomorrow? Can I see you then?"

"No."

His brows lifted. "Don't you want to at least check your calendar before you give me the brush-off?"

"No," she said again. "Because even if I have no plans—" and the sad fact was that she didn't "—I have no intention of making plans with you."

"Ouch."

"You know who I am," she reminded him. "So you know there are a lot of people in this town—not to mention your family—who'd have something to say if we started spending time together."

"I don't care."

"You don't have to care, because you're a Chandler and you live and work at West River Ranch," she pointed out. "I'm the one who'd have to listen to the snickers and bear the weight of community judgment."

He didn't deny that was true. Instead, he said, "I don't think we should give other people the power to decide what we want."

"I'm already a notch on your bedpost," she reminded him. "Shouldn't you be scouting for a new conquest?"

"I don't even have bedposts, and if I did, I wouldn't put notches—literal or figurative—on them. I've also never been given the brush-off by a woman who spent a night in my bed," he noted with a frown. "Were you disappointed in some way?"

"Now you're just fishing for compliments," she said accusingly.

"So you weren't disappointed?" he pressed.

"You know I wasn't," she told him.

"So give me a chance to not disappoint you again," he said, with a playful wink.

"I don't think so."

His smile faded. "I'm not going to beg you to go out with me."

"I would hope not," she said.

"But I might point out that the boy who made a positive

impression on your first day of high school deserves a second chance."

She refused to let him see that her resolve was wavering.

Because no matter how much she wanted to spend more time with him, there really wasn't any point. Because no amount of wishing or hoping could change who they were or the history between their families.

Instead, she only said, "Good night, Holt."

Then she walked into the house, closing the door behind her.

He should have gone straight home.

But for reasons he couldn't begin to fathom, when he left Tess's house, Holt found himself back at The Bootlegger, sitting on the same stool that he'd occupied the night before.

But the bartender was different tonight. Female. Brunette. Pretty. Perky.

She folded her arms on the bar and leaned forward to ask him what he wanted. The deliberate pose pushed her breasts together, giving the customers at the bar an eyeful of impressive cleavage visible above the low scoop neck of her top.

She flirted with Holt while she poured his whiskey and announced that she had no plans after work, if he wanted to stick around.

"What time does the bar close?" he asked, more out of curiosity than because he had any intention of accepting her offer.

"Midnight tonight," she said. "But Denim & Diamonds is open until two, if you wanted to head there for a drink afterward."

"Mornings come early on the ranch," he said regretfully.

Her smile only widened. "So could you, if you spend the night with me," she said with a wink.

Her blatant interest was a balm to his ego—still smarting from Tess Barrett's rejection. A reminder that he could have any woman he wanted. Or almost any woman.

The problem was, he only wanted Tess.

"I really do need to get some sleep tonight," he said.

She pouted, but her gaze was thoughtful as she studied him. "You're not thinking about sleep," she surmised. "You're thinking about a woman."

"You can hardly blame a man for such thoughts when a beautiful one is standing right in front of him," he said lightly.

"That's a pretty good line," she said. "But you didn't try very hard to sell it."

"Sorry," he said. "It's been a long day."

"She break your heart?"

"Who?"

"The woman on your mind."

He didn't bother to attempt another denial. "No."

"Dent your ego?" she pressed.

He had to smile at that. "Maybe. Yeah."

"Then maybe you need to get back on the horse again, cowboy."

"I'll give that some thought," he promised, pulling his wallet out of his back pocket.

He set some money on the bar to pay for the drink, including a generous tip, but—cognizant of Tess's admonition about drinking and driving—left the whiskey untouched and walked out the door.

Meg was pouring hot water into the teapot when Tess made her way inside—a telltale sign that she anticipated a long conversation, and Tess prepared herself to be grilled more thoroughly than the steak she'd had for dinner.

"How's Emma doing?" she asked, not only because she was hoping to postpone her friend's inquisition but also because she hadn't had a chance to talk to Meg since she'd left The Bootlegger the night before at the behest of the little girl.

"She's fine." Meg carried the pot and two mugs to the table. "She settled right down after her bath tonight."

"And last night?" Tess prompted.

"Just the usual separation anxiety," her friend confided, pouring the tea. "When she's awake, she understands that the bad man is gone forever. But sometimes her dreams take her back to that night, and if I'm not there when she wakes up..."

Tess reached across the table to squeeze her cousin's hand.

She knew all about *the bad man* and *that night*—when Meg learned that a restraining order was no defense against an unstable ex-husband with a gun. Both mother and daughter had been traumatized by what happened, but Tess worried that the little girl's ongoing nightmares held them both back from healing.

"What does Dr. Halstead say?"

"That the nightmares are her brain's way of attempting to heal from the trauma and she's doing great."

"Maybe you should call him in the middle of the night when Emma wakes up screaming."

Her friend managed a small smile. "Which happens much less frequently these days, so I guess we are doing better, if not great.

"And that's enough about that," Meg said firmly. "Now I want to hear about your night with Holt Chandler."

Tess covered her face with her hands and spread her fingers to peek out between them. "Are you judging me?"

"I'm not," her friend promised. "Or, if I am, I'm giving you top marks."

She had to smile at that, though her smile was weary.

"But I'm going to need some details before I can finalize your score," her friend teased. "And you should start at the very beginning."

"The beginning would be when he came into the bar last night, after you left, and sat down on the stool you vacated," Tess began her recital of the facts. "He then proceeded to have a few drinks, decided to stay at the inn rather than drive back to the ranch, invited me to his room and I said *yes*."

Meg sighed wistfully. "I guess some dreams do come true."

"That's what I thought last night, too," she admitted.

"And now?"

"Now… I almost wish that I'd left the bar when you did."

Meg frowned. "You're not honestly telling me that Holt Chandler is lousy in bed?"

"No," Tess said. "He was…amazing. But I left while he was still sleeping, and when our paths crossed at the hospital later, he pretended not to see me."

Her friend winced in sympathy. "Harsh."

Tess nodded. "I shouldn't have been surprised, but I was. And then I was so mad—or possibly hurt—I impulsively accepted Jordan Derringer's invitation to dinner."

"And then, when you got back from dinner, Holt was here… to apologize and tell you that he wanted to see you again?" Meg guessed.

Tess responded with another nod.

"So when are you seeing him again?" her friend prompted.

"I'm not."

"Why not?" Meg demanded.

"Because he's Raylan Chandler's grandson and I'm Tallulah Leonard's granddaughter," she said.

And the Chandler family had roots and respect in Whispering Canyon, while Tess's pedigree was dubious at best. Though her mother had been married to her father fifteen months before Sage was born—and Tess had followed a full two years later—she knew that she and her sister would forever be known as Tallulah Leonard's granddaughters and assumed to be women of questionable character and loose morals, like the woman who'd allegedly ignored Raylan Chandler's marital status when she set out to seduce him.

Nine months after their short-lived affair, Tallulah gave birth to his child and allegedly attempted to blackmail him to keep that fact a secret. A plan that backfired spectacularly when Raylan and Eleanor petitioned for custody of the baby.

Whether Tallulah couldn't bear the thought of losing custody of Wyatt or simply didn't want to lose the court battle with Raylan, she packed up and left town with the baby in the darkness of night. Raylan had hired a team of investigators to find his son, but Tallulah hadn't stayed in any one place long enough for them to track her down, and it was almost eight years later before she was located in Humboldt, Tennessee. By that time, Wyatt had two younger sisters—Abby, who was Tess's mom, and Sunny, who was Meg's mom—each with different fathers.

"Yes, you're Tallulah Leonard's granddaughter," Meg acknowledged. Her tone was brisk but not unsympathetic, because that was a branch they shared on the same family tree. "But you're also Tess Barrett. Smart and sexy, warm and kind, fun and loyal and so much more. And obviously he's aware of at least some of your amazing qualities, because he wants to see you again."

"I slept with him a couple hours after meeting him in a bar," Tess reminded her friend. "He wants to see me again because he thinks I'm easy."

Meg laughed at that. "If only he knew the truth."

"Well, I was easy with him," she confided. "Probably because I've never experienced such an intense attraction to anyone before. I swear, the first time he touched me, I got so overheated, I half expected my clothes to melt away."

"Tell me more," her friend urged.

So Tess obliged, because Meg was her best friend and there were some things that a woman just had to share with her best friend. But she didn't go into too much detail, and she didn't confide—didn't want to even think about—the fact that she and Holt had come together three times in the night…but they'd only had two condoms.

Chapter Six

Any thoughts Holt might have had about dropping into bed when he got home were waylaid by the discovery of his middle brother sitting in his living room, watching a baseball game on TV.

"Come on in. Make yourself at home," Holt said dryly.

"Thanks, I think I will," Flynn replied, not shifting from his position in the center of his brother's sofa, his feet propped up on the coffee table.

Holt made his way to the kitchen, where he opened the refrigerator and took out two bottles of beer. Returning to the living room, he offered one to Flynn. "What are you doing here?"

His brother responded with a gesture toward to the TV.

"Since when do you care about—" Holt glanced at the screen to see who was playing "—the Mariners or the Rangers?"

"I don't," Flynn admitted. "I just needed a distraction."

When he returned from Afghanistan, Flynn had chosen to move into a rustic cabin in the foothills, insisting that he didn't want anything fancy, just a place to lay his head. He'd later confided to Holt that most nights he didn't even sleep in the bed their mom had ordered to be delivered to the cabin, complaining that the mattress was too damn soft for a man accustomed to sleeping on the ground with a rucksack for a pillow.

It was a rare—and very limited—glimpse into the time he'd spent overseas. Aside from that, Holt knew very little about his brother's experiences in the army, but he knew that when he came home, riddled with bullets, the doctors hadn't been optimistic about his chances of survival. Flynn had surprised them all. But while his body had healed, his spirit still struggled with the fact that he'd come home without Ellis, the cousin who'd enlisted with him right out of high school.

Holt lowered himself into one of the chairs that flanked the sofa, frowning as he realized that his brother's presence in his living room had distracted him from a notable absence.

"Where's my dog?"

"At the main house with Grams and Willow."

"Sulking because I didn't come home last night," Holt surmised.

"No, being a guard dog."

"Because Gramps is in the hospital?"

"And because someone ransacked the house yesterday," his brother said in a matter-of-fact tone.

"For real?"

Flynn nodded. "While we were at the hospital."

Holt frowned. "Seems like an unlikely coincidence."

His brother nodded again. "In fact, I'd guess not a coincidence at all."

"Was anything taken?"

"Some of Grams's jewelry—the stuff she kept in that glass tray on her dresser—including her mother's locket. Not that it's worth a lot of money, but it meant a lot to her. Most of her valuable stuff—the pearl choker she wore when she and Gramps got married and the diamond ring he gave her for their fiftieth anniversary—was locked up in the safe. Either the thief didn't find it or couldn't get into it, because it was untouched."

"Thief—singular?"

Now his brother shrugged. "That's the theory, as there are several obviously valuable—but big—items that were overlooked."

"Easier to take if you've got someone to help you carry them," Holt mused. "I assume the sheriff was called?"

"Yeah," Flynn confirmed. "Not that Garvey did much. Took a look around. Asked for an inventory of missing items. Promised to notify the local pawn shops to be on the lookout for anything on the list."

"Good to know he's earning his salary," Holt said dryly.

"He also pissed off Grams."

"How'd he manage that?"

"Asked if the missing items were insured. Noted that everyone happened to be out of the house at the same time, implying it might have been an inside job."

"Jesus." Holt shook his head. "The man isn't just incompetent—he's an idiot."

"Grams responded with something like, 'Yeah, it was real convenient that my husband was shot.' Garvey wasn't even smart enough to backpedal. He continued pressing, saying it was odd that the family had had such an unfortunate run of luck and suggested they should install an alarm system."

"As if it was a random break-in perpetrated by some drifter wandering by." Which, of course, it wasn't. The main house at West River Ranch was far enough from the main road to discourage even routine canvassing or soliciting.

"Grams kicked Garvey out," Flynn continued. "But his questions got me thinking that maybe the shooting wasn't an accident."

"You can't believe someone was trying to kill Gramps," Holt protested.

"Maybe the intent wasn't to kill but to wound—to ensure the rest of us would follow the ambulance to the hospital, leaving the ranch vulnerable."

"Vulnerable except for half a dozen hands," he pointed out.

"Half a dozen hands occupied with usual ranch business who'd have no reason to be up near the house," his brother countered.

"You're suggesting not just a shooting and a break-in but a conspiracy," Holt realized.

"Just something to think about," Flynn said. "If you can tear your thoughts away from a certain sexy blonde long enough to think about anything else."

"What sexy blonde?" he asked, feigning ignorance.

Flynn's snort told Holt his brother wasn't fooled for a minute. "Your dog isn't the only one who noticed that you didn't come home last night."

"I'm touched you're keeping tabs on me."

Flynn snorted again. "I stopped at The Bootlegger last night to pick up food and saw you cozied up with her at the bar."

"I didn't see you there."

"Because you were cozied up with the sexy blonde."

"There were a lot of people there last night," Holt hedged. "I'm not even sure I remember a blonde."

"You don't remember Tess Barrett? The same woman you were talking to at the hospital yesterday afternoon?"

Holt's gaze narrowed. "How do you know Tess?"

"Now the wheels are turning," Flynn noted.

"If you've got something to say, say it."

"Some people might object to you spending time with Tallulah Leonard's granddaughter," his brother said.

"Are you one of them?"

Flynn shook his head. "My only concern is for Tess."

Holt's brows lifted. "So much for family loyalty."

"You're a Chandler, which means there's no shortage of people who've got your back," Flynn pointed out. "The same can't be said for Tess."

"I don't know about that," Holt said. "Her best friend-slash-cousin-slash-roommate seems like she'd go to the mat for her."

"Sure, because Megan grew up in Whispering Canyon, too, where, sixty years later, people haven't forgotten that Tallulah Leonard got knocked up by a married man and tried to blackmail him to keep quiet about the affair."

"That was hardly Tallulah's only—or even her worst—indiscretion."

"But they were *her* indiscretions, and yet her daughters and granddaughters continue to be judged for them."

"Which has nothing to do with me," Holt said.

"Or maybe it does, if you plan on seeing Tess again."

"I haven't closed the door on the possibility," he said, because no way was Holt going to admit to his brother that Tess had shut it for him.

"While you're thinking about it, think about what you want from her. If you're just looking for someone to mess around with, find someone else. Tess doesn't need the fallout of a failed relationship with Holt Chandler."

"Why are you assuming a relationship between us would fail?"

Flynn shrugged. "Your track record of failed relationships?"

"And why does it seem as if you know Tess better than I do?" he asked suspiciously.

"I don't know Tess at all," his brother said. "But I've gotten to know Megan a little bit in recent months."

Holt's brows lifted. "You've been fraternizing with a woman with a kid?"

Now Flynn shook his head. "It's not like that."

"What's it like then?"

"We met at a meeting, okay? And that's all I'm going to say."

"Sorry." Holt held up his hands, aware that his brother didn't like to talk about his occasional attendance at sessions for trauma survivors at a local church. "I didn't mean to overstep."

"You didn't," Flynn said tersely. "It's fine."

"Anyway, I think what we all need to focus on right now is being there for Grams and Gramps," Holt said, attempting to shift the conversation back to more neutral ground.

"A good plan," Flynn agreed with a nod.

And maybe, Holt thought, as he settled in to watch the end of the baseball game with his brother, by the time his grandfather was home from the hospital and the man who'd shot him was behind bars, Tess Barrett would be nothing but a pleasant—and distant—memory.

Almost three weeks later, Tess hadn't stopped thinking about the night she'd spent with Holt Chandler. It didn't seem to matter that, in all that time, she hadn't heard a single word from him. He hadn't stopped by the house again. He hadn't even called or sent a text message.

And that was fine, she decided. She hadn't expected to hear from him.

But she did hear that, on the Saturday after the shooting, Raylan Chandler was released from the hospital to continue his recovery at home. Rumors and speculation continued to run rampant around the subject of the shooting, but so far there didn't seem to be any solid leads or suspects.

Patricia Reeves had gone home the same day as Raylan Chandler, though Tess continued to see the knee replacement patient on Monday afternoons at Peak Performance Physical & Massage Therapy, where she spent most of her time when she wasn't at the hospital. Usually, it was Jordan who brought his grandmother in for her therapy, and though he never missed an opportunity to flirt a little, she could tell that his interest had waned. In fact, on her most recent visit to the clinic, Patricia had warned Tess that her grandson had been on a couple of dates with Kellie Hart, the creative genius behind local bakery ♥ Cakes. Tess assured the woman that she was happy Jordan was happy.

When Patricia had gone, after her usual appointment Monday afternoon, Tess's boss called her into his office. As the most junior associate at Peak Performance, she only had a handful of patients who'd specifically requested to work with her—a former high school teacher with frozen shoulder, a coworker of her mom's who suffered chronic headaches, a longtime friend of her sister's who had sciatica—which meant that she was often assigned to work with patients that the senior therapists couldn't fit into their schedules. Tess didn't mind, and she was always willing to pick up extra hours at the clinic.

She was a little surprised, however, to hear that she was being assigned to help with Raylan Chandler's rehab. And even more so to learn that his therapy would take place at West River Ranch—which greatly increased her chances of crossing paths with Holt.

Or maybe it didn't.

After all, Holt was involved with the cattle ranching operations at West River while Tess's duties only required her to be at the main house, presumably some distance from wherever the cows would be grazing.

Still, she was a little apprehensive about the possibility of seeing him again. Not that there were any hard feelings between them. In fact, there were no feelings at all. Nothing but the fading memories of a single night together.

Except that the memories weren't fading.

Not for Tess, anyway.

Every day, images of the sexy cowboy intruded on her thoughts. And every night, memories of their night together stirred in her dreams.

So maybe it wasn't any wonder that she didn't sleep well the night before her first trip out to the ranch. After hitting the snooze button one too many times, she woke up groggy and already behind schedule. Then, when she was filling her travel mug, she spilled coffee on the sleeve of her blouse, forcing her to change her top, which further delayed her departure.

Finally, at 10:02, she pulled into the long, winding driveway for a session that had been scheduled to start at 10:00.

"I apologize for being late," Tess said, as Eleanor Chandler ushered her into the living room, where a treatment table had been set up and her patient was waiting. "I didn't realize how long it would take to get here from town."

"You've been here before," Raylan pointed out to her.

She nodded. "A couple of times, I think. But the last was Mrs. Chandler's seventy-fifth birthday party, when I was sixteen."

"That was nearly ten years ago," he noted.

"Bite your tongue," Eleanor said.

"Biting my tongue doesn't make it not true," her husband responded, before turning his attention back to Tess again. "Your mama mostly grew up at West River Ranch, with her sister and brother."

"I'm aware of that," she assured him.

"And you and your sister spent a fair amount of time here when you were little, running around the yard, chasing the dog—or your cousins."

Memories—or at least snippets of what might have been memories—nudged at the back of her mind. Blue, blue skies. Soft green grass. Childish shrieks and giggles.

"I supposed we did," Tess agreed, though she wasn't entirely sure.

"Then I guess your interests changed," he mused. "And you decided you'd rather dance on your toes than ride horses."

She smiled at his description of ballet, though she didn't remember finding much pleasure in the dance classes.

I'd rather wear cowboy boots, she said, when Mom ushered her and Sage into the store to get their first ballet slippers.

And that's why you're taking dance lessons, Abby told her.

That doesn't make any sense, Tess protested.

It was a mistake to let you spend so much time at the ranch. You don't belong there.

Mrs. Chandler said we're welcome anytime.

Well, you're going back to school soon and you're going to be so busy with schoolwork and dance lessons and other things, you're not going to have any time to visit.

Tess cleared her throat. "I think Mom was concerned we were getting too comfortable here and wanted to ensure we knew our place."

And their place wasn't rubbing elbows with the likes of the Chandlers. A fact she'd let herself forget for the one night she'd spent in Holt's bed.

"Your place is wherever you make it," Raylan said. "Don't you ever let anyone else's ideas about that hold you back."

Which was easy for him to say. Because he'd been born with not just a silver spoon but a whole silver place setting in his mouth.

Of course, that wasn't his fault any more than her questionable pedigree was hers, Tess acknowledged, if only to herself.

"Since we're already behind schedule, we should get started on your therapy," she said now. "But first, let me assure you that I won't be late again."

"No need to worry about that," the old man said. "It's not like I've got anything else on my schedule for the day."

"And yet I'm sure you'll manage to make your way to the barn later to harass whoever happens to be around," his wife chimed in.

"Asking questions isn't harassment," he protested.

"It is when the form of the question implies criticism," Eleanor countered. "Your sons and grandsons and the other hands know what they're doing, and if they don't, then the fault lies with you for not teaching them right."

He scowled. "You know darn well I taught them right."

"I do," she confirmed. "Which is why there's no reason for you to go down to the barn to harass them."

"Obviously I'm not going anywhere until I've been put through the paces by my lovely therapist here," Raylan noted.

"Then I'll leave you to it and help Willow figure out lunch," his wife said.

"I'm going to be working up an appetite, which means I'll want more than a sandwich."

"You'll eat what Willow puts on your plate and say *thank you.*"

"Some of the roast beef leftover from last night would get a hearty thank-you," he said in a cajoling tone.

As the rancher's wife turned away, Tess saw a smile tugging at the corners of her mouth.

"I'm going to get a roast beef sandwich," Raylan guessed.

"Gotta keep the cattle ranchers in business," Tess said lightly.

The rancher chuckled at that, then winced as Tess began to probe his injured shoulder.

"Have you been doing the exercises they showed you at the hospital?" she asked, concerned by his obvious discomfort more than three weeks after his injury.

He nodded.

"And stopping if you experience any pain?"

"No pain, no gain."

"No," she said sternly. "Pain means you're putting too much stress on your already injured body. When it hurts, you need to stop. And when you stop, you need to ice. Do you understand?"

"Yes, ma'am."

She lifted a brow.

"Sorry," he said sheepishly. "Your tone reminded me of the way my mama used to sound when she scolded me for misbehaving."

"I know you want to push ahead with your recovery," she said, gently massaging the tissue, "but pushing too hard is only going to set you back."

"Yes, ma'am," he said again.

It was just like a woman to drop into a man's life again when he'd finally almost stopped thinking about her, Holt decided.

Not that Tess was at West River Ranch to see him, he acknowledged. She was here to help with the rehabilitation of his grandfather's injury.

The bullet wound in Raylan's arm was almost completely healed, the only evidence that he'd been shot a raw, puckered scar on his biceps. But the dislocated shoulder, despite having been put back into place, continued to give him trouble.

And of all the physical therapists in all of Whispering Canyon—which admittedly might not be all that many—Tess Barrett had been assigned to his grandfather's care.

Or possibly requested by the patient's wife, as his grandmother had been only too happy to share the news with Holt when he was at the main house a few weeks back.

So when he saw the orange Kia bumping along the rutted driveway—a ridiculously impractical vehicle on a ranch—he wasn't completely taken by surprise. And when he saw the same vehicle park by the main house and the female driver emerge, he'd assured himself that what felt like a punch in the gut was nothing more than hunger.

Still, he'd had to force himself to stay at the computer for another hour, updating the breeding records, before he headed to the main house to charm Willow into feeding him lunch. The week after that, he'd managed to manipulate his schedule again so that he happened to be at the house when Tess was there. Today, however, he was out riding fence with a couple of cousins, and it didn't look like they were going to be done anytime soon.

"What are you grumbling about?" Austin said.

"I wasn't grumbling," Holt denied.

"You were definitely grumbling," Greyson confirmed.

"Maybe because I hate riding fence."

"I don't think it's anyone's favorite job," Austin noted.

"I'd rather ride fence than castrate calves," Greyson said.

"That's a nasty assignment," Holt agreed.

"But it didn't sound like you were grumbling about fences," Greyson said, circling the conversation back again. "Not unless you've started naming the fences and this section is 'damn woman.'"

Austin chuckled at that.

Holt scowled.

"Any particular woman on your mind?" Greyson prompted.

"Nope." He offered the lie without compunction. He'd taken enough grief from Flynn after his brother saw him with Tess; he didn't need his cousins chiming in with unsolicited advice about a woman he'd mostly forgotten about, anyway.

"Sonofabitch," Greyson said now.

"What is it?" Holt asked.

"Have a look." He stepped back so that his brother and cousin could move in.

"Sonofabitch," Austin echoed, because it was apparent the wire fence here hadn't been damaged by weather or wildlife—it had been cut.

"To let cows out?" Holt wondered aloud. "Or to let someone in?"

Of course, there was no way of knowing the answer to that question. And as they refocused their attention on repairing the fence, conversation now centered on whether or not to tell their grandfather what they'd found.

In the end, they decided that they didn't want to give Raylan an excuse to saddle up and ride out to check the damage himself—especially as the damage was already being repaired—and risk aggravating an injury that he was still rehabbing.

Which brought Holt's thoughts full circle again.

Though the truth was, since the night they'd spent together, Tess was never far from his mind. So many details of that night remained achingly, temptingly, clear: the way she tilted her head when she was listening to him; the teasing glint in her gorgeous green eyes; the seductive promise in the curve of her lips; the fresh apple scent of her hair; the silky texture of her skin; the surprising strength in her slender limbs as they wrapped around him; the sexy sounds she made—sighs and gasps and moans—when he touched her; the way her body shuddered when she came.

And five weeks after the night they'd spent together, he still dreamed about her at night and woke up aching for her.

Chapter Seven

"Cookies from Gramma Lula," Tess said, holding up the Tupperware container in her hand when her mom opened the door.

"You should take them home for Meg and Emma," Abby said.

"I've got another container to take home. These ones are for you and Dad. Your favorite—white chocolate macadamia nut."

Abby's lips pressed together in a thin line, but she took the proffered container. "Thank you."

"You should give Gramma a call—thank her yourself."

"Maybe I'll do that," Abby said.

But Tess knew that she probably wouldn't. She understood that her mother's relationship with her mother was complicated, a result of their fraught and difficult history. Still, it hurt her to see her grandmother hurting, and she knew that Tallulah had been trying—for a lot of years now—to atone for the sins of her past.

But perhaps some transgressions were simply unforgiveable; some wounds so deep that not even the passage of time could heal.

"Tea?" Abby asked, already filling the kettle.

"Sounds good," Tess agreed, settling into her usual seat at the kitchen table.

"I wasn't expecting to see you today," Abby said, taking the seat across from her daughter.

"It's the first Friday of the month, which is when I usually come for an afternoon visit."

"When you didn't have any patients on Fridays," her mom noted. "And now you do."

"How did you hear about that?"

"I work at The Mug Shot Café. Not much happens in this town that I don't hear about."

"Then you must have heard that Raylan Chandler isn't expected to go to physiotherapy, like anyone else in Whispering Canyon. Instead, physiotherapy goes to him," Tess said. "And because I'm the most junior member on staff and the only one without regularly scheduled patients on Fridays, I was assigned to work with him."

"You think your boss wouldn't be making the trip out to the ranch himself if that's what Raylan Chandler wanted?" her mom asked, sounding amused.

Tess shrugged.

"If you're going out to West River Ranch, it's because Raylan asked for you."

"Why would he do that?" she wondered.

"He probably feels invested in you—and your sister—because he and Eleanor helped raise me and my sister," Abby said.

"Hmm," Tess said, considering.

"Did he ask how you like your job? Or what your plans are for your future?"

"Well, yeah," she admitted. "But those are the questions that most of my patients ask in the beginning. Then, after about the third session, they want to know if I'm dating anyone and, when I tell them I'm not, they suggest setting me up with a neighbor or a grandson—or a neighbor's grandson."

Her mom laughed at that. "I heard about your date with Jordan Denninger. And that he's now dating Kellie Hart, of Hart Cakes."

"I hope they're very happy together," Tess said sincerely.

"I also heard she's doing the cake for Raylan and Eleanor's

anniversary," Abby continued. "Which, by the way, you'll be getting an invitation to."

"How do you know?"

"Eleanor came into the café last week and mentioned that the whole family would be invited."

"*Our* whole family?"

Abby nodded.

"Even Gramma Lula?"

"Knowing Eleanor, it wouldn't surprise me."

"Will you go—to the party?"

Her mom shrugged. "I don't know."

Tess nibbled on a cookie. "You never talked much about growing up at West River Ranch."

"I didn't really see the point."

"Did you like living there?" she asked cautiously.

"I loved it." Abby picked up the pot to refill her cup. "And hated it."

"I guess that explains it," Tess noted dryly.

Her mom exhaled a weary sigh. "West River Ranch was—*is*—the most amazing place I've ever seen. The mountains. The valleys. The creek. The cattle. The horses. The house. When I lived there, Raylan and Eleanor were raising five kids and we each had our own bedrooms, though Sunny and I had to share a bathroom."

"That must have been quite the hardship."

Abby smiled. "The ten years we spent at the ranch were like a dream. Or maybe a fairy tale. Certainly, the house was a castle compared to most of the places we'd lived with Tallulah.

"But when you're a kid, there's nothing scarier than the unknown. So while our life with Gramma Lula wasn't ideal by any stretch of the imagination, it was at least familiar. In the beginning, I hated Raylan and Eleanor for taking us away. And later, I hated them for sending us back.

"We'd lived there since we were kids. It was the only home we remembered. The only stable home we'd ever had. And suddenly, when Uncle Wyatt was getting ready to go off to college, Raylan and Eleanor decided that it was time for me and Sunny to go live with Gramma Lula, who we'd only previously seen a few times a year."

"There had to have been a reason," Tess guessed. "Was that when Gramma Lula got sober?"

"That was the explanation they gave, but…there was other stuff going on at the time that made the explanation suspect."

"What other stuff?" she asked curiously.

Abby reached for a cookie, taking a moment to consider her response. "Raylan caught me and RJ in a…compromising position…in the barn."

Tess's jaw dropped. After she'd managed to close it again, she said, "RJ is…the middle son?"

Abby nodded.

Which meant that—

"You had sex with Holt's father?"

"No!" Her mother's cheeks flushed. "I was only sixteen—definitely not ready to have sex."

Tess exhaled a quiet sigh of relief.

"But there were all these hormones running rampant in my body, and he was—" a small smile played at the corners of Abby's mouth "—hot. Really, really hot."

Tess put her hands over her ears. "Please, spare me the details."

"There aren't a lot of details to share," her mom said. "It certainly wasn't as big a deal as Raylan made it out to be. But he was obviously worried that if we spent more time together, it would lead to something more." She shrugged. "And he might have been right about that. I'd never felt about anyone the way I felt about RJ.

"But I don't have to tell you that the Chandler men are charismatic," Abby continued. "You had your own crush as a teenager."

Tess nodded, unable to deny the truth to the mother who'd

held her while she cried after the last day of her freshman year, because Holt was graduating and she'd never again see him in the halls of Aspen Ridge High School.

"That was a long time ago," she said now.

"And you got over your schoolgirl infatuation, just like I did, and moved on," Abby noted proudly.

And Tess was feeling pretty good about that fact, at least until she pulled the grocery list out of her purse, intending to do the shopping on her way home, and saw that Meg had scrawled *tampons* on the bottom of the list. That was when Tess realized she hadn't had a period in…more than five weeks.

She was *almost* one hundred percent certain that she wasn't pregnant—there were all kinds of reasons that a period could be late, after all.

But she needed to be *absolutely* one hundred percent certain, so she made her own mental addition to the shopping list.

And then she drove to a pharmacy in Howlett's Pass, because she didn't dare risk buying a pregnancy test in Whispering Canyon.

Miranda Chandler was a big fan of family dinners. At least once a month, the entire family gathered at Raylan and Eleanor's house for a Sunday meal. Every other Sunday, Miranda summoned her sons to the table in their family home.

Holt never griped about having to make a command appearance at the weekly family dinner. Why would he? The food was always plentiful and tasty and, afterward, he invariably went back to his cabin with a plate of leftovers.

But tonight, the meal was delayed as they waited for Flynn to return from a trip into town. Boone's twins—never fond of sitting still for long—had been sent to play outside, and Holt had volunteered to go with them. He was currently tossing a ball for his dog, who could chase and retrieve all day, while the twins pushed toy trucks in the dirt—occasionally, deliberately, running the vehicles into one another, resulting in a cacophony of crashing and exploding sound effects.

"What have you got there?" Holt asked, when Flynn finally arrived with a bakery box in hand.

"Cupcakes."

Both boys' heads lifted.

"Cupcakes?" they echoed in unison.

"For *after* dinner," their uncle said firmly.

"Is it dinnertime now?" Gage asked.

"Probably as soon as you guys go in and wash up."

They left their trucks in the dirt and raced to the house.

"What are you sucking up for?" Holt asked suspiciously, when the boys had gone.

"I'm not sucking up for anything," Flynn denied. "I just thought Mom might appreciate a contribution to the meal."

"And that she'd be less likely to yell at you for being late. Again."

"I have a good reason for being late."

"What's that?"

Flynn gestured with the box. "I was picking up cupcakes."

Holt knew there was more going on than his brother was telling him, but he also knew that Flynn wouldn't say anything else until he was ready—which happened when they were all seated.

"Has anyone heard from the sheriff?" Holt asked, as platters and bowls of food were passed around the table.

His dad frowned as he transferred a couple pieces of fried chicken to his plate. "Not since he was here asking questions about the break-in."

"That was almost six weeks ago."

"Proof that Billy Garvey is the laziest damn sheriff in the whole state," Boone said.

"Language," Miranda admonished her oldest son, with a pointed glance at his twins.

"The only reason he's still sheriff is that no one can be bothered to run against him," Flynn remarked.

"Maybe that's something for you to consider," RJ suggested.

"I don't do politics," his middle son responded bluntly. "But I did see Sawyer in town today."

"Did he have any news?" Holt wondered.

"I'm not sure it's news," Flynn said, "but he gave me the names of a couple of witnesses who might have been nearby when Gramps was shot."

"Garvey never mentioned anything about witnesses," RJ noted. "What did they see?"

"That's a good question. Sawyer didn't know because Garvey didn't bother following up to take their statements before they went back to California."

RJ frowned. "So now we'll never know what—if anything—they saw."

"I could take a trip to Santa Cruz," Flynn said, as if he was just tossing the idea out there.

"You want to go to California?" Boone asked, surprised.

Flynn shrugged. "It might be our only hope of getting some answers."

"It might also be a wild goose chase," RJ cautioned.

"Well, I think it's a great idea," Miranda said.

Her husband frowned. "You do?"

"My only request is that you wait until after your grandparents' anniversary party," she continued.

"I can do that," Flynn agreed.

"Good."

And that was the end of that subject—at least until dinner was finished and the cupcakes had been reduced to crumbs. Then Boone hurried out the door with his boys, eager to get them home and into the bathtub before bed, and Flynn escaped with a vague claim of having things to do, leaving Holt to help tidy up the kitchen.

"Why would you encourage Flynn to chase off to California?" Holt asked his mom, as she wrapped a plate of leftovers for him to take home.

"I was wondering the same thing myself," his dad admitted.

"I would have thought it was obvious," she said. "Because as long as he's occupied tracking down potential witnesses in California, he's not thinking about reenlisting."

Tess glanced at her watch again.

Usually, Eleanor had the door open before she'd lifted a hand to knock, but no one had responded to her summons today. Even if the rancher's wife wasn't home, there should have been someone there to answer the door: Willow, the longtime housekeeper and one of Eleanor's best friends; or any of the numerous family members who occasionally stopped by; or Raylan, in anticipation of his weekly therapy.

She recognized the vehicles in the driveway from her previous visits, but she had no idea who they belonged to. She knew that Clayton, the eldest son, and his wife, Laura, lived in the main house on the ranch, though she hadn't crossed paths with either of them on any of her previous visits. No doubt because Clayton was usually busy with his ranching duties and Laura worked as a courthouse clerk in town.

Their eldest son, Austin, lived in the bunkhouse onsite; their second born, Dawson, was "God only knows where" on his recent cross-country tour with Canyon Creek Trio, playing his guitar and crooning to crowds of screaming fans; and their youngest, Greyson, had an apartment in town, near his law office.

RJ, Raylan and Eleanor's second-born, had another home on the property with his wife, Miranda. Boone, their first born—and Holt's oldest brother—had moved into the foreman's house with his wife, Nadine, when she was pregnant with their twins. Now it was just the widowed single dad and his boys who lived there.

Flynn, RJ and Miranda's middle son, had returned to Whispering Canyon six months earlier after a dozen years in the military. It had been Eleanor's suggestion that he move into an old cabin in the foothills. She'd understood that the former soldier needed space, and she'd hoped the cabin would give him that along with the comfort of still being close to family. It didn't take long, though, for everyone to realize that Flynn wasn't going to find comfort or peace until Ellis was home, too.

Ellis's parents were Wyatt and Kristin, who had their own home at West River Ranch. Wyatt was Raylan's youngest son, born as a result of a short-term affair with Tess's grandmother—and yes, it was strange for Tess to think that her uncle was Holt's uncle, too. Wyatt and Kristin's eldest, Colby, resided in the bunkhouse with his cousin and several other hands, while their youngest, Jackson, lived and worked in town.

All of this information had been imparted to Tess through casual conversations with Raylan and/or Eleanor during the rancher's physical therapy—or over the coffee and cookies that Eleanor insisted she stay for at the conclusion of the sessions when she'd discovered that Tess had no other patients on Fridays and, therefore, no reason to rush off.

Which was why Tess was annoyed to realize that her sole patient was AWOL. She tried calling the number on file and could hear the phone ringing inside the house, but her call went unanswered. She followed up by contacting the clinic to see if Raylan or Eleanor had canceled the appointment, but the receptionist at Peak Performance hadn't heard from either of them.

Muttering under her breath, she started back to her vehicle.

"Tess?"

Glancing up, she found herself face-to-face with "Holt."

"What are you doing here?" he asked.

"It's Friday."

He nodded slowly, as if uncertain as to why she was sharing that information. Then the confusion in his eyes cleared as he realized, "My grandfather was supposed to have therapy today."

She nodded. "Every Friday for the past four weeks and the foreseeable future," she told him.

"Clearly, he forgot—or at least forgot to cancel," Holt said.

"Because he took my grandmother to a cattle auction in Riverton."

"Good to know the romance is still alive after sixty-five years of marriage," Tess said. "Of course, it would have been even better to know before I made a pointless thirty-five-mile drive here from town."

"You're annoyed," Holt noted.

"You're perceptive."

"And not only at my grandfather," he realized.

"Do you know when they'll be back?" she asked.

He nodded. "Sunday afternoon."

"I'll see them on Tuesday, then," she said.

"Tuesday?" he said, surprised. "I thought his therapy was on Fridays."

"Starting next week, it'll be Tuesdays and Fridays. I'll call on Monday to remind your grandfather." She turned toward her vehicle again.

"Tess—wait."

She kept walking.

"Please."

Now she paused, albeit with obvious reluctance.

He breached the distance between them in a few quick strides.

"Since you're here and apparently have nothing else to do, why don't we saddle up a couple of horses and go for a ride?" he suggested.

"Because I don't want to go for a ride." She inwardly winced at the peevishness of her tone, because it wasn't Holt's fault that his grandparents weren't home. Other things might be his fault, but not that.

"That's not what you said when you and my grandfather were chatting last week," Holt noted.

"You were eavesdropping?"

"I didn't think you were having a privileged conversation in the living room of my grandparents' house," he said. "Anyway,

I heard him mention that you were welcome to borrow one of the horses anytime, and you said you'd like that."

"I was being polite."

"I don't think you were," he argued. "There was a definite note of wistfulness in your voice."

"What would you know about wistfulness?" she challenged.

"You think I've always gotten everything I ever wanted because I'm a Chandler?" he guessed.

"I think it's a pretty safe bet," she agreed.

"Well, you're wrong."

Tess shrugged, clearly unconvinced.

"And anyway, we were talking about what *you* want," he reminded her.

She was quiet for a long minute before she confided, "I used to love riding, but the truth is, I'm not sure I even remember how. It's been a lot of years since I've been on a horse."

"They say it's like riding a bike—except it's a horse."

She smiled a little at that.

It wasn't even a full smile, and still it punched like a fist to his gut, taking Holt's breath away.

Damn, she was beautiful.

Over the past few weeks, he'd heard bits and pieces of enough conversations between Tess and his grandparents to know that she was also smart and funny and kind. Unfortunately, she was also strictly off-limits to him.

His mother had made that clear the day after she saw Tess at the hospital. When she saw the way he looked at her, when Holt hadn't even realized he'd been looking.

Those Leonard girls are predators—always trying to get their hooks into Chandler men.

He knew, of course, about his grandfather's long-ago affair with Tallulah Leonard and that his uncle Wyatt was the result of that affair. But it seemed patently unfair to paint all the women in Tallulah's family with the same brush just because she'd enticed his grandfather to break his marriage vows. At least, that was the way the story had been told to him—that Raylan had been seduced by the wannabe homewrecker.

Even if it was true, Raylan was hardly blameless, though his mistress had borne most of the weight of judgment. From Holt's perspective, only Eleanor was without fault, though his grandmother denied that claim, insisting that she'd been going through a rough time and had shut her husband out, effectively driving him into the arms of the other woman.

Holt hadn't asked for the details of that *rough time*—truthfully, he didn't want to know—but later found out that Eleanor had nearly lost her life giving birth to his dad and had, in fact, lost the ability to have more children. The realization had devastated his grandmother, who'd dreamed of filling her home with children. Holt suspected her sense of loss had been further amplified by the fact that Raylan's infidelity resulted in another child.

But that was all ancient history. Certainly, his grandparents didn't seem to hold Tess's family background against her.

So why was his mother so opposed to him being with Tess?

And why did it matter when he obviously hadn't heeded her warning?

Because when he'd really needed to not be alone, Tess had been there. And he'd taken advantage of her warmth and compassion.

Not that she'd been unwilling. On the contrary, she'd been passionate and eager and so damn hot, he'd found himself fumbling like an awkward teenager. But if she'd noticed his distinct lack of finesse, she hadn't said a word.

Thankfully, he hadn't been so far gone that he'd forgotten to ensure her pleasure first. And pleasuring Tess had been an incredible pleasure for him.

But thinking about that night wasn't serving any purpose now, so he shoved the memories firmly to the back of his mind.

"So what do you say?" he prompted.

"I'll admit to being a little bit tempted," Tess said.

"And yet, you're still hesitating," he noted.

"Because I'm also confused."

"About what?" he asked.

"Why you're suddenly being so nice to me," she admitted.

"I'm always nice." It was an automatic reply—and not an entirely truthful one. And while a lot of women would have taken the statement at face value, giggling or fluttering their eyelashes in response, he should have expected a different reaction from Tess.

"You mean like the day after when our paths crossed at the hospital?"

Her pointed question hit its target.

"Didn't I already apologize for acting like an ass?"

"Yes, you did," she acknowledged. "But you didn't say *why* you acted like an ass."

He shrugged. "I was embarrassed."

Hurt flashed in her eyes. "I see."

"I don't think that you do," he said.

"You were embarrassed that you sank low enough to invite Tallulah Leonard's granddaughter to your bed," she guessed.

"No," he immediately denied. Then he sighed. "Although maybe that was part of it."

"Well, let me see if I can recall the chain of events from that night," Tess said. "I was at The Bootlegger first. You sat down beside me. You then proceeded to down four shots of whiskey and invite me to your room."

"All of that's true," he agreed. "Except that it was three shots of whiskey and you left out the part where you were sending out all kinds of come-hither vibes."

"I assure you, I have *never* sent out come-hither vibes," she said indignantly.

"Are you denying that you were into me that night?" he challenged.

"I think you've got your logistics twisted around," she said dryly.

And damn if her smart mouth didn't make his own want to smile.

"But no," she continued. "I'm not denying that there was some chemistry between us. I'm also not ashamed that I gave in to it."

"*Was* some chemistry?" he echoed. "I'd say there *is* some chemistry. And that spending one night together did nothing to satisfy my desire for you."

"Well, I can assure you there's not going to be a repeat performance, cowboy."

"As I wasn't at my best that night, I can agree that there won't be a repeat performance," he said, letting his lips curve just a little bit now. "And I promise the next time will be better."

"There's not going to be a next time, either," she told him.

"Never say never," he cautioned with a wink.

"And that's my cue to leave," she decided.

He caught her hand before she could take a single step and was surprised by the frisson of electricity that snaked through his veins. He'd been attracted to plenty of other women in his twenty-nine years, but he'd never felt such an immediate and powerful attraction as he'd experienced with Tess. "Please stay."

She hesitated. "I really don't know that this is a good idea."

"Taking a ride?" he wondered. "Or us?"

"Obviously I'm talking about the ride," she said. "Because there is no *us*."

"A subject for discussion another time," he decided.

"Holt…"

"I like the way you say my name."

She rolled her eyes, but he could see the hint of a smile teasing her lips. "With total exasperation?"

He grinned. "Let's go see if we can find you some boots in the tack room."

Chapter Eight

"Why can't I just wear my running shoes?" Tess asked.

"You can," Holt said. "But footwear with a heel will fit more securely in the stirrup, ensuring your foot doesn't slip out."

"And I thought cowboys just wore heels to make themselves look taller," she couldn't resist teasing.

"And now you know the truth," he lamented. "Without my boots, I stand at five eight and three quarters."

"Except that I've seen you without your boots."

In fact, she'd seen him without anything on—and suddenly they were both reminded—*again*—about the night they'd spent together six weeks earlier.

He tore his thoughts away from the memories to focus on the task at hand. Rummaging through the inventory, he found a pair of women's boots and offered them to her. "Try these."

"Whose are they?"

"I think they belonged to Karli—Austin's ex-wife."

"Austin was married?"

"It didn't last long," he said.

"Might be why they look brand-new," she mused, sitting on the wooden bench to take off her running shoes and try on the boots.

"How do they feel?"

She stood up and walked across the room, then back again. "A little big, but good enough," she decided. "Why would she have left them behind?"

"Karli was a city girl through and through," Holt said. "And scared to death of horses when she first came to live on the ranch. Though she eventually got over her fear, she never grew to love them—or life so far from Macy's and Starbucks."

"I'm a city girl, too," she reminded him. "Though my routines are more likely to take me to Tren-Dee Boutique and The Mug Shot Café."

"I'm guessing, then, that you don't know how to tack a horse?"

"Not a clue," she admitted.

"We'll save that lesson for another day."

It was hard to stay mad, Tess acknowledged, when you were riding on the back of a horse under blue skies with the sun shining and birds singing in the trees. In consideration of the fact that she hadn't ridden in several years, Holt set a leisurely pace, and as her mount—a mare named Goldilocks—trotted along beside his, she breathed deeply of air scented of pine and grass and horses.

In the distance, she saw cattle grazing under the watchful eye of a couple of men on horseback. The cowboys waved to Holt, and he lifted his hand in acknowledgment.

After about an hour in the saddle, they came to a stream where Holt suggested they dismount and allow the horses to drink.

"Who were those men who waved to you?" she asked, when her feet were on solid ground.

"Austin, Colby and Waylon. The first two are cousins, the last is a longtime hand," he explained, when she looked at him blankly. "And no doubt they'll all give me no end of grief for playing hooky today."

"I didn't ask you to play hooky."

"I'm not blaming you," he said. "It was absolutely, one hundred percent, my idea."

"Why?"

"Because playing hooky is always more fun than working," he said. "But also because it was an opportunity to spend time with you."

"Why do you want to spend time with me?"

He shrugged. "I like you."

"You don't really know me."

"So give me a chance to get to know you."

She didn't respond to that.

He took a step closer, tipping her chin up so she would meet his gaze. "What are you afraid of, Tess?"

Looking into his deep blue eyes, she could no longer deny that she *was* afraid. Because being with Holt made her want things she knew she could never have. And when she finally responded, she did so with complete honesty.

"That maybe I'll like you more than you like me."

"Or maybe I'll like you more than you like me," he countered. "Or maybe we'll each decide that we like the other a lot."

"Or not at all."

"Also a possibility," he acknowledged, sliding his other arm around her waist and drawing her closer. "In any event, I'd like to take the time to find out."

Though Tess continued to eye him warily, she didn't evade his embrace. And when her gaze dropped to his mouth, he thought that she might want his kiss as much as he wanted to kiss her. But as he dipped his head toward her, intending to do just that, Dark Knight butted his head against Holt's shoulder.

"What the hell?" He glared at the stallion as Tess did take a step away now.

The horse blew out an impatient breath.

Beside Dark Knight, Goldilocks let out a nervous whinny.

Which was when Holt realized he'd been so focused on Tess, he'd failed to notice the dark clouds that had rolled in.

"It looks like we might be getting a storm," he said, frowning at the sky.

"I guess that means we should be heading back," Tess said.

He thought he detected a note of disappointment in her voice and was glad to know that she'd enjoyed the ride, though he suspected her pleasure would dissipate quickly when the dark clouds overhead opened up.

"Too late," he realized, as the first drops of rain started to fall from the sky.

Holt boosted Tess into her saddle again before vaulting onto the back of the stallion.

"This way." He turned Dark Knight in the opposite direction from which they'd come.

She hesitated. "Isn't that the wrong way?"

"We need shelter," he told her. "Fast. And there's shelter this way."

Tess nudged her horse into motion.

Holt could have ridden Dark Knight harder and faster, but he didn't want Tess falling behind, so he made sure his mount kept pace with hers and, by the time they reached the cabin, they were both soaked through.

"The side door's unlocked—go on in," he directed, after helping her to dismount.

"What about the horses?" she asked, sounding worried.

It surprised him that she would consider the animals—who were much more capable of handling the elements than a slender woman without even a jacket—and pleased him, too. City girl or not, she clearly had a heart that cared about others, animals as well as people.

"I'll take care of them," he promised.

Satisfied by his response, she nodded and opened the door he'd indicated.

Tess stepped gratefully into the cabin and found herself in what seemed to be a mud/laundry room. She sat on the utilitarian bench beside the door to tug the borrowed boots off her feet, then set them aside, along with the hat Holt had placed on her head—also Karli's. Venturing a few steps farther, she discovered a stack of freshly laundered towels in an open cupboard beside the washing machine. She grabbed one from the top and rubbed it over the dripping ends of her hair. Her blouse, she noted with dismay, was not only plastered to her skin but almost completely transparent, revealing the delicate lace pattern of her bra.

"I see you found the towels," Holt noted, when he joined her in the mudroom a few minutes later.

"I did," she confirmed, grabbing another from the stack and offering it to him.

She froze, with her arm extended, when she spotted the hairy beast by his feet.

"Thanks." He dropped to his knees to rub the towel over the animal's wet fur. "Say 'thanks,' Buddy."

The dog barked.

Tess blinked. "Your dog's name is Buddy?"

"Yeah," he admitted. "But in my defense, I didn't name him."

"Who did?" she wondered.

"My nephews." He finished toweling off the dog and she handed him another for himself, which he draped over his shoulders before sitting to remove his boots and hat.

"How long have you had Buddy?" she asked curiously.

"About a year and a half, I guess."

"And what kind of dog is he?"

"Aside from a wet and smelly one, you mean?"

Buddy whined, as if he knew his character—or at least his physical form—was being disparaged.

"Aside from an obviously smart and loyal one," she said.

Holt shrugged. "The rescue couldn't say for sure, except that he's part Lab, possibly with parts of hound and retriever mixed in."

"I always said that if I got a dog, I'd get a rescue."

"They're the best," he said.

"For what it's worth, I think Buddy's a perfectly good name."

The dog barked and Tess patted his damp head.

"He's glad you approve," Holt said with a smile.

"What is this place?" she asked, when he rose to his feet and led her through another door, into the main part of the cabin.

"An old hunting shack."

"It's definitely not a shack," she noted, admiring the natural stone-and-wood construction and soaring ceilings with exposed timber beams. "And it doesn't even look so old."

"More than a hundred years," he told her. "My great-great-great-grandfather's brother built it, but my dad, my brothers and me did some renovations more recently."

She would have guessed a hunting cabin to be of basic construction and simple design, with bare wooden floors and tiny windows. Any furniture would likely be secondhand—a sofa with broken springs or a threadbare love seat, perhaps a battered table and mismatched wooden chairs for eating, a set of rustic bunks in the corner of the living area and a woodstove with a stack of logs ready for burning.

And the only part she would have been right about was that the floors were wood—made of random-width planks smoothly finished and polished and scattered with woven rugs. Instead of a woodstove there was a fireplace—a stunning river-rock design flanked on both sides by windows that stretched floor to steeply pitched ceiling.

The sofa and chairs were dark brown leather, the occasional tables crafted in the ever popular Mission style, the lamps made of wrought iron. A bronze-colored bowl in the middle of the coffee table was filled with pinecones. A couple of picture frames and a trio of chunky candles sat on the mantel and a soft Sherpa throw was draped over the back of the sofa, making her suspect that a woman—Eleanor, perhaps—had helped with the finishing touches.

The kitchen was completely updated, with granite countertops, stainless-steel appliances and a freestanding island. French doors opened off the eating area to a deck that wrapped around three sides of the cabin, all with endless views of rolling hills, evergreen forests and craggy mountains—including the infamous Two Sisters.

A flannel shirt was draped over the back of one of the stools at the island, an empty coffee cup on the counter, a stack of unopened mail beside it.

"S-someone lives here," she realized.

"Yeah."

She looked at him, then at the dog, now curled up on a big floor pillow by the fireplace. "You?" she guessed.

"Yeah," he said again.

"Why didn't you just s-say it was your cabin?"

"I wasn't sure you'd want to come here if you knew."

"Well, as you s-said, it's sh-shelter."

"You're shivering," he realized. "So the rest of the tour—not that there's much more—will wait until you're out of those wet clothes."

"Like that's s-something I haven't heard b-before," she said, but followed him willingly to the bathroom.

The floor here was covered in stone tiles, the cabinetry natural wood with open shelves and seagrass baskets. The bowl-style sink was made of hammered metal with a pump-style faucet. The stone-and-bronze textures and colors carried through to the backsplash and the fixtures in the glass-walled shower stall and separate freestanding bathtub.

"Did you d-design this?"

"No." Holt shook his head. "The granddaughter of a friend of my grandmother's is an interior designer who offered to take a look at the space and offer some suggestions."

Tess found herself wondering if the woman had offered more than suggestions, but no way was she going to ask him that question.

"I'll b-bet you were happy to take her s-suggestions," she said instead.

"Very happy," he agreed, reaching into one of the seagrass baskets to pull out a couple of towels. "Bath or shower?"

"Sh-shower," she said, though the prospect of sinking into the deep tub filled with scented bubbles was undeniably tempting.

"The temperature's preset," he said, opening the glass door to turn on the water. Then he pointed to another knob. "That one switches the flow from the waterfall showerhead to the handheld."

"G-got it," she said.

"Set your clothes outside the door and I'll hang them up to dry."

"What am I s-supposed to wear in the m-meantime?"

"I'll find you something," he promised. "Just give me a minute."

She nodded.

In less than the sixty seconds he'd requested, he was handing her a bundle of clothes that included a plain white T-shirt, flannel pajama bottoms and a pair of wool socks.

"Th-thanks."

"No problem." He stepped out of the bathroom again. "Now get naked and get warm."

She didn't need to be told twice.

As soon as he'd closed the door, she was stripping out of her wet garments. A difficult task with fingers numb from the cold and sodden fabric clinging to her body. And then, before she stepped into the shower—easily big enough for two people—she reached over to lock the door.

Not that she was really worried Holt might come in while she was showering, but the locked door gave her some protection against her own imagination running wild. Because while they'd already been naked together—and did all kinds of things the memories of which were enough to chase the chill from her bones—they hadn't shared a shower, and she suddenly found herself intrigued by the thought of running her soapy hands over his tightly muscled body.

When she was clean and warm, she snapped off the water

and slid open the door, reaching for the towel he'd hung over the rail. It was soft and thick, and she dried off quickly before she could get chilled again, then donned the clothes he'd given her and surveyed her reflection in the mirror.

The T-shirt was soft from countless washings—and worn so thin she could see her nipples through the fabric. With a silent apology to her host for invading his privacy, she exited the bathroom and ducked into the room across the hall that she correctly surmised was his bedroom. She glanced around, searching for a closet and trying not to stare at the king-size bed with leather headboard. She definitely didn't want to think about him in that bed or speculate how many women had shared it with him, though he'd obviously been telling her the truth when he said he didn't have bedposts upon which to notch his conquests.

She found the closet and removed a flannel shirt from a hanger, tugging it on over the T-shirt to hide the fact that her nipples were straining against the thin cotton. Then she rolled the cuffs of the sleep pants up so she wouldn't trip on them and made her way back down the hall.

"That's a cute look," Holt said, when she ventured into the living room in her borrowed attire.

"You picked it out," she reminded him. "And though I'm not going to win any fashion contests, I'm at least warm, so thanks."

"You're welcome." He continued to set candles around the room. Then, catching her quizzical expression, he said, "I'm not setting the scene for seduction, but storms like this can knock out the power, so I wanted to be prepared."

"Makes sense," she agreed.

"And while we do still have power, I'm going to take my turn in the shower."

When Holt was gone, Tess browsed the contents of his bookshelves and tried not to think about him now naked under the spray, though it wasn't easy to block her lustful thoughts and prurient longings. Spotting a recent bestseller that she'd wanted to read, she pulled it off the shelf and settled on the sofa, snuggled beneath the soft Sherpa throw.

She didn't realize how tired she was until she woke up to the sounds of someone rummaging around in the kitchen. Feeling suddenly self-conscious—and just a little bit queasy—she pushed the blanket aside and rose to her feet.

Holt was dressed in a clean pair of jeans and a navy hoodie that made his eyes look even bluer, with a pair of wool socks on his feet—just like the ones she was wearing—and stirring something in a pot on the stove.

As she moved closer, her stomach growled.

Audibly.

Holt glanced up, a wide grin spreading across his face.

"I thought you might be getting hungry," he said. "I know I am."

"I could eat," she agreed.

"How does homemade beef stew sound? I've got a loaf of crusty bread here, too."

"It sounds—and smells—amazing."

"Can I get you something to drink? Coffee? Tea? Coke? Sorry, I don't have any Diet Coke."

Just the mention of coffee made her queasy stomach lurch, and she shook her head.

"Water?" she suggested.

He filled a glass from the dispenser in the door of the fridge.

"Thanks," she said, when he set it on the island in front of her. "Can I do anything to help?"

"I appreciate the offer, but reheating stew doesn't require a sous-chef."

"If you don't give me a task, I'm going to wander around and be nosy," she warned.

"Didn't you do that when I was in the shower?"

"I was tempted," she admitted. "But I restricted myself to your bookshelves."

"Find anything interesting?" he asked.

"The latest Quinn Ellison."

"It's a good one," he confirmed. "I'm surprised you fell asleep reading it."

"Which says more about my own recent sleeplessness than the writer's talent," she assured him.

"Any specific reason you've been having trouble sleeping?"

"Yes," she admitted. "But not anything I want to talk about."

"Well, there are more bookshelves in my office, mostly filled with manuals, textbooks and binders of breeding records, if you need a more effective sleep aid than Quinn Ellison."

"Why do you have breeding records in binders? I would have expected that information to be more useful on a computer?"

"It is," he said. "But my grandfather is a little wary of technology and likes to keep paper records 'just in case.'"

"Something he has in common with my grandmother," she noted.

"You mean, aside from my uncle, who's also your uncle?"

"Aside from Uncle Wyatt," she agreed.

"At least sharing an uncle from opposite sides of the family doesn't make us family," he pointed out.

"Thank God for that," she agreed, moving closer to the windows that she imagined afforded breathtaking views of the mountains when it wasn't pouring rain.

She could see the same peaks from town, of course, but that view was somewhat obstructed by multistory buildings and streetlights. Here, there was nothing but nature. And right now nature was demonstrating that it was a powerful force, rain pouring down and lightning spearing across the sky as thunder rumbled in the distance.

She shivered and moved back to the kitchen.

"Sit," Holt urged. "Eat."

She glanced at the dog, who'd obediently dropped to his haunches and appeared to be waiting for a treat, then at Holt.

"Were you talking to him or me?"

"You," he said. "Though I guess it's Buddy's dinnertime, too."

He measured food into the dog's bowl, then joined Tess at the table.

She lifted her spoon and dipped it into the stew.

Holt dug into his meal with enthusiasm. And though Tess was hungry, too, she nibbled cautiously on the crust of her bread and took small bites of the meat and vegetables.

He finished his meal and carried his empty bowl and plate to the dishwasher.

"Is there something wrong with the stew?" he asked. "Did you want something different?"

"No, this is fine," she said.

"Because I saw you devour a cheeseburger and onion rings in half the time it's taken you to swallow a few mouthfuls of stew."

"My stomach's just been a little unsettled the last few days," she confided.

He frowned at that as he dropped a pod into the single-serve coffeemaker on the counter. "Are you sure you don't want anything else to drink?"

"I'm sure," she said, deliberately keeping her focus on her bowl as his java started to brew.

"I've got decaf, if you prefer."

"Water's fine," she said.

Holt lifted his cup to his lips, inhaling the fragrant scent of the coffee.

His gaze flew across the room when he heard chair legs scraping against the wooden floor as Tess pushed her stool away from the island. Her face had taken on a slight greenish tinge, he noted with concern, and a fine sheen of perspiration glistened along her hairline as she took slow, shallow breaths.

"Tess? Are you okay?"

She responded by racing down the hall to the bathroom.

The dog chased after her, assuming a *sit* position outside the door she'd slammed shut and through which Holt could hear the unmistakable sound of retching.

Buddy glanced at the door then Holt, whining softly.

Apparently, his dog expected him to take some kind of action, so he knocked, a little apprehensively. "Tess? Can I get you anything?"

"I'm fine." He heard the toilet flush, followed by water running. Then the door opened and she stood in front of him, refusing to meet his gaze. "Sorry about that."

"Why didn't you take a sick day if you weren't feeling well?" He forged ahead then without giving her a chance to answer his question. "It's a good thing my grandfather wasn't home for his physio session. He's an eighty-six-year-old man who doesn't need to be exposed to a stomach bug."

"I'm not sick," Tess assured him, moving past him to return to the kitchen.

Which didn't make any sense to Holt. Because healthy people didn't throw up for no reason.

Then he remembered Boone's wife occasionally bolting to the restroom when she was expecting the twins and his brother explaining that morning sickness was inaccurately named as it could—and did—strike at any time of day.

Holt looked at Tess again, noted that she was more pale now than green, and realized the truth. "You're pregnant."

Chapter Nine

Tess took a cautious sip of water from the glass in her hand. "Give the man a gold star," she said lightly.

Holt swore. And again, when his mind didn't seem able to move past that particular thought. Then he let loose with a creative string of curses that had her brows lifting.

"You're reacting rather strongly to news that has nothing to do with you," she remarked.

Nothing to do with him?

Relief crashed over him like a tsunami, nearly bringing him to his knees.

"You're saying…it's not my baby?" he said, almost desperate to believe it could be true. Partly because he was appalled to think that that he'd gotten a woman pregnant outside of a committed relationship and partly because he dreaded having to explain his involvement with this particular woman to his parents.

She shrugged. "Who knows?"

But her feigned nonchalance didn't fool him, and panic rose up inside him again as the memories of that night played back in his mind.

Because while Tess hadn't been a virgin, it had been apparent to Holt that she didn't have a lot of sexual experience. Not that it was obvious in any way that detracted from his enjoyment, but more that she seemed surprised by her own. As if, despite having willingly accepted the invitation to his room, she hadn't had high expectations. That fact, combined with Meg's comment about Tess not having had a date in six months and never staying out all night, confirmed his suspicions.

His gaze narrowed on her now. "I think *you* know."

And he did, too, even if every fiber of his being wanted to reject the possibility.

And now he was the one taking slow, shallow breaths.

Because Tess wasn't just pregnant—she was pregnant with *his* child.

She wouldn't meet his gaze, but the color in her cheeks confirmed his suspicions. The baby she was carrying was his—so why was she denying it?

"Do you have any saltine crackers?" she asked him now.

He went to the pantry and dug out a box. "Should I reheat your stew?"

She shook her head as she accepted the sleeve of crackers he offered. "This is fine. Thanks."

She nibbled on a few crackers, alternating with cautious sips of water. Holt gave her a minute—or maybe the minute was for his own benefit, as he attempted to make his head stop spinning.

"If I hadn't put the pieces together, were you going to tell me?" he asked her now.

She met his gaze defiantly. "I hadn't decided."

He scrubbed his hands over his face. "Hadn't decided if you were going to tell me? Or hadn't decided if you're going to have the baby?"

"Oh, I'm having the baby."

He swallowed the panic that rose in his throat.

She was having the baby.

His baby.

Which meant that—ready or not—he was going to be a father.

And he was very definitely *not* ready.

But that didn't matter, because he'd been raised to take responsibility for his actions, and that was what he was going to do.

"Well, then," he said, pleased his voice sounded calm and rational even if he was feeling anything but. "I guess the only thing left to decide is a date for our wedding."

Tess responded with a laugh, because he had to be joking.

"I'm serious," Holt said.

Though he hadn't cracked a smile, she remained unconvinced. "You can't honestly expect that I'd want to marry you."

He frowned at her reply. "Why wouldn't you want to marry me?"

She took a minute this time to consider her response.

"Maybe I should want to marry you," she finally said.

And truthfully, there was a part of her that desperately did—the part that was totally freaked out about the prospect of being a single mother.

Just like Tallulah.

As if the unkind comparisons to her maternal grandmother hadn't already plagued her in the past, when news of her pregnancy got out, there would be no escaping them. Because she wasn't just unmarried and pregnant, she was pregnant by a Chandler. Just like her grandmother sixty years earlier.

She pushed the uneasy truth aside to refocus on the conversation.

"But I have no intention of trapping you—or being trapped—in a marriage simply because we were careless one night," she continued. "And I know there's no way you want to marry me."

"At this point, it's not about what either of us wants but about what's best for our child," Holt said.

"I appreciate that you're trying to do what you think is the right thing, but—"

Her reply was severed by a deafening crack of thunder overhead that made her jump.

Then the lights flickered.

Once. Twice.

And the cabin went dark.

Holt had warned her about a potential power outage. It was why he'd set candles around the cabin. So while she wasn't really surprised by the event, she also wasn't pleased by the inopportune timing.

And she was a little unnerved to discover that it was really, really dark.

"Don't move," he said to her now.

She hadn't planned on it, as she couldn't see three inches in front of her face.

But she could hear the rain pounding on the roof.

And a low whimpering sound near the floor.

"Relax, you big baby."

"I'm relaxed," Tess said. *Lied.*

Holt chuckled. "This time I was talking to the dog."

"Oh." She heard a scraping sound—a match head being dragged across the striking surface, she realized, when a tiny flame appeared.

"Buddy's not a fan of storms," he continued, as he used the first candle to light several others that he'd set around the room. "Probably because it was on a night very much like this that I found him."

"*You* found him?" He'd mentioned that Buddy was a rescue, but she'd assumed he'd gone to the shelter and picked out a dog that someone else had rescued.

Holt nodded. "He was cowering beside a dumpster, in the parking lot behind the hardware store. Cold and wet and hungry.

"I planned to take him to the shelter," he continued. "I didn't have time to take care of and train a puppy. But when I put him in my truck, he crawled across the seat and into my lap, dropped his chin onto my thigh and looked up at me..."

"With puppy dog eyes?" Tess guessed.

"Yeah," he admitted. "And I was a goner."

And so was she, Tess realized.

Or at least in danger of falling head over heels again for the man who was still as innately kind as he'd been to her on her first day of high school.

"That's better," Holt said, setting the first candle back in its holder. "At least now we won't trip over the furniture."

Tess nodded, though she wasn't sure it was better at all.

Because suddenly the cabin wasn't just a refuge from the storm, it was cozy and romantic. And suddenly, she was achingly aware that she was alone with Holt—the man she'd seriously crushed on since her freshman year of high school. The man she'd shared a bed with for one night six weeks earlier and with whom she was going to have a baby as a result. The man she now suspected she could fall all the way in love with, if she let herself.

Thankfully, Tess was too smart to let herself fall in love with Holt. Because no one—least of all his family—would accept a relationship between them, which meant that loving Holt could only lead to heartache.

Another crash of thunder made her jump again.

He settled his hands on her shoulders, making her pulse leap and race.

"It's just thunder," he said, his hands sliding down her arms in an apparent effort to soothe that had the opposite effect.

She swallowed. "I know."

Buddy, recognizing a fellow fraidy-cat, pressed his trembling body against her legs, perhaps seeking—or offering—comfort.

"There's nothing to be afraid of here."

"I'm not afraid of thunder," she told him.

"Are you afraid of me?" he asked.

"No."

"Then why are you so jumpy?"

"Because you're in my personal space."

"You didn't have any objections to me being in your personal space a few weeks ago," he pointed out.

"And look where we are now," she said dryly.

A hint of a smile curved his lips. "I like having you here."

"I wasn't referring to the geographical location so much as our situational dilemma."

"You mean the fact that you're pregnant with my child," he guessed.

"About that," she said. "I appreciate that you're willing to take responsibility, but there's no reason for anyone to know it's your baby."

Now he frowned. "Would you prefer to have people whisper and speculate about who might be the father?"

She shrugged. "They're going to do that, anyway."

"Not if we're married," he told her. "If you're Mrs. Holt Chandler, they wouldn't dare."

He was probably right. At least in that they wouldn't dare speculate within his earshot. But they'd still whisper about Tess, and they wouldn't care if she heard what they were saying.

"I appreciate what you're trying to do," she said again. "Sincerely. But no one gets married because of an unplanned pregnancy in the twenty-first century."

"I'm sure that's not true," he argued. "But there's no reason we have to make any final decisions about anything tonight."

"You're not going to change my mind," she told him.

"Maybe you'll change mine," he said.

Tess eyed him warily.

"But since we're currently at an impasse, why don't we put the subject aside for now?"

"I can do that," she agreed cautiously.

"Good." He nodded. "I'm not sure the candlelight is adequate for reading and watching a movie is obviously out, but I do have some board games that might help us pass the time."

"Really?"

He opened one of the cupboards beneath the bookcases. "Pop Up Pirate, Crocodile Dentist and Hungry Hungry Hippos."

"An interesting selection," she mused.

"I have twin three-year-old nephews," he reminded her.

"Do they spend much time here?"

"Not a lot. But I quickly learned the importance of keeping them entertained so they don't try to climb the furniture or lasso the dog."

"And they like games where they shove swords into a barrel, get their fingers chomped or feed semiaquatic mammals?"

"You know your preschool games," he remarked with surprise.

"I have an honorary three-year-old niece," she told him.

"Right." He nodded.

"Any chance you've got a deck of cards in that cupboard? I noticed 'poker night' was written on the calendar in your kitchen, and I've always wanted to learn how to play."

He took a silver case out of the cupboard.

"Ooh, you're a serious poker player."

"Not really," he denied. "This was a birthday gift from my brothers, so that I could host our games here."

"It's nice that you like to spend time with them—socially—after working with them all day."

"I guess it is," he agreed, not having given it much thought before. "Although our monthly poker games have dwindled to three or four times a year because everyone has so many other things going on in their lives."

"That's about as often as I see my sister," Tess confided. "She moved to Colorado Springs for college and got a job there after graduation."

"Do you miss her?"

"Like crazy. But I've got Meg. And Emma."

"Meg has a sister, too, doesn't she?"

Tess nodded. "Nicole. But she took a job teaching in Alaska last year."

Holt took out a deck of cards, then closed the case again.

"Aren't we going to play with chips?" she asked.

"I thought we'd start simple," he said. "Play a few hands

so you learn the basics of the game before we add betting to the mix."

"But playing with stacks of chips looks like so much fun on TV."

"It's only fun until you lose your stack of chips," he cautioned, as he began to shuffle the deck.

"All right," she relented. "We'll play your way."

"A good idea, since you don't know how to play," he said dryly.

She tapped the table in front of her. "Hit me."

"That's Blackjack."

"Oh. What do you say in poker?"

"Most players don't say anything. They just wait for the dealer to deal."

"Okay."

"We're going to start with Texas Hold'em," he said, as he dealt two cards facedown to each of them. "Those are your hole cards. You pick those up to see if you've got anything good."

She frowned at the eight of clubs and queen of hearts in her hand. "How do I know what's good?"

"Two of a kind is always a good start. Also face cards and Aces—sometimes just having the highest card can win you a hand. Cards in sequence might build toward a flush."

"A flush?" she echoed dubiously.

He looked at her uncertainly. "Do you know *anything* about poker?"

"No," she admitted. "I've only seen it on TV when I'm scrolling through the channels looking for something more interesting to watch."

His lips twitched. "Give me a sec."

When he returned, he set a piece of paper on the table beside her.

"What's this?"

"Your cheat sheet."

She skimmed the notes he'd written, numbered one through ten, ranking poker hands.

"Question," she said. "How can I get three or four of a kind when I only have two cards in my hand?"

"We're not done yet," he told her.

"Okay."

He then placed three cards face up in the middle of the table. "This is called the flop. They're essentially community cards that all the players get to add to their hand."

"There's two fives. That's a pair."

He nodded.

"And that's good, right? Even if I have nothing else of value, I've got a pair?"

"You and everybody else around the table," he reminded her. "And if somebody else had a five already in their hand, that gives them three of a kind, which beats a pair."

She glanced at the cheat sheet, nodded.

He walked her through several hands, patiently answering her questions and correcting her mistakes, and then doing it all again.

"Can we play with the chips now?" she asked, when he gathered up the cards to shuffle.

"A reckless request from someone who hasn't won a hand."

"I'm not suggesting we actually back the chips with real money," she said. "I'm not that reckless."

"My mistake," he responded dryly.

"Is that a *yes*?"

"Why not?" he decided.

"Can I have the orange ones?"

"The orange ones represent a thousand dollars," he pointed out to her.

"But we agreed we're not playing with real money, so why does it matter?" Tess asked.

And that was how Holt ended up playing Texas Hold'em with Tess with high-value chips.

She was a careless gambler and a horrible bluffer, but she was clearly having fun, and her smile brightened up the room far more than the candles he'd lit. And when she laughed, the sound wrapped around his heart and squeezed.

Had he ever been so captivated by a woman?

He didn't think so and, truthfully, he wasn't entirely pleased to be so now. Especially as she'd previously expressed an unwillingness to give a relationship between them a chance.

And still he'd manufactured excuses to stop by his grandparents' house around lunchtime on Fridays, knowing she'd be there. Not that they ever exchanged more than a few words, if that, but he'd looked forward to those brief moments when their paths crossed just the same.

And now that he knew they were having a baby together, there wasn't any question in his mind that they were going to be together, though it was apparent that Tess still needed some convincing.

So it was a lucky thing that he'd invited her to go for a ride today—and that they'd been caught in the storm, which he knew was the only reason she was here with him now.

"Look at that." Tess put her hole cards face up on the table in front of the flop. "I got a straight."

"6-7-9-10-J isn't actually a straight."

"They're in order."

"But missing an 8."

"I had an 8 in my last hand."

"Which doesn't count for this one."

She pouted at that.

"But your 6-7-9-10-J are all diamonds," he pointed out to her.

She looked at the cheat sheet again, her expression brightening. "That's a flush."

"It is," he confirmed.

"And you've only got a pair of Jacks. That means I win."

He nodded.

Grinning, she scooped up the chips in the middle of the table. "And now I want to quit while I'm ahead."

Because he didn't want to dim her smile, he didn't dare point out that, though she'd won that hand, she definitely wasn't ahead—her stack of chips reduced to a fraction of its original sign.

"Did you have fun?" he asked instead.

"So much fun," she said. "Thanks for teaching me to play."

"I wouldn't rush off to Vegas for a tournament next weekend," he cautioned.

"Vegas isn't my style," she assured him. "But I learned something much more important than four of a kind beats a full house."

"What's that?"

"You're patient and encouraging and kind—all traits of a good parent."

"So this was a test?"

"No," she immediately denied. "Just an observation."

"Well, I hope you're right. But at the very least, I plan to be an involved parent—if you'll let me."

"I have no intention of standing in your way."

"You don't?"

"Just because I don't want to marry you doesn't mean I can't appreciate the importance of my child having a father in her life."

A flash of lightning lit up the sky then. A brilliant, jagged fork that speared across the inky black darkness to stab the ground below. A crack of thunder immediately followed.

"Mother Nature's in a mood tonight," Tess mused, gently rubbing the dog, who'd snuggled close to her.

"It doesn't look like this storm going to let up anytime soon," Holt acknowledged.

She sighed softly, but not so softly that he didn't hear it.

"I'm sorry you feel stuck here," he said.

"I'm sorry you're stuck here with me," she told him.

"I'm not." He lifted his hand to brush a wayward strand of hair away from her face. As his fingertip traced the shell of her ear, she shivered.

His grandfather often remarked that Holt had the magic touch when it came to dealing with skittish horses. His brother Boone had noted that his magic touch worked with most women, too. But Holt had never known a woman as skittish as Tess Barrett.

Maybe she had reason to be wary. His mom had been fairly dismissive of Tess at the hospital, and while he was willing to cut her some slack because he knew she'd been worried about Raylan—as they'd all been—he'd sensed, even then, that there was something more behind her attitude.

Yes, his grandfather had an affair with Tess's grandmother, but that was like a hundred years ago—or at least sixty. In any event, that affair happened long before his mother was part of the family—and even longer before either he or Tess had been born.

And now that they were going to have a baby together, he figured that any areas of commonality were more important than their differences.

"We were good together, Tess."

"You were drunk and I was lonely—that's hardly a recipe for happily ever after."

"I'm definitely not drunk now," he told her.

"Our situation is complicated enough, don't you think, without adding anything else to the mix?"

"The attraction is there, whether you want to acknowledge it or not," he pointed out.

"I have no doubt you've experienced attraction with any number of women without feeling compelled to propose marriage to them," she countered.

"It's true that I've never proposed to another woman," he said. "It's also true that I've never slipped up with another woman."

"Slipped up?" she echoed.

"Forgotten to use protection," he clarified.

"Never?" she said dubiously.

"Never," he confirmed.

"Not even when you were seventeen years old and fooling around with Lauren Ritter in the back of your new Jeep Wrangler?"

His brows lifted. "How did you know about me and Lauren? And my Jeep?"

"We went to the same high school," she reminded him. "Everyone knew about you and Lauren. And you and Marcy—who was Lauren's best friend until you and Lauren became you and Marcy. And then you and Harper. Or was it Sloane after Marcy?"

"It seems you paid more attention to my social life than your classes."

"I helped out with the yearbook," she told him. "The chronology of your romantic partners was immortalized in the pages of the Aspen Ridge Record. Though, for what it's worth, your cousin Jackson went through more girls that year than you did—though it appears there was some overlap between you."

"Can we get back to my original point?" he asked her.

"Which was?"

"That I've never had unprotected sex with another woman. And never means not ever. Not even once. Not even when I was seventeen."

"Well, good for you," she said.

"So maybe I didn't slip up the night we spent together."

"You're saying that you somehow miraculously found a third condom and we didn't have unprotected sex? In which case this pregnancy is either a figment of my imagination or proof of immaculate conception?"

He rolled his eyes. "I'm saying that maybe this baby was meant to be. Maybe we were meant to be."

"I never would have pegged you for a romantic," she said.

"Certainly no one's ever accused me of being one before," he acknowledged. "But maybe finding out that I'm going to be a father has given me a different perspective on things."

Chapter Ten

"You found out two hours ago," Tess remarked dryly. "I don't think the reality of impending fatherhood has sunk in yet and, when it does, you'll be grateful that I didn't accept your impulsive proposal."

"Impulsive doesn't mean insincere," Holt told her.

"My answer's still *no*."

He was sure he'd never met a more stubborn woman than the one he was looking at right now.

"We're having a baby together, Tess," he reminded her.

"No," she said again, shaking her head. "*I'm* having a baby."

"*My* baby," he clarified.

"Are you one hundred percent certain of that?" she asked, a deliberate note of challenge in her voice.

Holt held her gaze unwaveringly. "Yes, I am."

"Well, no one else will be," she told him.

And that, he suspected, was why she'd raised the question of paternity rather than wait for him to do so. Because she'd grown up in Whispering Canyon, known to one and all as Tallulah Leonard's granddaughter—which meant that she was accustomed to the snide remarks of those who believed they were better than her simply because their skeletons remained in the back of their closets and hadn't been paraded in front of the whole town.

"Nobody else matters," he said, wishing he could convince her it was true.

"Maybe they matter to me," she said. "Maybe I don't want to be another Leonard girl trying to get her hooks in a Chandler man."

"No one would dare say such a thing about my wife," he promised.

"I'm not going to marry you, Holt. I can't."

"Are you already married?"

She shook her head. "No."

"Then there's no reason you can't," he said reasonably.

"You don't want to marry me, Holt. You just think it's the right thing to do."

"It *is* the right thing to do."

"What did you have in mind? A short-term marriage so that our child is born legitimate and then we go our separate ways? Or would you martyr yourself to be a husband to me and a father to our child 'til death do us part?"

"Child*ren*," he said, emphasizing the plural.

She swallowed. "Please don't tell me twins run in your family."

He couldn't help but chuckle at her horrified expression.

"They don't," he said.

She exhaled an audible sigh of relief.

"I only meant that I'd like our child to eventually have one or two siblings."

"Don't you understand that I'm trying to let you off the hook?"

"Being married might not be so bad," he mused.

"That's hardly a resounding endorsement."

"In fact," he continued as if she hadn't spoken, "it could be very good—and not only because we could more easily share the responsibilities of childcare."

"You're talking about sex," she guessed.

"Not only sex—though if we were making a list of pros and cons, I'd definitely put that in the pro column."

"We're not making a list because—" She paused to stifle a yawn.

"You're tired," he realized. "You should go to sleep."

"I'm just waiting for the storm to pass—and my clothes to dry—so I can go home."

"I know this isn't what you want to hear, but you're not going to make it home tonight," Holt told her.

"Why not?"

"The river always runs high in spring, because of the snow-melt from the mountains. Add in the amount of rain we've gotten today, and it will be threatening to overflow its banks, which makes the road to the main house impassable."

As if on cue, his phone chimed, signaling receipt of a text message.

Holt picked it up and glanced at the screen.

Where are you?

The message, typically abrupt, was from his cousin Austin.

Holt replied:

Home.

Good. Stay put. River's rising fast.

Holt knew that meant the road from his cabin to the main house would soon be impassable, as he'd just explained to Tess.

Are you home, too?

Austin replied with a thumbs-up emoji.

Flynn?

Another thumbs-up.

Holt swiped to close the messaging app.

"Everything okay?" Tess asked.

"Just my cousin confirming that we're stuck here until morning."

"So I'm going to have to sleep here," she realized.

He nodded.

"But…there's only one bedroom," she protested.

"Yeah, but it's got a king-size bed."

"I'm not sleeping with you, Holt."

"It's a king-size bed," he said again.

"Still not sleeping with you."

"Okay," he relented. "You take the bed. I'll take the sofa."

She looked skeptically at the five-and-a-half-foot sofa, then at his six-feet-plus frame. "I don't think that's going to work," she said. "*You* take the bed. *I'll* take the sofa."

"You're pregnant. You're not sleeping on the sofa. Besides, I'm not ready to go to sleep yet."

She yawned again.

"And you obviously are." He picked up the flashlight he'd set on the table, turned it on and put it in her hand. Then he took her gently by the shoulders and steered her in the direction of the bedroom. "Go to bed, Tess."

"Any chance you've got a spare toothbrush?" she asked.

"In the medicine cabinet. You'll find toothpaste there, too."

"Thanks."

She stopped protesting and went to bed.

When Tess had gone, Buddy following closely at her heels, Holt extinguished the candles he'd set around the room and sat in the dark, watching occasional flashes of lightning through the windows.

He remembered his English teacher in high school talking about how storms were symbolic of change. At the time, Holt had scoffed at the idea, but there was no denying that his life was changing.

He was going to be a dad.

Now that the initial panic had subsided—mostly—he could acknowledge that it was both a terrifying and exhilarating realization. And maybe a little more terrifying than exhilarating at this stage, so it was a darned good thing he'd never slipped up at seventeen—he would never have gotten past the panic stage.

But he wasn't a kid anymore.

Tess wasn't a kid, either, but he suspected that she might still be reeling from the discovery of her pregnancy—even if she'd already made the decision to have and keep their baby. And since that decision had been made, no way was he going to let her do it alone.

He was going to step up, to be a husband and a father, but first he had to convince her to give him—to give *them*—a chance. Since further efforts toward that goal would have to wait until the morning, though, he stretched out on the sofa to try to get some sleep.

Unfortunately, Tess was right. The logistics of fitting his seventy-four-inch frame on a sixty-six-inch sofa were challenging.

And uncomfortable.

No way was he going to wake Tess to ask her to move to the sofa—or ask for her permission to sleep in his own bed. Instead, he decided this was one of those instances where it would be better to ask for forgiveness after the fact.

The power was back on by the time he headed to his bedroom, and when he pushed open the door, the light from the hall spilled into the room, illuminating the woman sleeping in his bed. She was on her side, practically clinging to the edge of the mattress. Buddy was curled up on the bottom of the bed, by Tess's feet.

The dog lifted his head when Holt stepped through the door and obediently hopped to the floor when his person gestured for him to get down.

She'd taken off the flannel shirt and sweatpants—both folded neatly on the chair beside the bed—which meant that she was only wearing his T-shirt. And maybe wool socks.

And he was about to crawl under the covers with her.

But first, he put a couple of spare pillows on the bed, creating a foam wall between them.

And fell asleep wishing that she was in his arms.

Tess woke up aware that she wasn't in her own bed—and definitely wasn't alone.

She kept her eyes closed as the events of the previous day flooded back to her. The horseback ride with Holt. The almost-kiss by the creek. The storm. The pregnancy revelation. His unexpected proposal. Her refusal.

She'd accepted the offer of his bed, though, and before she'd fallen asleep, Buddy had hopped up with her, curling up by her feet at the bottom of the mattress.

But she didn't think it was Buddy in bed with her now.

A suspicion that was confirmed when she opened her eyes and found herself looking at a man's chest.

A familiar, hard man's chest.

"Good morning," Holt said huskily.

"Um…" She wasn't entirely sure what else to say. "How did you end up in my bed?"

"Technically, it's my bed," he reminded her. "And when I got in it last night, you were way over on that side. But I made a pillow wall between us, anyway, to ensure I stayed on mine."

He was on his side, she realized.

And so was she.

On his side and in his arms.

But he didn't seem to mind.

She cleared her throat. "So where's the pillow wall?"

"You tore it down."

"*I* tore it down?"

"Well, I assumed so, as the pillows are on your side," he pointed out.

Glancing at the floor, she realized he was right about that, too.

Unable to dispute the evidence, she said instead, "I thought ranchers kept early hours."

"I couldn't abandon my houseguest," he said reasonably. "Also, my arm is trapped."

She could feel it beneath her. The firm biceps muscle cushioning her cheek.

She immediately lifted her head and shifted it to the pillow. "Sorry."

"No need to apologize," he told her.

His mouth was barely a whisper from hers. His eyes dark and intent. She knew he was thinking about kissing her. But she also knew he wouldn't do it. Not without some kind of sign or signal from her.

"But maybe you want me to apologize for not staying on the sofa," he suggested.

"No. I don't want you to apologize," she said, and breached that scant distance to touch her mouth to his.

It had been a mistake to kiss him, Tess realized.

But apparently she was destined to make mistakes with Holt Chandler, because as soon as she was kissing him, she wanted more. She wanted his hands on her and his body intimately joined with hers, reminding her of the pleasures that she'd never experienced with another man.

She knew what people thought about her. She wasn't oblivious to the whispers that followed her around town. Ironically, her bad-girl reputation wasn't based on anything she'd ever done but solely on the fact that she was Tallulah Leonard's granddaughter. A relationship she could hardly do anything about—and wouldn't even if she could.

Tess's mom had dealt with the same whispers growing up. Despite the fact that she'd lived at West River Ranch for many of her early years, in the care of Raylan and Eleanor Chandler, she'd still been known as Tallulah Leonard's bastard daughter.

As a result, Abby had impressed upon her daughters the importance of ensuring their behavior was always above reproach. Whenever they went out with friends, she'd remind them to never be alone with a boy, because rumors were often more damaging than truth, and a boy's boastful claims were always given more credence than a girl's denials, especially when that girl was a Leonard. They were cautioned not to let their hormones overrule their common sense, not to believe the lies boys would tell and to never ever *ever* have unprotected sex, because getting pregnant would only confirm what people thought they already knew.

Tess had taken her mother's advice to heart, so much so that she hadn't dated at all in high school. Meg had been subjected to similar warnings from her mother, which might have been one of the reasons that Tess and Meg were not only cousins but also best friends. Because they'd both grown up feeling ostracized by all the other girls who didn't want to even do group work with them for fear the "Leonard girls" reputation would rub off on them.

As a result, Tess went off to college with no dating experience and promptly fell head over heels for the first man who showed any interest in her. But still, she was careful, because being away from home didn't miraculously silence the echo of her mother's warnings in her mind.

Thankfully, Jonathon was wonderfully patient with her. After almost a year of dating, he asked her to marry him. And six weeks after that, she finally let him convince her that two people who'd already given their hearts to one another shouldn't be afraid to share their bodies.

Making love with Jonathon had always been…satisfactory. Certainly, he'd tried to please her, and if the earth never trembled, Tess figured she simply wasn't capable of feeling the kind of earth-shattering climax enjoyed by the heroines in the romance novels she liked to read.

But apparently it wasn't satisfactory for him, because only a few months later, he'd ended their engagement. Tess had been devastated—but also relieved, because she'd realized that she didn't want to spend the rest of her life having satisfactory sex.

A year after that breakup, she decided to try again with another long-term boyfriend. This time, her expectations were a little more realistic. This time, she only wanted to feel a connection. And the sex was…satisfactory again.

That relationship lasted a few more months and then Callum decided it was time to move on.

Holt was the first man she'd slept with since she said goodbye to Callum. She'd had no expectations when she'd gone to his hotel room six weeks earlier, but he'd nevertheless shown her that she was capable of feeling everything she read about in those romance novels—and more.

"Are you sure about this, Tess?" he asked, when she reached between their bodies to touch him intimately, clearly communicating her desire.

"It's the only thing I am sure about right now," she told him.

Apparently that was all the encouragement Holt needed, because he took her mouth again, kissing her long and slow and deep, sending hormones ricocheting through her body.

According to one of the pregnancy articles she'd read online, increased arousal was a common side effect for some women. She took solace in that knowledge, trusting that her passionate responses to Holt's every touch were natural physiological reactions.

Such as when he slid a hard thigh between hers, and the exquisite friction elicited a low moan of longing deep in her throat.

"More." She murmured the plea against his lips as her hips rocked against his, the hard evidence of his arousal setting off sparks that raced like fire through her veins.

He answered her request by easing a hand between their bodies, his fingers deftly zeroing in on the ache at her center, making her whimper.

She wanted—needed—to feel his hot, naked body against her. Inside her.

He stopped kissing her only long enough to dispose of her—*his*—T-shirt, then his tongue swept inside her mouth again, tasting and teasing. Her hands caressed his shoulders, his arms, his chest—would she ever get enough of his gloriously muscled body?

His knees bracketed her hips as he straddled her, holding her immobile while he explored with his hands. His lips. His tongue.

Oh, the things he did with his tongue.

Things that made her sigh and moan…and then left her completely breathless.

When she managed to catch her breath again, she reached for him, stroking the hard length of him through the thin cotton of his boxer briefs, then dipping inside to wrap her fingers around him, making him groan.

She loved touching him. Loved seeing how he reacted to her touch. She knew he'd been with a lot of women—women who undoubtedly had a lot more experience (and a lot fewer hang-ups) than she did—but she refused to let that knowledge hold her back. Because those women were the past, and she was the one here with him now.

He quickly dispensed with his briefs, and she quivered with anticipation, spreading her legs wide for him, eager—almost desperate—for the joining of their bodies. It thrilled her—and maybe even scared her a little—how quickly her body responded to him. How much she yearned for him.

He lowered himself over her, the tip of his erection nudging at the soft flesh between her thighs.

"Condom," he suddenly remembered, drawing back to reach toward his nightstand.

"Kind of like closing the barn door after the horse has escaped, don't you think?" she said lightly.

He paused, then chuckled softly. "I guess it is."

But she was reassured to know that using protection was as deeply ingrained a habit as he'd told her.

He pushed the drawer shut again and refocused his attention.

"Now...where was I?" he asked, tapping a finger against his chin, a playful glint in his eye.

"Right about here," she said, hooking her ankles at his back to pull him closer.

"Here?" he said, and entered her in one long, deep thrust.

Her only response was a moan as she tilted her hips to take him deeper. This time, *he* moaned, a throaty sound of satisfaction. Then he began to move, his rhythm slow and steady, and she felt the pressure begin to build low in her belly again.

She clutched at his shoulders, her nails biting into his skin, as he adjusted his rhythm. Driving faster. Harder. Deeper. His breath rasped out of his lungs, shallow pants that told her he was close to his own release. But still he held back, waiting for her.

He didn't have to wait long. She was already lost in a storm of desire, so many sensations battering at defenses, dragging her under, drowning her in pleasure. Then and only then did he find his own, emptying himself inside her.

Several minutes passed before he shifted his weight off her, but even then, he didn't release her. Instead, he wrapped his arm around her middle and tucked her close. And Tess found her eyes drifting shut as she fell back to sleep, her heart beating in tandem with his.

"I did it again," Tess lamented, when Meg and Emma returned home after the little girl's weekly swimming lesson Saturday afternoon.

"Ooh," her friend said. "I feel a Britney Spears song coming on."

Tess rolled her eyes.

Smiling, Meg turned her daughter toward the laundry room. "Go put your bathing suit and towel in the washing machine."

"Then can I watch *Paw Patrol*?" Emma asked hopefully.

"Then you can watch *Paw Patrol*," her mom confirmed.

When the little girl had skipped away, Meg shifted her attention to her friend. "Now, tell me more. And if it turns out that *it* is anything other than hot, sweaty sex with Holt Chandler, I'm going to be very disappointed."

"You're not going to be disappointed," Tess promised.

"Let's go into the kitchen so I can put the kettle on for tea," Meg suggested.

While her friend did that, Tess retrieved two mugs from the cupboard.

"Okay, details," Meg demanded, when they were settled at the table.

"I had hot, sweaty sex with Holt Chandler and I'm pregnant."

Meg bobbled her cup, splashing hot tea. "Damn."

Tess jumped up to get a towel. "Are you okay?"

"Fine." She mopped at the table. "But how could you possibly know that you're pregnant already? Unless..."

Tess nodded. "Last time."

"Well." Meg cautiously sipped her tea. "Congratulations?"

Tess laughed. Then her eyes filled with tears and she began to cry.

"Oh, yeah. I remember the flood of emotions," Meg said with sympathy. "Joy and panic. Excitement and panic. Panic and panic."

She nodded. "That about sums it up."

"Does Holt know?" her friend asked cautiously.

"Yeah."

"And?" she prompted.

"And...he offered to marry me."

"I hope you said *yes*."

Now Tess shook her head. "I said *no*. After I laughed."

Her friend's brows lifted. "How did *that* go over?"

"He was...surprised. Possibly annoyed. And definitely not happy. Because according to him, getting married is the best thing for our baby."

"But you're not convinced," Meg surmised.

"I barely know the guy," Tess pointed out. "And he definitely doesn't know me."

"I think it says something about his character that he wants to step up and do the right thing, and I don't think you should dismiss his proposal out of hand."

"It wasn't really a proposal," Tess said. "And I'm not going to marry a man I barely know just because the one night we spent together had unplanned consequences. Well, one night prior to this morning," she clarified, her cheeks flushing as she recalled making love with him in his cabin.

"Ooh, morning sex."

"Can we focus, please?"

"Right. Sorry. You're not going to marry a man you barely know because of unplanned consequences."

Tess nodded.

"And I will fully support you and do anything I can to help you," her friend promised.

"Thank you," she said, her throat tight.

Meg pushed away from the table then to wrap her arms around Tess and hug her tight. "That's what best friends are for."

She nodded again, more grateful than words could express to know that she had the very best one in her corner.

Chapter Eleven

Holt was sitting in one of the Adirondack chairs on her porch when Tess arrived home after work the following Monday. Ramona Martin was, coincidentally, on her porch, cleaning her front windows.

He immediately rose to his feet as she started up the walk.

"The neighbors are going to start talking," she warned.

"You can tell them I'm a delivery driver for the flower shop," he suggested, as he offered her the bouquet in his hand.

She accepted the bundle of colorful blooms, pleased by the gesture but also a little wary. "Poppy's drivers wear red baseball caps."

"I'm a new hire." He winked. "Haven't earned my cap yet."

She tucked the flowers under her arm and reached into her purse, then handed him a five-dollar bill.

"A tip?" he guessed.

"It is customary," she noted.

"How about I trade you this—" he tucked the bill into the side pocket of her purse "—for five minutes of your time so that I can apologize properly? Preferably inside."

"Why?"

He nodded toward the adjacent house. "Because your neighbor has been pretending to clean her front window since I got here."

A quick glance over her shoulder had Ramona Martin

squeezing the trigger on the bottle in her hand to spray the glass again.

Tess pulled out her key and unlocked the door.

"Sorry about the toys," she said, as she stepped over an assortment of dolls. "Emma doesn't always have time to tidy up before she goes to preschool."

"Probably something I'm going to have to get used to, anyway," he noted. "Although more likely cars than dolls, because it's likely our child will be a boy."

"Boys can play with dolls. And girls can play with cars," she pointed out. "And why do you say it's likely our child will be a boy?"

"Because there hasn't been a girl born in the Chandler family in five generations."

Five generations?

"I didn't know that," she admitted, standing on tiptoe to reach the cupboard above the refrigerator, looking for a vase.

Holt easily plucked one from the shelf and set it on the counter. "Which is why it's important for us to spend time together, so that we can get to know one another better."

"I thought you said you were here to apologize," she said, turning on the tap to fill the container with water.

"I am," he confirmed.

"What are you apologizing for?"

"Assuming you'd jump at the opportunity to marry me just because I asked."

"A lot of women in this town would have jumped," she acknowledged, snipping the stems of the flowers. And she might have been one of those women, if she'd believed he actually wanted to spend his life with her and wasn't only asking because she was pregnant with his baby.

"And I assumed you were one of them because…because you were right—I don't really know you," he admitted with seeming reluctance.

"Finally something we agree on," she said.

"Which doesn't mean that I've given up on the idea of marriage," he told her.

"It would never work, Holt," she said, arranging the colorful blooms in the vase. "Because we're two people from different worlds who just happen to be having a baby together."

"Our worlds aren't so different."

Her smile was wry. "Only someone from your world could say that and sound as if he really believed it."

"I'm a cattle rancher and I've seen you eat a burger—there's common ground right there."

"You're not just *a* cattle rancher," she protested. "Your family owns and operates one of the most successful ranches in the state—maybe the country."

"Are you suggesting that you'd feel differently if West River Ranch was struggling? Because let me assure you, the cattle industry is fickle and fortunes can turn on a dime."

"I'm pointing out that you wouldn't even be asking for this chance if not for the fact that we had a *whoops!* moment during the one night we spent together."

"Then let me point out to you that we were very much living in the same world that night—and in that world, the attraction we felt for each other was pretty intense. Don't you think that should count for something?"

"By my calculations, sad plus lonely equals reckless decisions."

"And the morning after the storm?" he challenged. "What do your calculations say about that?"

"Pregnancy hormones plus proximity equals another reckless decision."

Holt shook his head, clearly exasperated. "Is it really so hard for you to admit that you're attracted to me?"

"Maybe it is," she allowed. "Or maybe—attraction aside—there are just too many reasons that we don't work."

"I'd say the baby you're carrying proves that we do."

"That's a circular argument and I don't have the energy to go around and around again."

"Are you working too hard?" he asked, immediately concerned. "Maybe you should cut back your hours."

"I'm not working any harder than usual."

"But you're growing a baby now."

"Thanks for the reminder," she said dryly.

"I'm overstepping," he realized.

"A little bit," she agreed.

"Okay. I'll go." He kissed her sweetly on the forehead before making his way back to the door. "I just wanted you to know that I'm here, if you need anything—someone to go riding with…an extra body at the poker table…a father for your baby."

She chose to ignore his parting remark, saying only, "Thank you for the flowers."

Then she closed and locked the door at his back—and wished she could as easily banish the silly teenage dreams that had once inspired her to write his name in hearts on the inside cover of all her notebooks…and that continued to linger in her heart.

Flynn was scowling when he opened the door. "What are you doing here?"

"I need some brotherly advice," Holt told him.

"Boone was busy?"

"Ha."

"It was a legitimate question," Flynn said, but he stepped away from the door so Holt could enter. Buddy padded in beside him, confident in his welcome. "Beer?"

"Sure." He followed his brother to the kitchen, where Flynn pulled two bottles out of the fridge and offered one to him. "Thanks."

He twisted off the cap and glanced toward the small table. "You still only have one chair?"

"I'm still only one person," Flynn pointed out.

"Apparently you never plan on bringing a woman here," Holt remarked mildly.

"Any woman willing to come home with me would have to be as screwed up as I am, and that would not be a good combination."

"You should reach out to Veterans Affairs," he suggested, not for the first time. "Find someone to talk to."

And Flynn responded the way he always did: "Talking isn't going to fix anything."

Holt held back a sigh as his brother reached into a cupboard and pulled out a dog biscuit. Buddy immediately assumed the *sit* position, then trotted off with his treat.

"Should we go into the living room and watch the…wall?"

Flynn shrugged and followed.

"You really need to get a TV," Holt said.

"I don't want a TV."

Holt sipped his beer, trying to find the right words to introduce the topic of conversation.

"Should I get a crowbar to pry it out of you?" Flynn wondered.

He gave up his search for the right words and just blurted out, "I asked Tess Barrett to marry me."

His brother gave no outward indication that the announcement surprised him. He merely considered it for a moment before saying, "So you slept with her and now she's pregnant?"

"That sums it up," Holt confirmed.

"Are you happy about the baby?" Flynn asked now.

"Getting there," he said. "And believe me, nobody's more surprised about that than me. Except maybe Tess."

"So when's the wedding?"

"As soon as I can convince her to say *yes*."

Apparently *that* surprised his brother, because Flynn's brows disappeared beneath the hair that flopped over his forehead. "She turned you down?"

"Yeah," Holt admitted.

Now his brother chuckled.

"Why is that funny?"

"Because it's probably the first time in your life a woman has refused you anything—and probably nothing has ever mattered more."

"You have a warped sense of humor," Holt grumbled.

"Undoubtedly," Flynn agreed. "Time in a war zone has a way of changing a man's perspective on a lot of things."

Holt couldn't deny that was true, but he also knew his brother wasn't likely to divulge any more information than that, so he returned his attention to his own predicament. "I don't understand why she doesn't want to marry me."

"Clearly you're not as irresistible as you seem to think."

"I don't think I'm irresistible," he argued, perhaps a little testily. "But I do think getting married is the right thing to do under the circumstances."

"Even without your wealth of experience with the female gender, I know that isn't a proposal to warm a woman's heart," his brother told him.

"I took flowers to her tonight, but they didn't seem to aid my cause. Do you have any better ideas?"

Flynn snorted. "You definitely came to the wrong brother. Boone's the one who did the marriage and family thing—at least for a while."

"And he's still grieving for Nadine, which is why I came to you. Also, you guessed about the baby," Holt confided. "And I promised Tess I wouldn't tell anyone until she was ready to share the news."

"So you're already lying to her." His brother shook his head. "Not a good start to your relationship."

"I had to tell someone," he said in his defense. "Although, according to Tess, she'd be perfectly happy if no one knew I was the father of her baby."

Flynn's brows lifted again. "She said that?"

"Yeah."

"So maybe you should be grateful she's letting you off the hook," his brother suggested.

"I don't want to be let off the hook." Holt frowned. "I don't even like calling it a hook, as if it's something that snagged me unawares."

"Didn't it?"

"I didn't plan to be a father—or a husband—at this point in my life. Probably not for another five—or even ten—years, at least. Hell, maybe never. Who knows? But the reality is, I'm going to be a father and I want to do it right."

"Try to look at it from her perspective," Flynn suggested. "And consider why she might be reluctant to jump into marriage with a guy she doesn't even know if she's compatible with—except in the most obvious way."

"I figure that's a pretty good start."

"Not to mention that you can be an involved parent without having to marry her," his brother continued.

"I know it's the twenty-first century, but people will still judge her for getting pregnant," Holt pointed out.

"With her family history, it's inevitable," Flynn agreed.

"Doesn't seem fair, though."

"Of course, it's not fair. But growing up as Tallulah Leonard's granddaughter in Whispering Canyon, I'm sure Tess learned long ago that life isn't fair."

"Maybe that's the key," Holt mused.

Flynn frowned. "What's the key?"

"Getting Tess to see that our child can have a very different life depending on whether he's born to Tallulah Leonard's granddaughter—or my wife."

Eleanor was opening the door before Tess could lift her hand to knock Tuesday morning. "I'm so sorry about last week," she immediately apologized.

With everything that had happened since then, Tess had almost managed to forget the events that precipitated her excursion with Holt. “Did you have a good time at the auction?” she asked the rancher’s wife now.

“We did,” Eleanor confirmed. “And though we got some rain, it wasn’t anything like the storm here.”

“I’ve never seen anything like it,” Tess admitted. “Though maybe that’s because I usually close the blinds and snuggle up under the covers when a storm hits.”

“But you were stuck at Holt’s cabin this time,” his grandmother noted, seemingly unconcerned by the fact. “And he refuses to put up any window coverings.”

“Hard to blame him,” Tess said. “If I had a view like that, I wouldn’t want to shut it out, either.”

“Plus, he’s so far removed from civilization, he doesn’t need to worry about anyone peeking in his windows,” Eleanor remarked. “Aside from the occasional moose or bobcat or grizzly, that is.”

“Yikes.”

“Anyway, Holt seems happy out there. I don’t think he even minds when he’s stranded by the river rising, though I’m sure it was inconvenient for you.”

“We managed,” Tess assured her.

“I hope he was a good host. And a gentleman.”

“He was a very good host, especially considering I was an uninvited guest.”

“Well, he did invite you to go riding. At least, that’s what he told me.”

“I think he felt sorry for me, because Mr. Chandler stood me up,” Tess confided.

A smile teased the corners of Eleanor’s mouth. “You think he felt sorry for you?”

“Why else would he have taken me out?”

“Since you asked, I’ll tell you that I think my grandson might have a little bit of a crush on you. That day at the hospital, even as worried as I was about Raylan, I could see there was a bit of a spark between you and Holt.”

Tess laughed. "I'm sure you're mistaken about that."

"Maybe I am," the rancher's wife allowed. "Or maybe that's why Holt comes up with some excuse to interrupt his work and stop by the house every day that you're here."

"Speaking of work," Tess said, attempting to shift the conversation. "Has Mr. Chandler been keeping up with his exercises?"

"I've heard him muttering and groaning, so I know that he has."

"Good, because I've got a few new ways to make him mutter and groan today." But as Tess headed to the living room, Eleanor's words—*I think my grandson might have a little bit of a crush on you*—echoed in her mind and lifted her heart.

Tires & Tune-Ups was *the* place in Whispering Canyon for automotive parts and service. When the repair shop originally opened, some sixty years earlier, it was simply called Winchester's, the name of the original owner. Then Winchester's son took over and grew tired of answering calls from customers thinking it was a gun shop, so he changed the name to Winchester's Auto Repair. By the time Winchester's grandson took over, the shop's namesake had passed on and the business was rebranded again. Aside from the name and the number of bays, not much else had changed over the years—at least, not so far as Tess could tell, and her dad had worked there for longer than she'd been alive.

On one side of reception was a waiting area, with plastic chairs arranged around a long glass table covered with supermarket tabloids and actual print copies of the local news. The other side was filled with columns of tires stacked halfway to the ceiling. At the far end was a desk, where Stan Stickells usually juggled the phone lines at the same time he calculated invoices and greeted or dispatched customers.

Tess gave herself a minute, to see if her stomach would react negatively to the familiar scents of tire rubber, motor oil and stale coffee. But apparently—having already ditched its contents once earlier that morning—it was unbothered by the smells. After exhaling a quiet sigh of relief, she realized that the voice she heard at the back of the reception area didn't belong to the shop's owner but her own father.

"We'll see you at eleven o'clock on Friday… That's right—I've got you booked in for an oil change and tire rotation with a note to check the noise coming from the backend, which I suspect is your muffler… No, I can't be one hundred percent certain without actually inspecting the vehicle, but I promise we'll take care of it for you on Friday… Yes, ma'am, eleven o'clock… Thank you." A second line was ringing before he'd ended the call on the first. "Tires & Tune-Ups. This is Roger—how can I help you?"

Tess waited patiently for him to answer a question about all-weather versus all-season tires before she stepped up to the counter.

"I'm looking for the boss," she said.

"And you found him." Her dad grinned. "Stan's on holidays this week and left me in charge."

"Darn," Tess said, obviously teasing. "I was hoping he might be able to squeeze my Kia in for an oil change."

"You wouldn't need to beg favors if you called and made an appointment like most of our customers," Roger admonished gently.

"You're right," she agreed.

"So how long has the service light in your dash been on?"

"Just a couple weeks."

He sighed. "I know I raised you better than that."

"I don't usually have to drive too far, but now that I'm making weekly trips out to West River Ranch, I figured I should get the oil changed."

"If you don't take care of your engine, it can fail you—whether you're just over at the Market Pantry grabbing a few groceries or halfway to Billings to see Canyon Creek Trio."

"I can't remember the last time I made a trip to Billings," she told him. "Or went to a concert."

"You're missing my point."

"Regular maintenance is required to keep my vehicle running," she said, echoing the words he'd spoken to her countless times.

"So you do hear what I say," he noted. "You just choose to ignore my advice most of the time."

"Can you squeeze in my Kia?" she asked hopefully.

"Only if you let me take you for breakfast while the guys are changing your oil."

"Sounds like a win-win to me."

Half an hour later, Tess was sitting across from her dad at The Corner Diner, digging into a thick Belgian waffle topped with bananas and strawberries and a generous dollop of whipped cream.

"Still a fan of dessert for breakfast, I see," Roger noted with a smile.

"I like eggs and bacon well enough," Tess said. "But this is better."

Roger scooped up a forkful of scrambled eggs. "We don't do this often enough."

"Every five thousand miles."

"Or a couple of weeks after the five-thousand-mile mark," her dad retorted.

Tess shrugged, unrepentant, as she chewed a mouthful of waffle and fruit.

"Can I ask you a question?" she said, when she paused between bites of breakfast.

"Always."

"When you were first dating Mom—did you have any… concerns?"

"Only that she'd figure out she could do a lot better than me," Roger responded.

"There's no one better than you," Tess said loyally.

He winked across the table. "Lucky for me, your mom believes that, too."

She answered with a smile, then her expression grew serious again. "What I'm really trying to ask is—were you ever bothered by the fact that she was Tallulah Leonard's daughter?"

Roger dumped a packet of sugar into his coffee, stirred. "From the first minute I laid eyes on Abby, I was head over heels and absolutely nothing else mattered."

"Really?" she said dubiously.

"Really," he confirmed, lifting his mug.

She stabbed a slice of strawberry with her fork, considering.

Her dad sipped his coffee. "Does this have anything to do with you dating Holt Chandler?"

"I'm not dating Holt Chandler," she denied. "Why would you think I was?"

"I heard he was at your house three times last week."

"Which makes me think Ramona Martin had her car in for service recently," Tess guessed.

"She needed new brakes—front and back," he said, returning his attention to his eggs.

"She needs to mind her own business."

"She's the block captain of your Neighborhood Watch," he pointed out.

"A position she only volunteered for because it gives her an excuse to stick her nose into everyone else's business," she grumbled.

"Perhaps," Roger agreed. "But most people know her well enough to believe only fifty percent of what she says—which is why I figure Holt Chandler was probably only at your house one-point-five times last week."

A reluctant smile curved her lips.

"So...are you dating him?" her dad pressed.

"No." Tess pushed the remnants of her waffle around on her plate. "Maybe."

He seemed troubled by her response. "Is he hassling you?"

She shook her head. "No."

"You're sure about that at least?"

Now she nodded. "I'm sure."

"You like him?" he asked cautiously.

"Probably more than I should."

"Why would you say that?"

"Because he's a Chandler."

"Any man—even a Kennedy or Rockefeller—would consider himself lucky to snag the interest of my little girl."

"Your little girl is twenty-six years old," she reminded him.

"I know very well how old you are—and when you're attempting to shift the topic of conversation."

She sighed. "The truth is, I don't know what's going on with Holt."

"When you figure it out—if there's anything to figure out—you might consider bringing him around to the house for a proper introduction," her dad suggested.

"I'll do that," Tess promised.

Holt had been a regular customer at Tires & Tune-Ups for as long as he'd had a driver's license and, over the years, he'd gotten to know the owner quite well. During that same time, he'd been introduced to various other employees, though he'd never taken particular notice of any individual and certainly had never made a trip into town for the sole purpose of seeking one out.

Walking into the shop, he was inexplicably nervous, not unlike when he'd been in high school and eager to make a good impression on his prom date's parents. But it wasn't the meeting with Roger Barrett that had his stomach in knots so much as the potential fallout from Tess when she learned that he'd taken it upon himself to meet her father. But they were going to have a baby together—not that he intended to share that information with the baby's grandfather just yet—and he felt strongly that he should lay the groundwork for the news of their imminent wedding, assuming he managed to convince Tess to accept his proposal.

"Mr. Barrett?"

Roger glanced up, his gaze immediately narrowing. "What can I do for you, Holt Chandler?"

He should have expected that Tess's father would know who he was, but he'd come here with the intention of introducing himself and the other man's immediate recognition threw him off his stride.

"I'm looking for new tires for my truck," he said, switching gears and gesturing to the Ford F-150 parked in front of the shop.

"Let's go take a look."

Holt led the way, then stood there, feeling foolish, as Tess's father walked around the vehicle.

"Looks to me like you've got four perfectly good tires," the other man remarked.

"Yeah, but it was all that came to mind in the moment," he admitted.

"So why don't you tell me why you're really here?" Roger suggested.

"I just wanted to introduce myself, sir. And to tell you that I've been seeing your daughter."

"You might have stopped by a couple weeks ago if you wanted to tell me something I didn't already know."

"Tess told you that we're...dating?"

"No," her dad said. "But you can't share a burger at The Bootlegger and then leave your vehicle—a very nice truck, by the way—parked outside her house and expect people won't talk."

Holt winced. "She won't be happy to hear that."

"She wasn't," Roger agreed. "But she wasn't surprised, either."

"I'm sorry if my attention has made her the topic of gossip," he said sincerely.

"Sorry enough to walk away from her?"

"No, sir. If there are people who have a problem with us being together, there's nothing I can do about that, but I hope you're not one of them."

"I trust my daughter to make the decisions that are right for her," Roger said evenly. "And I'm trusting that you'll respect her decision, whatever that might be."

"Yes, sir."

Tess's dad nodded. "Then perhaps our paths will cross again soon."

"You can count on it," Holt told him.

Because promising to respect Tess's decision didn't preclude his best efforts to influence that decision in his favor.

Chapter Twelve

Eleanor Chandler had led a privileged life. As Raylan Chandler's wife, she was known to—and respected by—almost everyone in town, leaving her free to go wherever she wanted, confident that she would be welcomed.

Her usual confidence wavered just a little as she pulled up in front of 32 Maplecrest Drive, but she steeled her spine, fluffed her hair and marched determinedly up the concrete path to knock on the wood door.

After a long moment, the door finally opened and she found herself face-to-face with her husband's former mistress.

Even sixty years later, it was easy to see why Raylan had been drawn to the other woman. Though Tallulah Leonard had lived a hard life, she was still attractive. Her previously blond hair was now gray and styled in a blunt cut that skimmed her shoulders. Her face was heavily lined, but her eyes—green like Tess's—were clear and bright. She was wearing minimal makeup—a touch of mascara to darken her lashes and a dab of gloss to shine her lips—and maximum jewelry—silver teardrop earrings that seemed to drip with colored stones, a collection of bangles on each wrists, an assortment of pretty rings on her fingers and even a chunky silver band on one thumb, though the ring finger on her left hand was conspicuously bare—a bold and unapologetic statement of her single status. Her (possibly authentic) vintage Rolling Stones concert T-shirt and faded denim leggings hugged her feminine curves, making Eleanor wonder if Tallulah worked out or had simply been blessed with exceptional genes.

Eleanor straightened her shoulders, aware that she was being subject to a similar examination by the other woman.

"You lost, Mrs. Chandler?" Tallulah finally asked, in lieu of a more traditional greeting.

"My name's Eleanor," she reminded her. "And no, I'm not lost."

"Then maybe you should tell me why you're here."

"I'd prefer to do so inside, out of earshot of your neighbors, if you don't mind."

"People in this town need to learn to mind their own business," Tallulah grumbled.

"Why would they start now?"

Her response earned a half smile from her husband's former mistress as she moved away from the door.

Eleanor stepped inside, not sure what to expect.

She'd been there before, of course. In fact, she and Raylan had picked out the house, wanting to ensure that Tallulah could raise her daughters in a good neighborhood. They'd paid for it, too, and were still on title as the owners. Until now, Eleanor hadn't given any thought to how that might make the other woman feel, to live in a home belonging to someone else, to worry that she might be turned out on a whim.

It hadn't been a power play but a necessity. Back then, Tallulah was an alcoholic who would sell (and had sold!) her grandmother's antiques for a bottle of bourbon.

She'd been sober for more than forty years now, but no one gave her credit for that. Instead, they continued to focus on the mistakes she'd made in the past, the woman she'd been way back when.

Eleanor could see now that Tallulah hadn't just lived in the house but taken care of it. It was clean and bright, the carpet relatively new, the walls recently painted. And beneath the scent of lemon polish, she thought she detected a hint of something sweet.

Vanilla, maybe?

No, something stronger and richer, she decided.

More like chocolate than vanilla.

"You're in," Tallulah noted, when Eleanor closed the door at her back. "So why don't you tell me what you want?"

"A cup of tea?"

"There's a café down the street."

It was a simple statement of fact, nothing in Tallulah's words or tone giving any hint of what she might be thinking or feeling.

"I thought we might have a cup of tea together," Eleanor said patiently. "There are some things we need to talk about. Please."

The other woman turned and headed down the hall. Eleanor followed her to the kitchen.

The room was a little outdated, she noted. The appliances old and the cabinets worn. Nevertheless, it was as spotless as what she'd seen of the rest of the house, despite the fact that Tallulah had done some baking earlier—as evidenced by the plate of brownies on the table, no doubt the source of the chocolate scent she'd detected.

"What kind of tea do you want?" her reluctant host asked.

"Whatever you're having is fine."

"I prefer coffee," Tallulah said, clearly not interested in meeting Eleanor halfway.

"Coffee works, too," she said easily.

Tallulah brewed two cups and carried them to the table. "You want cream or sugar?"

Eleanor would have loved some of each, but the other woman's tone suggested that she drank hers black and so she decided to do the same. "No, this is fine," she lied. "Though I wouldn't say no to one of those brownies, if you were offering."

After an almost imperceptible hesitation, Tallulah nudged the plate closer to her visitor.

"Thanks," she said, pulling back the plastic wrap and helping herself to a square.

"What is it you think we need to talk about?" Tallulah asked, when Eleanor had finished the first decadently rich and perfectly gooey brownie and was contemplating a second.

She helped herself to another brownie—because why not?—before she responded. "Are you aware that your granddaughter Tess has been spending time with my grandson Holt?"

"Now I understand," Tallulah said bitterly. "You want me to remind her of her proper place."

"Tess is a bright and beautiful young woman whose place should be wherever she wants to make it," Eleanor said.

The other woman frowned at that. "You're saying you don't have a problem with a possible romance between my granddaughter and your grandson?"

"Why would I?" she challenged. "They're both adults."

Tallulah sipped her coffee. "How does Raylan feel about it?"

"I suspect he's oblivious. Though Miranda isn't, and I get the impression that she has some concerns."

"Who's Miranda?" Tallulah asked.

"Holt's mother—and RJ's wife."

"What's her issue with Tess?" Tallulah demanded to know.

"I don't think she has an issue with Tess so much as the fact that her husband was—at least for a while—in love with Tess's mom," Eleanor confided.

"They were just kids," Tallulah said dismissively. "In lust more than love, I'd guess."

"Maybe," she allowed.

"Trust me. Chandlers might fall into bed with Leonards, but they don't fall in love with them."

Another statement of fact, but this time, Eleanor detected just a hint of something that might have been hurt beneath the surface of the other woman's words.

"I've seen Holt and Tess together," she said now. "And I think there's a real connection between them."

"Well, good for them," Tess's grandmother decided.

"But I'm worried that the history between our families might get in the way," Eleanor admitted.

"No way to change what's in the past," Tallulah noted.

"No," she agreed. "But we can choose to take a different path forward."

"Could your path be a little more direct to the point?" the other woman suggested impatiently.

Eleanor fought against the smile that wanted to tug her lips. "The point is that Raylan's planned a party to celebrate our sixty-fifth anniversary."

"I suppose I should say congratulations, though being stuck with the same man for six and a half decades doesn't seem like something I'd want to celebrate," Tallulah noted.

"It's June twenty-eighth," she continued. "I'm hoping you can be there."

Tallulah snorted out a laugh. "You've got to be kidding me."

"I'm not," Eleanor assured her.

The other woman took a minute to consider her response before she shook her head. "Well, thanks for the invite, but no thanks."

"I want Tess to know that there's no reason for her to feel guilty for wanting to make a future with my grandson, if she does, and the best way to do that is to show her that there are no hard feelings between us."

"I'm not sure there are no hard feelings."

"A few years back, you told me that you'd let go of your anger along with the bottle," Eleanor reminded her.

"There are lots of hard feelings aside from anger," Tallulah pointed out. "Dislike, distrust, resentment."

"Fair point," Eleanor acknowledged with a nod. "But I have to assume your feelings for your granddaughter are at the other end of the spectrum."

The other woman swallowed her last mouthful of coffee,

then set her mug on the table. "There isn't anything I wouldn't do for her—or any of my grandchildren."

"Then you should at least consider my invitation, for Tess."

"I appreciate what you're trying to do, really, but I can't imagine she wants to be there any more than I do. Whatever might be going on between her and RJ's son—"

"Holt," Eleanor interjected.

Tallulah shrugged, as if his name didn't matter—as if *he* didn't matter. And though the dismissive gesture raised Eleanor's hackles, she reminded herself that the other woman had always gone on the offensive when she was feeling defensive.

"Whatever might be going on between them right now will no doubt have fizzled out long before the end of June," Tallulah said.

"What makes you so certain?" she asked curiously.

"Because he's a Chandler and she's a Leonard and history has a way of repeating itself."

"You have my number," Tess said, when she found Holt waiting on her porch again Wednesday afternoon. "You could call or send a text message if you wanted to talk."

"But I couldn't give you these—" he offered her another bouquet of flowers "—through a phone call or text message."

"Thank you," she said. "But you have to stop this."

"I'm just the delivery man," he said, tapping the brim of the red baseball cap he was wearing. "Though I should probably tell you that the guy sending the flowers seems pretty crazy about you."

"Or maybe he's just crazy," she countered, sliding her key into the lock.

"You might consider taking pity on him and going out with him," he suggested. "Just once."

"I don't think he's the type of guy to be satisfied with just once."

His lips curved then. "You could be right about that."

"Which is why I've been careful not to encourage him."

"Sometimes a smile can be encouragement enough."

"I'm not smiling," she told him. But she gestured with her head as she stepped over the threshold, silently inviting him to follow.

"But you want to," he said, closing the door at his back. "Because you find me frustrating but also charming..."

She pressed her lips together when they started to curve. "Still not smiling."

"Even so, I don't think he's going to give up."

"He will. Eventually," she said confidently. "When he goes broke buying flowers or grows bored with the chase."

"Neither of those things is going to happen before your neighbors start talking," he warned.

"My neighbors are already talking," she acknowledged.

He winced. "I'm sorry."

"If you were really sorry, you'd stop showing up at my door."

"Have dinner with me tonight and I promise you won't see me tomorrow."

"Having dinner together will only add fuel to the fire," she warned. "As soon as people hear about my pregnancy, they'll speculate that you're the father."

"I *am* the father," he reminded her unnecessarily.

"But I don't want anyone to know that."

"And I want everyone to know, so it appears that we're at cross purposes."

She sighed. "Why are you doing this, Holt?"

"You know why."

"I'm trying to give you a chance to live your life without being tied to me for the next eighteen years."

"Maybe I want to be tied to you. Actually—" he wiggled his brows suggestively "—that sounds like it could be a lot of fun."

"You don't want to be tied to me," she said, ignoring his innuendo. "You only want to do the right thing."

Before he could respond to that, the door opened again.

"Shoes off," Meg said firmly to her daughter.

"I'm not wearin' shoes," Emma replied. "I'm wearin' boots 'cuz it rained today."

"Boots off," the little girl's mom clarified.

The boots obviously came off quickly, because a few seconds later, Emma was in the kitchen.

"Auntie Tess!" She raced toward Tess, who lifted the little girl into her arms to receive a smacking kiss on the cheek.

"This is a surprise," Meg said, noting Holt's presence when she followed her daughter into the room. "Not just my best friend but my best friend's baby daddy."

Emma's head swiveled. "Baby?" she echoed in a hopeful tone.

"Now you've done it," Tess said to her friend.

"*Baby*'s just a term of affection," Meg explained to her daughter. "Like when I call you *baby* sometimes."

"Oh," Emma said, obviously disappointed now.

"You should probably just call me Holt," he said to the little girl.

"Whatsa Holt?" she asked.

"It's my name."

"I'm Emma."

"It's a pleasure to meet you, Emma."

She giggled. "He's funny."

"A barrel of laughs," Tess said dryly, setting the wiggling child's feet on the floor.

"Can we have s'ghetti for dinner?" Emma asked, bouncing on her toes in front of her mom.

Meg looked at Tess. "Does that pass the smell test?"

"As long as we skip the garlic bread."

"But I *love* garlic bread," Emma said.

"You can have garlic bread," Meg told her daughter. To Tess she said, "I'll make it without the garlic."

"Smell test?" Holt said curiously.

"There are a few specific scents that seem to trigger my nausea," Tess admitted.

"Like coffee."

She nodded. "And garlic and peanut butter."

"Peanut butter?"

She shrugged.

"Are you staying for dinner, Holt?" Meg asked.

"If that's an invitation, I won't turn it down," he said.

Meg looked at her friend.

Tess shrugged again.

"It's an invitation," Meg said.

"Then yes, thank you."

"Well, that was unexpected," Meg mused, when Holt had gone. "And the flowers were certainly a nice touch."

"He can be incredibly thoughtful and charming," Tess acknowledged.

"But?" her friend prompted.

"But…" Tess's response trailed off on a sigh.

"It would help if you actually told me what you're thinking," Meg said. "Because as hard as I try, I can't read your mind."

"I guess I'm just wondering why he's doing any of this," she admitted.

"What is it you think he's doing?"

"Pretending this unplanned pregnancy hasn't sent his whole world into a tailspin and insisting that he wants to be part of the child's life," she said. "Why can't he act like a normal guy and breathe a sigh of relief that I'm willing to let him off the hook?"

"Maybe he's hooked on you," Meg said.

"He's Holt Chandler."

Meg set her glass down and snapped her fingers. "*That's* who he is. I thought he looked kind of familiar."

Tess ignored her friend's sarcasm.

"If I had my way, no one would need to know that he's the

baby's father," she said. "And yes, I know people will talk, but they've been talking about me my whole life."

"And is that really something you want your child to experience?" Meg asked gently.

"Of course it's not what I want, but marrying Holt would be even worse, because people would assume that I either trapped him or married him for his money. Or both."

"Obviously this is a decision only you can make, but I feel compelled to point out that you can't know how hard it is to be a single parent if you haven't been there," her friend said. "When you're a single parent, there's no one else to share the day-to-day responsibilities. And I'm not just talking about feedings and diaper changes—though an extra set of hands there would be helpful—but the weight of the responsibility.

"When you're a single parent, you're the one responsible for making every decision. Is it too cold to take the baby outside? Is his bath water too warm? Is the floor too hard? Is the crib mattress too soft?

"And when the baby refuses to sleep, there's no one to take a turn walking with him. No one to drive you to the hospital when his fever spikes. No one to reassure you that his incessant crying isn't proof that you're the worst mom in the world."

"I get it," Tess said.

"No, you don't," Meg told her. "Until you've lived through each of those scenarios, you don't have a clue."

"I know I don't have a clue," she admitted. "But I'm panicked enough without you pointing out all the things I don't know and reminding me that I'm completely unprepared to be a mom."

"I just want you to understand that being a single parent isn't a choice most of us would make. So if you have the opportunity to raise your child with his father, I think you need to give it some serious consideration."

"Okay," she relented. "But why do you keep saying *he* and *his*?"

"Because the Chandler family hasn't born a girl in five generations," Meg said, repeating what Holt had told her.

"My baby could still be a girl," she insisted.

"Maybe," Meg allowed. "But boy or girl, your baby deserves a dad."

"And I'm happy to let Holt be a part of his child's life, if that's what he wants."

"What if he's not satisfied with visitation?"

"I can't imagine he'd want to share custody."

"Shared custody is probably the most common arrangement these days," Meg cautioned. "But you need to consider that he might decide he doesn't want to share his child—not even with the mother."

"What are you saying—that he might go after primary custody?"

Meg looked at her. "Tess, he's a Chandler. You can't tell me the thought hasn't at least crossed your mind."

"He wouldn't," Tess said, though an icy finger of fear raked down her spine.

"I bet our grandmother didn't think Raylan would sue for full custody of her son, either—until he did."

Now Tess's whole body went cold.

"I'm not trying to scare you," Meg said gently. "I'm just trying to make you see that there are a lot of different ways this could play out."

"Obviously I have some things to figure out," she said. "And thankfully, I'm only seven weeks along so I've got some time to do so."

"While you're figuring things out, you might want to rethink Holt's proposal."

"I already told him I'm not going to marry him."

Meg gestured to the vases around the room. "I think all the flowers in here prove that he hasn't given up."

"Because he's not used to hearing a woman say *no*."

"That might be part of it," Meg allowed. "Another part might be that the man wants a real chance to have a relationship with the mother of his child."

"I'm not opposed to having a relationship in which we co-parent our child," Tess said.

"Okay, I've got another question for you," Meg said.

"Another one—this must be my lucky day."

Meg ignored her sarcasm, asking instead, "Why are you so adamantly opposed to marrying a man you've been in love with since you were fourteen, with whom you enjoyed fabulous sex and are now expecting a child?"

"I had a crush on him when I was fourteen," Tess clarified.

"A crush you never got over."

She sighed, unable to deny it was true. "Maybe because I'm afraid that, if I spend too much more time with Holt, I could easily fall in love with him."

"Believe me, there are worse things than being in love with the father of your child."

Tess knew that was true—and that her friend had found that out the hard way.

"I know there are worse things," she acknowledged gently. "But I don't want to be the only one in love, grateful for any crumbs of affection that might fall in my direction."

"It's possible that he could fall in love with you, too," Meg pointed out.

Possible, maybe, Tess acknowledged. But she was afraid to let herself hope. Because it wasn't only her heart that she would be risking now, but her baby's, too.

After Raylan's usual therapy at West River Ranch on Friday, Tess stopped by to see her grandmother.

"Lula? Are you home?"

"In the kitchen," her grandmother called out.

Tess toed off her shoes inside the door and made her way to the back of the house.

"Mmm," she said, sniffing the air. "Something smells good."

"Oatmeal raisin cookies just came out of the oven," Lula said, carefully transferring them from the baking sheet to a cooling rack.

"Is the church having a bake sale?" Tess asked, noting that there were also brownies, pecan tarts and chocolate cupcakes.

"No," her grandmother admitted.

Which meant that she was stress baking.

In her previous life—as Lula referred to it—she would have drowned her sorrows or worries or whatever in the bottle. But she'd been sober for more than four decades now, and when she found herself stressed, she busied herself in the kitchen instead of seeking solace from alcohol.

"What's going on, Gramma?"

Lula frowned. "You know I don't like when you call me that."

"I know you don't like it," Tess acknowledged. "But I don't know why, because you are my grandmother."

Lula turned away to stir the chocolate melting in the double boiler. "That title isn't a birthright."

"I don't know," Tess said, nibbling on a warm cookie. "According to my fifth grade social studies teacher, the mother of my mother is my grandmother."

"Well, I wasn't much of a mother to yours," Lula reminded her, turning off the element beneath the pot before shifting her attention to the next recipe.

Tess took the bag of oats out of her grandmother's hands and set it aside.

"Scotty likes oatmeal chocolate chip cookies," Lula said, naming one of the little boys who lived next door.

"I'm sure he'll be just as happy with oatmeal raisin."

Lula shook her head. "He doesn't like raisins."

Tess gave up arguing with her grandmother and turned to fill the sink with hot, soapy water so that she could wash the already used mixing bowls and utensils. "Aside from the bake-a-thon, how was your day?"

"Fine." Lula mixed brown sugar with the oats.

"Did you have any visitors today?"

"I have one right now."

"How about earlier?" Tess prompted.

"It sounds like somebody already told you that the sheriff was here," Lula noted, as she combined the wet ingredients with the dry.

She nodded. "Meg saw his car in your driveway when she was on her way to pick up Emma from preschool."

"Is that why you're here?"

"I just want to know if he's hassling you," Tess said.

"He's got no reason to hassle me," her grandmother said, dropping spoonfuls of dough onto a baking sheet.

"Which isn't really an answer."

"Billy Garvey's father was sheriff before him," Lula pointed out. "He might have had reason to hassle me, because I had a tendency to be drunk and disorderly back then, and Alvin certainly took pleasure in doing so. Of course, he was always a lousy sheriff and his son's only following in his footsteps."

"What did Billy want from you, Gramma?"

"Nothing more than to pick at old scars," Lula said dismissively, sliding the tray into the oven.

"I need more than that," Tess said.

Tallulah sighed. "He just reminded me that I was a lousy drunk and a lousier mother and that Raylan and Eleanor Chandler had my kids taken away from me. Then he speculated that the old wound might still be festering, filling my soul with poison and hate. Maybe enough to finally do what I threatened to do some fifty years ago."

"He can't honestly think that you might have shot Raylan Chandler."

"Like I said—picking at old scars."

"Well, he has no right. And I'm going straight to the sheriff's office now to give him a piece of my mind."

"He has an obligation to investigate the shooting," Lula

noted. "And once upon a time, I did threaten to kill the man. Garvey wouldn't be doing his job if he didn't look in my direction, and now I have to believe he's done looking. But if you go storming into the sheriff's office, he might start to think there's something to his cockamamie theory."

"Cockamamie?" Tess felt a smile tug at the corners of her mouth. "Someone's been using her word of the day calendar."

Lula shrugged. "It's an easy way to expand my vocabulary."

"Did you tell the sheriff his theory was cockamamie?"

"I didn't use the word, but I did annotate with scornful laughter."

"Well, at least that's something," Tess decided.

"You don't have to worry about me," her grandmother said. "I'm fine."

"You're baking as if you intend to give Sara Lee a run for her money."

"Are you saying that you don't want any cupcakes, then?"

"Of course, I want cupcakes," Tess said. "I'll take some of the brownies and pecan tarts, if you're giving them away, too."

"To share with Meg and Emma?" Lula guessed.

"If I have to," Tess said, making her grandmother chuckle as she began to pile the requested items into a Tupperware container.

When the oven timer dinged, Tess slid a baking mitt onto her hand to remove the tray of cookies. "Mmm, these ones look and smell just as good as everything else."

"They're particularly tasty when they're still warm from the oven," Lula said. "I'll make some coffee to go with them."

Before Tess could protest that she didn't want any, her grandmother had dropped a pod into the maker. In almost no time, coffee was pouring out of the spout and into the cup below. Even as the scent teased Tess's nostrils, it churned her stomach.

"Excuse me," she said to her grandmother, then raced to the bathroom.

When she returned several minutes later, Lula was nibbling on a cookie and sipping her coffee.

"I made you peppermint tea," she said, indicating the cup on the opposite side of the table.

"Thanks." Tess slid into the vacant seat.

"So—" Lula nibbled another bite of cookie "—is it Holt Chandler's baby?"

Chapter Thirteen

Tess was taken aback by her grandmother's question. And though she was tempted to hedge or deflect, the knowing glint in Lula's eye warned that such efforts would be futile. Instead, she asked, "How did you guess?"

"I saw Eleanor Chandler the other day, and she mentioned that there was something going on between her grandson and my granddaughter."

"Where did you see Eleanor Chandler?"

Gramma Lula waved away the question. "That's not important."

"Did she seem bothered by the fact that something was going on between Holt and me?" Tess asked cautiously.

Her grandmother took another bite of her cookie. "The opposite, in fact."

"Hmm," she mused.

"Does he know about the baby?"

Now she nodded.

"He offer to marry you?"

She nodded again.

Lula popped the last bit of cookie into her mouth. "Am I going to get an invite to the wedding?"

Tess sipped her tea. "There's not going to be a wedding."

"You said no?" Lula's tone was incredulous.

"Of course, I said no," Tess told her. "And I thought you, of all people, would support my decision."

"Because I never married any of the men who knocked me up?"

"Well, yes," she admitted. "And because you always said that marriage was nothing more than indentured servitude of women."

Gramma Lula sighed. "Didn't your mom ever read the story about the fox and the grapes to you when you were a kid?"

"The one about the sour grapes?"

Her grandmother nodded. "It's possible I might have a different opinion of marriage if I'd had the chance to walk down the aisle."

"Are you saying—do you think I should marry Holt?"

"I think you'd be a fool not to at least consider it," Lula said. "And I know your mother didn't raise any fools."

"I already said no," Tess reminded her. "It's possible he's changed his mind by now."

"Then he's a fool."

Tess wasn't amused when she found Holt on her porch—again—when she returned home after her visit with her grandmother Friday afternoon.

"This really isn't a good time," she told him.

"Rough day?" he asked, offering her yet another bouquet of flowers along with a tower of tea boxes wrapped in cellophane and tied with a big red bow.

The cheery blooms did give a little boost to her spirits and the assortment of herbal teas tugged at her heart, though she had no intention of telling him so. "Not as rough as my grandmother's."

"You want to invite me in to tell me about it?" he asked hopefully.

"I really just want my dinner and bed." She sighed. "Except that I planned to pick up pizza on my way home and forgot, so I guess it will just be my bed."

His brows lifted.

"Definitely *not* an invitation," she told him.

"Meg and Emma aren't home tonight?"

"They have dinner with her parents on Fridays."

He nodded. "So what do you like on your pizza?"

"Usually I'll eat almost anything," she said. "But in light of my recent…sensitivities…probably just pepperoni."

"Okay. You go put the flowers in water—I'll go pick up the pizza."

"You're sure you don't mind?"

"I offered, didn't I?"

She nodded. "Thank you."

An hour later, she was sitting across from him, the pizza box empty, nibbling on a brownie.

Holt didn't nibble. He popped a whole brownie into his mouth.

"So good," he said, with a mouth full of chocolate.

"You should try a pecan tart."

"I already did," he admitted. "Best I've ever had."

"My grandmother stress bakes," she confided to him now. "And the sheriff stopped by to see her today."

"What did Billy Garvey want with her?"

"He questioned her about your grandfather's shooting."

Holt frowned. "He thinks she had something to do with it?"

"I don't know what he thinks, but the fact that your grandfather was shot and my grandmother was questioned about it should be all the evidence you need that a relationship between us could never work."

"I don't see that it has anything to do with us," he countered.

"It's only one of the many reasons there can never be an us," she told him.

"There already *is* an us," he argued.

"No," she denied. "There's a *you* and there's a *me* and there's a *baby*, but there's *not* an us."

"Our baby deserves a family, Tess."

She had to swallow the lump that rose up in her throat before she could respond. "I understand that you want our child to have a family, but are you willing to give up your own in exchange?"

"What are you talking about?"

"Holt, your mom is never going to approve of a relationship between us."

"She'll come around," he said.

"I'm not so sure about that," Tess said. "But at least I now know that she doesn't hate me because I'm Tallulah's granddaughter."

"She doesn't hate you," Holt interjected.

"She hates me," Tess said again, because she had no doubt about Miranda's feelings, "because I'm Abby Leonard's daughter."

Holt frowned at that. "Are you telling me that my mom has some kind of history with your mom?"

"No. I'm telling you that your *dad* has a history with my mom."

Holt was still pondering Tess's claim when he headed to his parents' house for Sunday dinner with his family.

Tonight his mom had promised a traditional roast dinner, which meant a prime cut of Chandler beef with all the usual accompaniments: mashed potatoes, gravy, carrots, corn and Yorkshire pudding.

When Holt walked through the door, Buddy at his side, Gage and Zane immediately abandoned their crayons and coloring books in the middle of the living room floor to tackle the dog. Buddy lowered himself to the floor, a resigned—and not entirely unwilling—recipient of their attention.

"Maybe I should get a dog," Boone mused.

"You don't need a dog, you need a nanny," Miranda said.

Holt knew it had been a struggle for his brother to parent on his own after the death of Boone's wife, almost two years earlier. He'd muddled through the first six months with a lot of help from Miranda and Eleanor and Willow, and then he'd acknowledged that they all need more structure and stability in their lives and he'd hired a nanny.

Cassie had stayed with him for almost eight months, and the boys had thrived under her care and attention. Then Cassie's sister in Bozeman had gone through a nasty divorce and she'd moved to Montana to help with her kids.

Since then, Boone had hired several more nannies, but none of them had stuck around for very long. It wasn't that the twins were too much to handle—though Holt could attest to the fact that they gave it their best effort at times—but that West River Ranch was far off the beaten path for anyone who lived in town. And though the rancher had offered accommodation as part of the deal, he had yet to find anyone who wanted to work and live so far away from town.

"What happened to Shauna?" his mom asked now. "She seemed to like it out here."

"Unfortunately, she was more interested in being their stepmother than their nanny."

"Oh." Miranda considered this revelation as she set plates around the table. "Well, she wasn't unattractive. And she was good with the boys. Maybe getting married again—"

"Stop," Boone said.

"I'm just saying—"

"Look who's here," RJ said, as his middle son walked through the door.

Miranda sent her husband a look of annoyance.

"Am I late?" Flynn asked, his gaze flitting around the tension-filled room.

"Actually, I'd say your timing was perfect," Holt told him.

Miranda huffed out a breath. "I only want what's best for my son. For all my sons."

"And your roast beef is the best," RJ said, touching his lips to her cheek.

Her expression softened even as she swatted him away with the napkins in her hand. "Go get it out of the oven, then," she said, before turning her attention to her grandsons. "Come to the table for dinner, boys."

"Yay!" The twins abandoned the dog to race to the table.

"Hands," Miranda admonished.

"Our hands are clean," Zane said, holding his palms up to show her.

"They might not look dirty, but you've had them all over that smelly dog so they need to be washed before you come to the table."

"Buddy's not smelly," Gage said, returning to wrap his arms around the animal's neck and press his face into his fur. "He smells like…roses."

Holt choked on a laugh.

"Then please go wash the smell of roses off your hands," Miranda said.

"But—" Zane began.

"Get your butts into the bathroom and wash up," Boone interjected.

The boys exhaled audible weary sighs, but they trudged to the bathroom to do their father's bidding.

When everyone was gathered around the table, conversation shifted to more neutral topics with occasional requests of "more roast beef, please" and "can you pass the potatoes?"

Buddy took up his usual position under the table, by the twins' chairs, where he knew he'd be the beneficiary of bits of food "falling" off the table.

When almost everyone had cleared their plates, Gage slid out of his seat to climb onto Boone's knee. Dropping his head onto his dad's shoulder, he said, "I'm tired."

"I'm tired, too," Zane said, climbing onto Boone's other knee.

"Looks like you're three-for-three," Miranda remarked.

Boone nodded. "We should probably head out right after ice cream."

"Ice cream!" Gage agreed.

"Ice cream!" Zane echoed.

The twins' grandmother frowned. "I don't think we have any ice cream."

The boys' identical hopeful expressions morphed into identical pouts.

"But we've got some in the freezer at home," Boone said, before the pouts could turn into tears.

"Can we go home now, Daddy?" Zane asked.

Boone looked at his mom, as if for her permission.

She sighed. "Yes, you can go home," she said. "And I'm sure you don't need me to tell you that it's not a good idea to give them ice cream too close to their bedtime."

"Nope," Boone confirmed, rising from his seat with a child in each arm.

"Well played," Holt murmured, as his eldest brother headed out with his sons.

Flynn nodded. "Once again, he skips out of KP."

"But he also skipped out before the food was packed up, and I'll gladly do the pots and pans in exchange for leftovers," Holt said.

"Speaking of," Miranda said, "I stopped by your cabin Friday afternoon with leftover lasagna."

"Yeah, I found it in my fridge. Had it for dinner last night—thanks."

"What did you have on Friday?"

"Pizza."

"I would have gone into town with you for pizza," Flynn said.

"I had a much prettier date," Holt told him.

"Tess?" his brother guessed.

He nodded.

"You were out with Tess Barrett Friday night?" Miranda asked.

"Actually, we had pizza at her place," he said.

"I thought I made it clear that I didn't want you spending time with that woman."

"I'm twenty-nine years old, Mom. I don't think I need your permission to go out with a girl I like."

His mother's mouth thinned.

Flynn, no fool, grabbed his plate of roast beef and veggies. "Thanks again for dinner, Mom," he said, and slipped out the door.

Miranda barely acknowledged his departure, immediately turning back to Holt to say, "So you're dating her now?"

He wasn't sure that was the right description for their relationship, but he nodded anyway. "Yes, I am."

"No." She shook her head. "You have to stop. Right now."

"Why?" Holt asked, baffled by her insistence.

"Her grandmother seduced your grandfather and made him break his wedding vows."

Holt had a hard time imagining anyone making his grandfather do anything he didn't want to do, but he knew better than to say so. "Haven't we moved beyond the point where we visit the sins of the father upon his son? Or, in this case, the sins of the grandmother upon her granddaughter?"

"How appropriate that you would mention the sins of the father," she said, an unmistakable note of bitterness in her voice.

He frowned. "What's that supposed to mean?"

"Ask yours," she said.

And then, as the man in question walked into the kitchen, she moved past him and out the door, letting it slam behind her.

"What was that about?" RJ asked.

"I was hoping you could tell me."

"I was branding calves with you most of the day—I have no idea what's got a bee in her bonnet."

"I asked her why she objected to me spending time with Tess and she went off on a tangent about Gramps cheating on Grams and then told me to ask you about the sins of the father."

RJ opened the refrigerator and pulled out a bottle of beer for his son. Holt accepted it and twisted the cap off. His dad took a second bottle for himself and did the same.

"I could use some help here, Dad," Holt said.

"With Tess?"

"I think I could bring Tess around to the idea of a relationship with me if she wasn't so convinced that my family doesn't like her. And I'm having a little trouble understanding how you can decide you don't like her when you don't even know her."

"There's a history between our families," RJ reminded his son.

"I'm aware," Holt said. "But that was sixty years ago."

"Actually…there's some more recent history, too."

"Of which I'm obviously unaware," Holt realized.

RJ swallowed a mouthful of beer. "You know that your mom and I started dating in high school?"

"Yeah. I've heard the story probably a hundred times."

"Well, there's a part of the story that you don't know," RJ confided. "We broke up for a while when I came home after my first year of college, and the reason we broke up is that I developed feelings for another woman."

…your dad has a history with my mom.

As Tess's words echoed in the back of his mind, he realized the truth. "Abby Leonard."

His dad nodded.

"You dated Tess's mom?" Holt pressed, seeking clarification of their history.

"No." RJ shook his head. "Not really. Your grandparents would never have approved of that."

"Because she was Tallulah's daughter?"

"More because she was living here and being raised by them."

"And Mom's still mad that you had a crush on Tess's mom—but never really dated her—years before you were married?"

"It appears that way," RJ agreed.

"So what are the chances that she'll finally get over that and accept Tess as part of my life?" he wondered aloud.

"Not worth betting on."

But his dad didn't know what was at stake—or that Holt was already all in.

Holt glanced at the screen of his phone, surprised to see Tess's name on the display. They'd exchanged several text messages in the nine days that had passed since he learned of her pregnancy and even spoken a few times, but Tess had never initiated a call, which immediately made him wonder if something was wrong.

He snatched up the device before the second ring had finished. "Tess. Hi."

"Hi," she replied, sounding uncharacteristically uncertain. "Am I calling at a bad time?"

"Not at all," he assured her. "What's up?"

"You asked me to keep you posted—with respect to the baby," she reminded him. "So I'm letting you know that I have a doctor's appointment on Thursday."

"Is everything okay?" he asked cautiously.

"Everything's fine. I mean, as far as I know. This is just a regular monthly checkup, but it's also my first ultrasound. The doctor said they usually schedule one sometime around seven or eight weeks to take some measurements of the baby to confirm due date and check the heart rate." She paused for a moment before she continued, "I was calling to see if you wanted to be there."

"I do," he said, pleased that she'd reached out and genuinely excited for a first glimpse of their baby. "Thursday, you said?"

"Yeah. Ten o'clock."

"Whispering Canyon Medical Clinic?"

"No!"

He was taken aback by her vehement response.

"The doctors there are good enough to operate on my grandfather but not to deliver our baby?"

"The doctors at WCMC are the best," she assured him. "But rumors would spread like wildfire if I was seen at the local maternity clinic—with or without you."

"I didn't think about that," he admitted.

"Dr. Robson is an ob-gyn in Howlett's Pass."

"It will take at least thirty minutes to get there, park, et cetera," he noted, mentally calculating. "Should I pick you up around nine fifteen?"

"Picking me up would also fuel the fire," she said. "I'll meet you there at nine forty-five."

"I understand why you don't want to announce your pregnancy to all of Whispering Canyon right now, but regardless of what happens between us, I am going to be part of our baby's life, so people might as well get used to seeing me as part of yours."

She was silent for a minute—for so long, in fact, he wondered if he'd pushed too hard and she was regretting that she'd made the call.

But when she spoke again, it was to say, "Okay. You can pick me up at nine-fifteen."

"I'll see you then," he promised, punching a triumphant fist into the air.

"Your range of movement is much improved, Mr. Chandler," Tess noted, pleased with the progress her patient had made in recent weeks.

"It feels better, too," the rancher confirmed.

"Obviously you've been doing your exercises even when I'm not here."

"Gotta be in tip-top shape to dance with my bride," he said.

"It's been a lot of years since I was a bride," Eleanor chimed in.

"You'll always be my bride," her husband said. "My one and only."

"And you've always been a smooth talker," she noted.

"You're coming to the party, aren't you, Tess?" Raylan asked now.

"Oh. Um..." She wasn't sure how to answer his question as she had yet to decide one way or the other.

"You got an invitation, didn't you?" he demanded.

"I did," she confirmed. "And I appreciate that you thought of me, but I'm not sure it would be...appropriate."

"You got an invitation," Raylan said again. "You should come. Maybe take a turn around the dance floor with one of my handsome grandsons—I've got nine you can pick from." The twinkle in his eye faded a little then. "And eight of them will be there."

"I'll keep that in mind," Tess promised.

"You do that," he said. "And if you're done with me for now..."

"I am," she confirmed.

"I'm gonna ride out with Clayton to see if we can find any evidence of the wolves Hank claims he saw last week."

"If Hank says he saw wolves, he saw wolves," Eleanor told her husband.

He nodded. "That's what I'm afraid of."

"You be careful out there," she cautioned.

"Always," he promised, and touched his lips to hers before he headed out the door.

"And I need to be heading back to town," Tess said to Eleanor, when Raylan had gone.

The rancher's wife looked disappointed. "Willow made pasta salad for lunch."

Tess glanced at her watch again.

"I don't want to keep you, if there's really somewhere else that you need to be," Eleanor said. "But if there's not, I'd appreciate your company."

"It's hard to say no to pasta salad," Tess said.

The other woman smiled, obviously pleased by her response, and hooked an arm through Tess's to lead her to the dining room.

"Can I ask you a question?" Tess asked, when she was seated across from the rancher's wife at the table.

"Of course."

"Why are you always so nice to me?"

"Is there any reason I shouldn't be nice to you?" Eleanor asked.

"You mean aside from the fact that Tallulah Leonard is my grandmother?"

"Which isn't something you had any control over."

"I love my grandmother," Tess said. "But I know what she did to you—to your family—and that you have legitimate reasons to hate her."

"Hate is an unproductive and unhealthy emotion," Eleanor said. "Though I will admit I'm not a member of Tallulah's fan club, I don't hate her."

"I don't think she has much of a fan club," Tess said dryly.

"In any event," the rancher's wife continued. "You bear absolutely no responsibility for what happened between your grandmother and my husband." Then she sighed regretfully. "Unfortunately, I can't say the same for myself."

"What do you mean?" Tess asked cautiously.

"I'm not excusing what Raylan did. Cheating is never okay," Eleanor said firmly. "But I do understand that he was seeking something I couldn't give him at the time. There were…complications…after RJ was born—the result being that I'd never have another child, which destroyed my dream of filling our house with children.

"When I found out that Raylan had dallied with a woman in town—a younger woman—and that she was pregnant…" Eleanor paused, obviously still pained by her husband's betrayal, even more than sixty years later. "His cheating was like a knife to my heart. To learn that his mistress could give him what I no longer could…it was like twisting that knife.

"He was ashamed to admit the affair and embarrassed that he'd been careless about birth control, but he never denied his guilt or responsibility for the child."

"And you ended up raising not only Wyatt but his two sisters, too."

Eleanor nodded. "To be honest, I struggled with the decision to seek custody of all three children—not certain if I was truly doing what was best for them or trying to fulfill my own dreams."

"Whatever your motivation, I'm sure—based on what my mother told me about her mother's struggles—you did what was best for them. She also said that you were more of a mother to her than Tallulah ever was."

"Abby called me Mama once," Eleanor confided. "She was about nine years old at the time, and hearing that word from her, seeing her look at me with trust and love, filled my heart with so much joy—immediately followed by so much pain and guilt. Because she had a mother, and I had no right to take her place.

"At the time, Tallulah wasn't capable of being responsible for herself never mind her children, but she was still the woman who'd carried them in her womb and brought them into the world.

"The next day, I went to Tallulah and promised that if she could get sober—and stay that way for a whole calendar year—I wouldn't oppose her application to regain custody of Abby and Sunny."

"Apparently it took her a while to get sober," Tess noted. "Because my mom said she was sixteen when you sent her and Sunny away."

Holt's grandmother winced. "I was afraid the girls would see it that way, but it wasn't what we intended. It wasn't even what we wanted, but it seemed the best solution at the time."

"Because of what happened between my mom and Holt's dad," Tess guessed.

"She told you about that?"

"She didn't go into details, but yes."

"We thought we were doing the right thing. It was obvious that they had feelings for one another, but Abby was barely sixteen, and we worried that he was taking advantage of her. That was our biggest concern. Really our only concern," Eleanor said, holding Tess's gaze. "Abby being a Leonard was never a factor."

Chapter Fourteen

"You're getting a late start today," Ramona Martin said, when she stepped outside Thursday morning and saw Tess sitting on the steps of the porch next door.

"I took the day off," she replied.

"In that case, an early start," the other woman amended.

Tess ignored her not-so-subtle prying and simply said, "Enjoy your yoga class."

"I always do," Ramona assured her, fluttering her fingers before settling into her car.

Tess breathed a quiet sigh of relief when she pulled out of her driveway, grateful that her nosy neighbor wouldn't be there to see Holt Chandler at her house again.

Gratitude soon shifted to worry when she realized that she hadn't confirmed their plans with him the night before. Maybe something had come up. Or maybe he'd changed his mind about wanting to be there for the ultrasound—or wanting to be part of their child's life.

When she'd seen the plus sign in the window of the pregnancy test, that answer had immediately been followed by so many more questions. One of which was—should she tell Holt? She hadn't yet settled on an answer to that question when the decision was taken out of her hands. He'd guessed the truth of her condition and hadn't completely freaked out. At least not outwardly.

Of course, it was entirely possible that his outward calm was nothing more than a facade. Tess thought she'd done a pretty good job pretending she wasn't freaking out, though she definitely was. And while the possibility of sharing the joys and responsibilities with someone else was definitely appealing, she was concerned that she might start to count on Holt to be there and end up being let down when he changed his mind about wanting to be a father to their baby. About wanting her. Because every man she'd ever known—aside from her own father—had let her down.

But then, less than three minutes after Ramona's car had disappeared from sight, Holt pulled up in front of the house. He immediately hopped out of the driver's seat and came around to open the passenger door for her.

"You look surprised to see me. Did you forget that you invited me?" he asked, obviously teasing.

"No. Of course not. My mind was just wandering."

"Anything you want to talk about?"

She shook her head as she fastened her seat belt.

"Well, I'm here for you," he said, as if privy to her innermost thoughts and fears. "Whatever you need. Every step of the way."

She didn't doubt that his intentions were good and that he meant what he was saying right now. But there were still seven months until the baby arrived, and she knew it was entirely possibly that he'd grow bored with the idea of being a father long before then.

But he was here now, and she was grateful.

"Good morning, Tess," Dr. Robson said by way of greeting when she entered the exam room. "How are you doing today?"

"I'm doing okay," Tess said.

The doctor shifted her attention. "I'm Belinda Robson—and I'm guessing that you're Dad."

Holt nodded and offered his hand. "Holt Chandler."

"It's a pleasure to meet you," she said. "And always a comfort to know that an expectant mom has a supportive partner."

"I'm happy to do what I can," he said.

"I'll bet you're both excited to get a first look at your baby, but before I ask the ultrasound technician to come in, I'm going to go through the usual checkup stuff with Mom." She looked at Tess then. "Is it okay if Dad stays for this part or do you want him to wait outside?"

"He can stay," Tess said.

The doctor nodded and proceeded to chat with Tess while she checked her weight and monitored her blood pressure.

"You're down almost two pounds," the doctor noted.

"Morning sickness."

"Every day?"

"Most days," Tess said. "But never at the same time of day."

"Of course not," the doctor noted with a smile. "Because then you might be able to prepare for it."

"I've learned to avoid specific trigger foods, though—coffee, garlic and peanut butter."

The doctor jotted notes.

"Nausea and/or vomiting?"

"Both."

"How many times a day are you throwing up?"

"Never more than once."

"You're taking your prenatal vitamins?"

Tess nodded.

"And eating healthy? Drinking lots of water?"

More nodding.

"Blood pressure's good," the doctor noted, removing the cuff from Tess's arm. "Any swelling in your feet or ankles?"

"Nothing noticeable."

"Okay, then." The doctor closed the folder. "Now it's your turn—do you have any questions for me?"

"I've heard it's important to stay active during pregnancy," Tess said. "But are there any restrictions on physical activity?"

"I'd steer clear of abdominal workouts—crunches, planks, et cetera—and anything that keeps you lying flat on your back for extended periods." She glanced at Holt now, taking in his cowboy boots and hat. "Horseback riding is generally safe through the first trimester, if you're an experienced rider, but beyond that, the baby will have moved above the pelvic girdle, a position that leaves him or her more susceptible to traumatic injury if you fall or are thrown off."

"Good to know," Tess said.

"Other than that, no restrictions," the doctor concluded. "And because a lot of patients are hesitant to ask, I'll just come right out and assure you that sex is absolutely on the approved list of exercise during a low-risk pregnancy like yours."

Holt watched as Tess's cheeks filled with color and, at the same time, felt a telltale warmth climb up his throat and into his face.

"Any other questions?" Dr. Robson asked.

"No," Tess said quickly. "I think that about covers it for today."

"Good." The doctor smiled. "Make sure you book a follow-up appointment at the desk for next month after your scan—which Marcy will be in to get started on right away."

Silence fell.

"Well, that was informative," Holt said, after the doctor had gone and a long, tense moment of silence had fallen between them.

"Aren't you glad you decided to come today?" Tess asked, laughter dancing in her eyes.

"Actually, I am. Because I want to be a supportive partner."

"And I appreciate that," she said.

"Of course, it would be a lot easier if we were married."

Her amusement quickly faded. "I'm not sure that's true, but I'll admit that I'm glad you're here now."

"Are you nervous about the ultrasound?" he asked.

"A little."

"Me, too," he confided.

"Why are *you* nervous?" she wondered.

"Because up until now, our baby was—at least for me—more of a concept than a reality."

"The anytime-of-day morning sickness made this pregnancy very real for me," Tess admitted.

"I'm sorry about that."

"I'm not sorry," she said. "Not about any of it."

A brisk knock on the door preceded the entry of the ultrasound technician, wheeling a portable cart ahead of her. "Good morning, good morning."

"Good morning," Tess echoed.

But Holt didn't respond to the greeting. He was staring, apparently speechless, at the ultrasound technician who, Tess realized now, was none other than Marcy Duncan—one of his many high school girlfriends.

Marcy glanced over, the easy smile on her face freezing when she recognized him.

"Oh. Wow." Her attention shifted to Tess. "This is…unexpected."

"So much for your plan to come to Howlett's Pass to avoid sparking rumors," Holt said to Tess.

"No one will hear anything from me," Marcy was quick to reassure them both. "I have a legal, ethical and professional duty to protect patient confidentiality and privacy, and I will always do so. But if this is too awkward for you—either of you—I can see if there's another technician available."

Holt looked at Tess.

She shrugged. "It doesn't bother me. Then again, *I* didn't sleep with her."

To Holt's surprise, Marcy laughed.

"If *you* had, we might still be together," she said, with a wink for Tess.

It took Holt a minute to connect the dots, and even then, he wasn't entirely convinced he had the full picture. "Are you saying…"

"Yep," she confirmed. "And now you could spark rumors in

Whispering Canyon, too. Which is one of the reasons I moved to Howlett's Pass years ago."

Marcy gave him another minute to consider that revelation before she said, "So…are we going to get a first look at your baby today?"

"We are," Tess confirmed.

The technician nodded, already setting up beside the bed on which the expectant mom was sitting. "Go ahead and lie down, then," she said. "Push your leggings down below your hipbones and lift your shirt up to expose your belly."

Tess followed her directions, and Holt moved around to the other side of the bed, so as not to interfere with the procedure. He reached for Tess's hand and was surprised when she let him link their fingers together.

Marcy finished transcribing the patient information from the chart to the computer, then squeezed some gel onto Tess's belly and began to spread it around with a transducer.

Tess squeezed Holt's hand tighter as an image appeared on the screen.

"There's your baby," Marcy said.

Holt leaned closer. "Where?"

Holding the probe against Tess's belly with one hand, Marcy pointed to the screen with the other. "This—" she gestured to the large outline "—is the amniotic sac. The fluid here protects the baby. This—" now she indicated a smaller, darker circle within the amniotic sac "—is the gestational sac. And inside the gestational sac—" she shifted her finger again "—is your baby."

"How big is she right now?" Tess wondered.

The technician glanced at the measurements she'd already taken. "One-point-five-eight centimeters. About the size of a kidney bean."

"That's…tiny," Holt noted.

"She's got a lot of growing to do over the next seven months," Tess agreed.

"Or *he* has a lot of growing to do."

"There's no way of telling if it's a boy or a girl, at least not through an ultrasound at this stage," Marcy said. "But I can give you a picture to take home, if you want."

Tess nodded. "Yes, please."

While the pictures were printing, Tess used the towel Marcy gave her to wipe the remnants of the gel off her belly, then pulled up her leggings and tugged down her shirt.

"Congratulations," Marcy said, as she handed a copy of the photo to each of them. "Sincerely."

"Tess?" Holt said questioningly, when the technician had gone. "Are you okay?"

She could only shake her head, too choked up to speak.

Thankfully, he didn't press her to respond. Instead, he sat on the exam table next to her and took her in his arms. And suddenly, the tears that she'd been holding back would be contained no longer.

Holt didn't say anything more, he just held her while she cried. Eventually the tears subsided, and she dabbed at the remnants on her cheeks with the corner of the towel Marcy had given her.

"I'm sorry," she said to Holt now. "I don't know what came over me, all of a sudden, I just felt..."

"Overwhelmed?" he guessed.

She nodded.

Overwhelmed was a good word to describe the way her heart was suddenly overflowing with love for the tiny life she carried inside—and the enormous, irrational fear that she was going to somehow totally screw up her child's life.

She already knew she would do anything for her baby. Anything to give him or her the best possible life. But did that include marrying the man whose shirt she'd soaked with her tears?

Assuming that he still wanted to marry her and wasn't

tempted to run fast and far away from the emotional woman who'd soaked his shirt with her tears.

"I can understand that," he said. "And I'm only thinking about how my life will change when the baby is born, while your life has already changed."

"Nothing matters more to me than giving my baby the best possible life."

"*Our* baby," he reminded her.

"Our baby," she confirmed.

"Feeling better now?" he asked, when she hopped down from the exam table.

"I'm not sure."

"Okay, then—how do you feel about ice cream?"

"Ice cream?" she echoed dubiously.

He shrugged. "Whenever I was upset as a kid, my grandmother would scoop up a bowl of ice cream."

"I'm not a kid," she told him.

"But you're having a kid."

She managed to smile even as her eyes filled again. "Hard to argue with that kind of logic."

So after they stopped at the reception desk to make an appointment for Tess's next checkup, Holt took her hand and led her to an ice cream shop down the street.

"You can learn a lot about a person from their favorite ice cream flavor," he said, opening the door for her.

"Seems like a lot of pressure to put on a scoop of vanilla," she said lightly.

"I should have guessed you were a vanilla aficionado," he said, after they'd ordered their ice cream—vanilla in a cup for Tess, chocolate in a cone for Holt.

"Why?" Tess sat at a table by the window. "What does it supposedly tell you about me? That I'm predictable? Boring?"

"On the contrary," he said. "Vanilla lovers are generally impulsive and idealistic risk-takers."

"I don't think anyone I know would describe me as either impulsive or a risk-taker."

"And yet, I seem to recall that you accepted an invitation to my hotel room one night eight weeks back."

She couldn't dispute that.

"And what does chocolate say about you?"

He grinned. "That I'm charming and flirtatious."

"Well, that's certainly true enough," she agreed.

"Also, men who like chocolate ice cream are known to be loyal husbands and excellent fathers."

"Now you're just making stuff up," she said.

"Am I?" he challenged. "Because the only thing my brother Boone loves more than chocolate ice cream is his kids."

"You can't make a generalization on the basis of one specific example," she protested, spooning up her last bit of ice cream.

"Chocolate's my dad's favorite, too."

"Or two specific examples." She licked the spoon and dropped it into the now empty cup.

"And I'm already head over heels for our baby."

"I'll give you that one," she relented, as Holt popped the last bite of cone into his mouth.

He took her hand again as they retraced their steps toward the clinic, where his truck was parked, and was pleased when she didn't try to pull it away.

"Solitaire or cluster?" he asked, pausing by the display window of a jewelry store.

"Is my answer to that question supposed to reveal some more deep insights about me?"

"Only about the kind of engagement ring you'd like."

She eyed him warily. "Are you talking about a hypothetical engagement at some future point in time?"

"We can go with that scenario for now," he agreed.

Her gaze slid to the window. "Probably a solitaire," she finally said. "Definitely nothing flashy."

"What about that one?" he said, tapping a finger against the glass.

"Apparently we have different definitions of flashy," she said dryly.

He chose another ring at random. "That one?"

"A little less flashy," she acknowledged.

"Let's go in and see if they've got anything you actually like," he suggested.

"What? No," she protested.

But he was already nudging her through the door.

An elegantly dressed salesperson crossed the room to greet them. "Welcome to Goldsmiths," she said. "Are you looking for anything in particular today?"

"Just browsing," Tess said.

At the same time Holt responded, "An engagement ring."

Patricia—according to the name on gold plate pinned to her jacket—shifted her focus to Holt, her smile widening. "Right this way."

They followed her across the room.

"We're looking for a solitaire, but nothing flashy."

"We're not looking for anything," Tess muttered under her breath.

He heard her, of course. And ignored her.

"A diamond by its very nature is flashy—it's why we love them," Patricia said, unlocking a display case. "But I think I understand what you mean."

She pulled out a tray. "These are some of our most popular styles—round, princess, emerald, oval and marquise," she said, indicating each column of rings in turn.

"Thoughts?" Holt asked.

"I think I already said *no*," she reminded him. But her gaze had lingered on the column that had been identified as princess.

Patricia's pleasant smile never changed, though her eyes widened slightly at Tess's remark.

Holt indicated the princess-cut ring in the middle, what he

would call a modest-size stone. "Can we take a closer look at that one?"

"Of course." Patricia unrolled a dark velvet cloth over the glass display case and set the ring on top of it. "This is a one-point-two carat princess-cut stone, colorless and internally flawless, set in a platinum band."

"I'm not sure what all of that means," Holt admitted. "But it's beautiful."

"Yes, it is," the saleswoman agreed. To Tess she said, "Would you like to try it on?"

"No," she immediately denied.

At the same time Holt said, "Yes, please."

"I thought we were having a hypothetical conversation."

"We were," he agreed. "And now I'm asking you, for real, to marry me."

"We've talked about this," she reminded him.

"Should I give you two a minute?" Patricia asked now.

"Yes, please," Holt said again.

The saleswoman slipped away.

"Holt—"

Whatever else she'd wanted to say was cut off when he touched his mouth to hers.

"Marry me, Tess."

The words were whispered against her lips, tempting her beyond reason.

But giving in to temptation was what had gotten them into this mess, so instead of saying *yes,* she said, "Why do you want to marry me?"

"I want to be a father to our baby."

"You'll be her father whether or not there's a ring on my finger."

His brows lifted. "Her?"

She flushed. "I don't know. But Meg keeps referring to the baby as *he* so I've started saying *she*—because I don't want to say *it.*"

"Boy or girl, I truly believe our baby would benefit from having a mom and dad who were married and living together." He picked up Tess's left hand then and slid the ring onto her third finger. "It fits," he mused. "Might be a sign from the universe."

"A sign that I have average-size fingers." But her gaze lingered on the ring.

He lifted her hand to touch his lips to her knuckle, just below the diamond. "Or that you're meant to say *yes* to my proposal."

"Would you listen to me if I said *yes*? Because you haven't listened any of the times I've said *no*."

"Try me," he urged. "Say *yes* so that we can get married and raise our baby together."

Tess remained silent, staring at the ring on her finger.

He reached into his pocket now and pulled out his Ace—the ultrasound photo of their baby. He set it on top of the display case, and looking at the little bean in the picture—*their baby*—she felt her heart pinch with longing.

"You've mentioned, on more than one occasion, that I'm a Chandler and you're a Leonard. And you're probably right that I've had an easier life because my name carries some weight in Whispering Canyon. While that's not something we usually have any control over, in this case you do, Tess." He pointed to her name in the upper corner of the photo. "You get to choose whether our baby will be born a Barrett or a Chandler. You get to decide what his birthright will be."

Tears filled her eyes, further blurring the image.

"That's not fair," she protested.

"I'm not interested in playing fair," he said. "I'm interested in protecting you and our child, and getting married is the best way for me to do that.

"But beyond that, I want you to be my wife, Tess. And I want our baby to belong to both of us.

"Now it's up to you to decide what you want—for yourself

and for our child. And I hope you'll decide it's to be my wife, so that you and our baby can share my name. I hope you'll say *yes*."

He wasn't promising that their life together would be all sunshine and rainbows, but he was offering a chance for them to be a family, and that was everything she wanted—even when she'd been afraid to admit it. The opportunity to raise their child with all the rights and privileges inherent in the Chandler name was only icing on an already tempting cake.

"Yes," she said.

"Yes?" he echoed, a smile slowly spreading across his face.

She nodded.

He whooped in triumph. Then he lifted her in his arms and spun her around.

"We're getting married," he announced to everyone in the store. Which, thankfully, was only three more customers and two other salespeople.

Patricia reappeared then, as if on cue. "Have you made a decision on the ring, then?"

"We have," Holt confirmed. "And we're going to need wedding bands, too."

Chapter Fifteen

"Next stop, City Hall for the marriage license," Holt said, as they exited the jewelry store.

"Now?" Tess asked, when he turned toward the municipal building.

"Right now," he confirmed. "We need a license to get married, and if we get one today we can get married today."

"Today?" she echoed, stunned.

"There's no waiting period in Wyoming," he told her.

"It sounds like you've already looked into this."

"The day you told me you were pregnant," he confirmed.

"I appreciate your enthusiasm, but don't you think we should maybe take a minute to catch our breath?"

He paused on the sidewalk and turned to face her. "How many minutes do you need?"

"I don't know. But I know I don't want to be wearing a T-shirt and leggings on one of the most significant days of my life."

His expression shifted from wary to understanding then. "You're beautiful, Tess. Always. But I understand what you're saying so—" he gave her a quick kiss "—give me five minutes. And your phone."

"Why do you need my phone?"

"Please," he said.

She shrugged and took her phone out of her purse, unlocking it before handing it to him.

"Thanks."

After Holt had made his mysterious phone call, they went to City Hall to get their marriage license. When they walked out of the building, Tess was stunned to see Meg and Emma standing at the bottom of the steps.

Meg was wearing a pale blue dress with a square neckline and slim skirt; Emma's dress was a similar color but with tulip sleeves and a full skirt.

"Your tasks," Meg said.

Holt took the envelope she handed to him and slipped it into his pocket.

"We'll meet you back here at four o'clock."

"That's why he needed my phone—to call *you*," Tess realized, as Holt wandered off.

"Of course," her friend said. "Who else would he call to be the maid of honor at your wedding?"

"I can't believe he called you." Tess's eyes grew misty. "Even *I* didn't realize how much I needed you here."

"So maybe the man knows you better than you give him credit for," Meg mused. "And just because you're getting married spur of the moment doesn't mean you have to forgo all the traditional bells and whistles."

"Are you the bell or the whistle?" Tess asked Emma, who was twirling on the sidewalk and watching the skirt of her dress flare out.

"I'm the flower girl," Emma announced, still twirling. "And this is my versy dress."

"*Anniversary* dress," Meg enunciated for her daughter. Then, to clarify for Tess, "For Raylan and Eleanor's party."

"Ah." She nodded. "Well, you both look very nice."

"When do we get the flowers, Mama?" Emma asked.

"When we're ready to walk down the aisle," Meg told her.

"I'm ready now," the little girl insisted.

"Well, Auntie Tess isn't," Meg said. "And nothing happens until the bride is ready."

"We're going shopping?" Tess guessed.

"We are," her friend confirmed. Then to her daughter, Meg said, "Come on, Twirly Girl. We have to see if we can find a dress for Auntie Tess that's as pretty as yours."

"I'm not Twirly Girl—I'm the flower girl," Emma reminded her mom, but she took her proffered hand and they set off.

Obviously Meg knew exactly where she was going, because in less than three minutes, she was reaching for the handle of a door on a boutique called The Bridal Path.

An immaculately dressed woman with auburn hair in a neat chignon met them at the door. "You must be Tess," she said, offering her hand and a warm smile. "I'm Courtney and I'm so happy we've been chosen to help you get ready for your big day."

"It's a pleasure to meet you," Tess said, as she was drawn further into the shop.

"Your maid of honor guessed at your dress size," Courtney said, smiling at Meg before her gaze returned to skim over Tess. "Pretty accurately, I think."

"She would know," Tess remarked. "She's always stealing clothes out of my closet."

"Not stealing, borrowing," Meg chimed in to clarify.

"Stealing's bad," Emma said solemnly.

"She also gave me some ideas about what she thought you might like, design-wise," Courtney continued.

"Big puffy sleeves and lots of satin bows."

Courtney slid Meg a mildly reproachful look. "A bride is often jittery enough on her wedding day without anyone stirring her up."

"Sorry," Meg apologized, though the sparkle in her eyes belied her contrite tone.

"I've preselected a few gowns for you to try," Courtney said, guiding Tess back to the fitting room. "But if there's nothing that appeals to you, you're welcome to comb through the racks."

Apparently Meg did know what Tess liked, though, because

the very first dress that Courtney revealed took her breath away. It was a halter style gown of delicate lace layered over a silky slip with a sweetheart neckline and slim skirt.

Courtney gave Emma a coloring page and crayons to keep the little girl occupied while the adults helped Tess dress. A somewhat time-consuming task considering the number of buttons that ran down the back of the gown.

While Meg was finishing with those, Courtney asked the bride's shoe size then returned with a pair of lace covered low-heeled pumps.

"Now the big reveal," she said, guiding her to the center of the room where she was surrounded by mirrors.

"Wow," Meg said, blinking the tears that filled her eyes.

"*Wow* is what a bride wants on her wedding day," Courtney agreed, smiling.

"What do you think, Emma?" Tess asked.

The little girl looked up from her coloring page. "Can you twirl?"

Tess laughed. "I think I'll leave the twirling to you."

"Okay," Emma agreed.

"Twirling aside," Meg said. "Do you like Auntie Tess's dress?"

Emma studied her for a minute, then nodded. "It's very pretty."

"That's *wow* in three-year-old language," Meg assured the bride.

"How does it feel?" Courtney asked now. "Any gaping or pinching?"

Tess shook her head. "No, actually, it feels good."

"It's rare for a bride to not need any alterations," Courtney said. "But this dress fits as if it was made to your measurements."

"Including your suddenly bigger boobs," Meg added under her breath.

"Did you want to try any of the other gowns?" Courtney asked.

Both Tess and Meg shook their heads.

"No," the bride said. "This is it."

"It's perfect," her friend agreed. "Now take it off—next stop is hair and makeup."

Holt knew that he'd pretty much strong-armed Tess into accepting his proposal, so he wanted to do something nice for her to make the day special. Although a part of him was tempted to hurry her off to a justice of the peace to make things official before she could change her mind, he realized that she'd likely envisioned something different for her wedding day.

Which was why he'd conscripted Meg to help out. He knew Tess had already trusted her best friend with the news of her pregnancy, so he figured she could be counted on to keep their nuptials a secret, as well.

He wasn't as confident about Emma, who'd been cast in the role of flower girl, but he couldn't help smiling as she twirled down the aisle of the "marriage room," tossing rose petals in the air along the way. Out of the corner of his eye, he saw Flynn smiling, too, and was glad he'd tapped his brother as the second witness for their ceremony.

Meg stepped forward next, offering the groom an apologetic glance in response to her daughter's antics. Then her gaze shifted from Holt to Flynn, and he felt his brother go completely still beside him.

Holt only had a few seconds to ponder that before the tempo of the music changed and Tess was there.

He hadn't anticipated how seeing her walk down the aisle in a white dress would affect him. Suddenly, she wasn't just Tess, the mother of his child. She was a stunningly beautiful bride.

His bride.

He started to feel a little lightheaded.

"Breathe," Flynn whispered, which was when Holt realized that air had stopped flowing in and out of his lungs.

So he drew in a breath, then exhaled slowly. He even managed to smile back when Tess's lips curved in a tentative smile.

He didn't know how to describe the dress she wore. Halter style, he thought it might be called, with delicate lace layered over a silky slip that dipped between her breasts and hugged her hips before falling all the way to the floor. Her hair had been styled in loose curls that tumbled over her bare shoulders, and she carried a handful of pale pink flowers.

As soon as she reached the end of the aisle, the ceremony began: "We are gathered here today to witness the joining in legal matrimony of Holt Chandler and Tess Barrett..."

Holt listened to the officiant recite the usual formalities with only half an ear, the rest of his focus on Tess. When instructed to join hands, she first gave her flowers to Meg, then reached toward him. Her fingers trembled a little, and he gave them a gentle squeeze of reassurance.

Though he'd been the one to push for marriage from the start, he'd nevertheless worried that he might have second thoughts when they got to the point of no return, as they were now. But he didn't feel trapped—not by the circumstances and definitely not by Tess. What he felt, instead, as he exchanged vows with this beautiful, passionate, amazing woman, was damn lucky.

"I now pronounce you husband and wife." The officiant winked at the groom. "You may kiss your bride."

Holt didn't need to be told twice.

He dipped his head and brushed his mouth over Tess's.

When her soft lips yielded to his, he forgot that this moment was a formality—much like the signing of the marriage certificate—and let himself sink into the kiss.

After several moments, Flynn muttered, "Get a room."

Holt finally lifted his mouth, his lips curving as he looked at his wife. "That's the best idea I've heard all day."

* * *

Tess shouldn't have been surprised to discover that Holt had already booked a room for their wedding night. Despite the haste with which the wedding had come together, it seemed as if he hadn't missed a trick. There had even been a photographer onsite to take formal wedding photos during the ceremony and after.

And after saying goodbye to Meg and Emma and Flynn, the bride and groom made their way to the Courtland Hotel, where the elevator whisked them to the honeymoon suite on the top floor.

"This is quite a bit fancier than The Outlaw Inn," she noted, looking around the suite.

"I considered taking you back there, because I have very fond memories of our first night together." Then he smiled. "I have very fond memories of the first night you spent in my cabin, too—or at least the morning after—and I'm looking forward to many more nights and mornings there with you."

"At the ranch," she realized.

"Well, yeah," he said.

"That's probably something we should have discussed before we exchanged vows," she noted.

"I didn't realize it was something that needed to be discussed."

"I live in town. I work in town."

"Are you suggesting that I should move to town to live with you and Meg and Emma?"

It was a ridiculous idea, of course.

They were married now, which meant they would live together and, as he didn't have roommates—aside from Buddy—it made sense that she would move out to West River Ranch.

Except that everything in her life was changing and she wasn't ready for everything to change.

"Tess," he prompted gently. "Tell me what you're thinking."

"I'm scared," she admitted.

"Of what?"

"Of giving up my whole life for you and being left with nothing when things don't work out."

He tipped her chin up, forcing her to meet his gaze. "I'm not asking you to give up your life. I'm asking you to build a life with me—and our child. And any other children we might have."

"You keep talking about other children and this one's still only a tiny bean in my belly," she pointed out.

"Maybe I'm jumping the gun a little," he acknowledged.

"You're definitely jumping the gun."

"But I'm excited about our life together."

"Really?" she said dubiously. "Because I'm terrified."

"Being excited doesn't mean I'm not scared," he said. "But I'm also determined to do whatever it takes to make our marriage work so that we can give our child—" he winked "—and any future children—a proper family."

"Everything's just happening so fast," she murmured.

"It's a little late to be getting cold feet."

"We seem to be doing everything out of order."

"Can I make a suggestion?" he asked.

She nodded.

"Let's enjoy the moments we have right now and not worry about what might or might not happen in the future, okay?"

"I wish I could, but my mind is spinning and—"

The rest of the words stuck in her throat when he covered her mouth with his.

This time, the kiss wasn't a formality. There wasn't anyone watching. No reason to pretend that his kiss didn't make her blood heat in her veins, spreading warmth and desire through her body.

"Why did you do that?" she asked, when he finally ended the kiss.

"Two reasons," he said. "One, because I wanted to kiss you.

And two, because you once admitted that you can't think when I kiss you and I wanted you not to think for a minute."

Her cheeks flushed. "I can't believe I told you that."

"Kissing you has the same effect on me," he told her. "I can only think of one thing—and that's how much I want you."

"I want you, too," she admitted.

"Turn around, then, so I can unzip your dress."

"It's not a zipper," she warned, presenting him with her back. "It's about a hundred tiny buttons."

He gently gathered her long tresses in his hand and pushed the bundle of hair to one side so he could access the row of fasteners.

If she'd exaggerated the number, it wasn't by much. And each tiny pearl-like button was secured by a delicate satin loop.

"Who did up all these buttons?" he asked.

"Meg."

"And probably laughed at the thought of me having to undo them," he muttered.

"She did say something about it being a unique kind of foreplay."

It was certainly that. As he made his way down the row, the two sides of fabric began to part, exposing a tantalizing column of pale skin. He continued to work the buttons but dipped his head to touch his lips to her back and felt her shiver in response.

He kissed her again, this time letting his lips skim down the bumps of her spine.

"Holt..."

"Mmm."

"My dress," she prompted.

"I'm working on it," he promised.

"Maybe you could work—" her breath hitched "—faster?"

"Are you in a hurry?"

"A little bit."

He finally finished with the buttons—or at least enough of them that he could peel the top down to her waist and push it over her hips, allowing her to step out of the dress now pooled at her feet. She turned to face him then, wearing only a pair of lace bikini panties and sexy heeled sandals.

"I think I'm going to like being married to you," he said.

"I'd like it if you got rid of some of your clothes," she told him.

"I'll get there," he promised. "But I'm your husband now, which means I call the shots and you have to do what I tell you."

She lifted a brow as she untucked his shirt to slide her hands beneath it. "I don't think so, cowboy."

"It was right there in the vows," he said, as she unhooked the fastening of his pants. "You promised to love, honor and obey."

"There was nothing about *obey* in our vows," she assured him, tracing the contours of his abs with her fingertips.

"Hmm." His brow furrowed as he pretended to think back. "Maybe I didn't slip the officiant enough cash."

"This is a partnership." Her hand moved downward now, beneath the waistband of his briefs, to wrap around him. "Not a dictatorship."

"What did you say about my—"

Laughing, she pressed her other hand to his mouth, muffling the rest of his question. She'd shared so many new experiences with him over the past few weeks, and this was new, too, Tess realized. Being able to laugh with an intimate partner, relax with him and have fun with him.

Grinning now, he picked her up and carried her to the bed. Then he hooked his fingers on the sides of her panties and pulled them down her legs, tossing them aside so that she was only wearing the sandals. Then he discarded his own clothing and spread her legs apart to kneel on the bed between them.

"I'm going to touch you now," he said. "In all the ways that I've been dreaming about touching you since the first night we were together."

"So touch me," she urged.

"I will." His hands slid up her torso to cup her breasts. "I am."

She sighed as his thumbs rubbed her already peaked nipples.

Then he replaced his hands with his lips, suckling first one breast, then the other, making her whimper.

"There's just one rule," he told her. "One rule you have to abide by. Can you do that, Tess?"

She was already breathless, mindless, willing to agree to anything. She nodded.

He kissed her then, and whispered against her lips, "No screaming."

She nodded again, and he focused his attention on giving her the pleasure he'd promised. And more. So much more that she quickly forgot his one rule—and definitely didn't abide by it.

And he didn't mind at all.

Chapter Sixteen

"I heard your phone beep about a dozen times," Tess said, when she'd managed to catch her breath again and was able to speak.

"Really?" Holt's response was muffled by her hair. "I couldn't hear anything over the sound of your screams."

She felt her cheeks flush. "It was your fault."

"No." He lifted his head then so she could see that he was grinning. "It was my pleasure."

"Don't you think you should check your messages?"

"No," he said again, but he did reach for his phone to turn off the sound.

"Aren't you worried that it might be something important?"

"Whatever it is, it can't be as important as focusing on my bride on our wedding night," he told her.

"Speaking of… Did I thank you for reaching out to Meg and making arrangements for my dress and the flowers and the cake?"

"All I did was reach out to Meg," he said. "She did the rest."

"Well, thank you, anyway."

"No thanks necessary."

"Why did you do it?" she asked him.

He shrugged. "Maybe because, in the lead-up to my grandparents' sixty-fifth anniversary, I've been inundated with stories about their courtship and their wedding and I realized that I wanted to be able to tell our child about our wedding day someday, and I didn't want it to be that we stumbled into City Hall on an ice cream sugar high."

"When I said *yes*, that's what I thought I was saying *yes* to," she confided.

"But is that the kind of wedding you envisioned whenever you envisioned your wedding?"

"I never had grand expectations," she told him. "Though I hoped for something a little better than when I exchanged vows with Liam Bell by the sandbox at Blackstone Park, wearing shorts and a T-shirt with a Band-Aid on my knee and a bouquet of wilted arnica in my hand."

His brows lifted. "You never mentioned that you were married before."

"It was a long time ago," she said dismissively.

"How long?"

"I was in second grade and head over heels."

"For Liam Bell?"

She nodded.

"Isn't he the bassist for Canyon Creek Trio?" he asked, naming the popular Country-Western band of which his cousin, Dawson, was a founding member, guitarist and lead vocalist.

"He is," she confirmed.

"And how long did your wedded bliss last?"

"Not even until dinnertime." She sighed wistfully. "Liam walked me home from the park and we announced our marriage to my parents, who pointed out that Trent's father being an ordained minister didn't actually qualify his son to perform legally binding wedding services."

"Any other previous marriages I should know about?" Holt asked now.

She shook her head. "No… But I was engaged once."

"Something else you might have mentioned," he mused.

"Also a long time ago."

"Third grade?"

"College, actually," she confided. "But I didn't date at all in high school, so Jonathon was my first real boyfriend—after Liam, of course."

"Of course," he agreed. "But why didn't you date in high school?"

"I'm Tallulah Leonard's granddaughter," she reminded him. "The only boys who wanted to go out with me were boys who thought they could get into my pants—and I wasn't letting anyone into my pants back then."

"So Jonathon was your first boyfriend…and first lover?" he guessed.

She nodded. "But we didn't sleep together until we were engaged—and then we broke up a few months later. According to Jonathon, the prospect of bedding a virgin was a lot more exciting than the reality."

"Do you want to wait here while I track down Jonathon and kick his ass?"

She managed a smile. "He's not worth it."

"I'm not going to disagree with that," Holt said. "But honey, if he made you feel in any way inadequate, he needs to have his ass kicked."

"I have a better idea," she said.

"What's that?"

She leaned close to whisper in his ear.

A slow smile spread across Holt's face. "Okay," he agreed, wrapping his arms around her and rolling her beneath him. "We'll go with that."

"I'm not sure this is a good idea," Tess said, as Holt handed his keys to the valet.

It was two days after their impromptu—and still secret—wedding and they were about to make their first public appearance together, the prospect of which had his new wife feeling distinctly uneasy, notwithstanding their agreement to keep the news of their nuptials—and her pregnancy—to themselves a while longer.

He took her arm and led her up the steps of the Whispering Canyon Country Club. "You don't think sixty-five years of marriage is cause for celebration?" he asked, deliberately misinterpreting the reason for her discomfort.

"You know I wasn't referring to the party but your insistence on bringing me here."

"My grandparents will be thrilled to see you," he assured her.

"And your parents?" she prompted.

Not as likely to be thrilled, he acknowledged, if only to himself.

To Tess he said, "They need to get used to us being together."

"But maybe tonight isn't the most appropriate time to make them aware of that fact."

"There's no time like the present," he said, lifting their joined hands to touch his lips to the back of the hand upon which he'd placed her rings—though tonight they were hanging on a chain around her neck.

"You promised to be discreet," she reminded him.

"Can I help it if I want everyone to know that the most beautiful woman in this room is mine?"

"You can turn off the charm—I already said *I do*."

He grinned. "You did, didn't you?"

"And we agreed to keep the news of our wedding quiet until after the party."

"I haven't said a word," he pointed out.

"The only person you've talked to so far, aside from me, is the valet."

"That's about to change," he noted, as he spotted the happy couple making their way toward them.

"Holt. Tess." Eleanor greeted them both with hugs and kisses. Raylan shook his grandson's hand before embracing Tess, taking advantage of the moment to whisper in her ear, "Guess I know which one of my grandsons you'll be dancing with tonight."

"Maybe all of them," she said, with a wink.

He chuckled, then said to Holt, "Hold tight to this one."

"That's the plan," he agreed.

Several servers were making their way through the crowd—and it was a crowd, Tess noted—and Holt automatically plucked two flutes of champagne from a tray and handed one to Tess.

Meg appeared out of nowhere and deftly removed the glass from her friend's hand. "Oh, thank goodness," she said. "I'm parched."

As she took a sip of the bubbly wine, realization dawned.

"I forgot you're…not fond of alcohol," Holt said, immediately contrite. "Can I get you something else to drink instead?"

"Sparkling water, if they have it," Tess said gratefully. "Still, if they don't."

"I'll be right back," he promised.

"So," Meg said, pulling her friend out of the crowd—and out of earshot of anyone else. "How's married life?"

"I've been married all of—" she glanced at her watch "—fifty-two hours."

"And?" her friend prompted, making Tess laugh.

Holt didn't make it to the bar before he crossed paths with his mother. And judging by the pinched expression on Miranda's face, she wasn't in a celebratory mood.

"Good evening," he said, dutifully dipping his head to kiss her cheek.

"I had high hopes it would be," she said. "And then you brought that woman here—to a family celebration."

Though he gritted his teeth at her reference to Tess as *that woman*, he managed to respond evenly. "She was invited."

"A courtesy, nothing more," Miranda insisted. "And I'm sure it wouldn't have crossed her mind to accept the invitation without your encouragement."

"You're right," he acknowledged. "Tess was reluctant to come, because she didn't want to make you uncomfortable."

"And yet she's here," his mother noted. "Why? You can't expect me to believe that you have real feelings for that—"

"Careful," Holt interjected, his tone deceptively mild. "That's my wife you're talking about."

He'd never seen anyone's face drain of color before—hadn't actually thought it was possible—until he saw the effect his words had on his mother. And though he knew Tess wouldn't be pleased that he'd broken his promise to keep their recent nuptials a secret until after the weekend, he had to trust she'd forgive him, considering the circumstances.

"No." The denial was a barely audible whisper. "Tell me you're joking. That you didn't marry her."

"I can't tell you that, because I did."

Miranda sank into a nearby chair. "When? *Why*?"

"Two days ago—right after we saw our baby on an ultrasound for the first time."

"She's pregnant?"

He nodded.

His mother laughed, but the sound was filled with bitterness rather than amusement. "I can't believe you could be so careless. So *foolish*."

"I'm not going to claim that we planned for this to happen," Holt said. "But we're very much looking forward to our future together as a family."

"Obviously she managed to convince you that the baby's yours, but I'm not so naive."

"The baby *is* mine," he said firmly. "And I'd advise you not to question the fact again."

"Or what?" she challenged.

"Or you'll forfeit the opportunity to know your grandchild."

RJ, returning from the bar with a beer for himself and a glass of champagne for Miranda, quickly picked up on the tension between his wife and their son. "Is there a problem here?"

Instead of responding to the question, Miranda said to Holt, "Why don't you tell your dad your happy news?"

"You have happy news to share?" RJ prompted.

"Tess and I are married," Holt said. "And we're going to have a baby."

RJ's surprised expression quickly gave way to joy as a smile spread across his face.

"That's wonderful news—on both counts," he said, drawing his son into his embrace. "Congratulations, Holt."

"Congratulations?" Miranda echoed incredulously. *"That's* your response?"

"An appropriate and sincere one," RJ said.

"Thanks, Dad."

"This isn't cause for celebration," Miranda said. "It's a disaster."

"A baby is a blessing," her husband insisted.

"She trapped him into marrying her."

RJ looked at his son questioningly.

"I'm the one who pushed to get married," he told his dad.

"Please tell me you at least had a prenup," his mom said.

"*Christ*, Miranda," RJ said, shaking his head.

"Don't pretend the thought didn't cross your mind," she shot back at him.

"And on that note," Holt said, "I'm going to excuse myself to go find my bride."

It didn't take him long to locate Tess. And his mood, already low as a result of the interaction with his mother, dipped further when he found his wife in conversation with Jordan Denninger by the cake table.

"Holt," the other man said.

"Jordan." He accepted the proffered hand only because it would be rude not to and he didn't want to make a scene at his grandparents' anniversary party.

After a brief shake, he took back his hand and slid his arm around Tess's waist, drawing her close to his side.

"And this is Kellie Hart," she said, introducing him to the other woman he hadn't even noticed was standing there. "The creative genius behind this stunning cake and Jordan's girlfriend."

Holt nodded, acknowledging that the message had been sent and received.

"I'm grateful to Mr. and Mrs. Chandler for giving me the opportunity to make the cake for their celebration," Kellie said. "And to be here to be a part of it."

"It was nice to meet you, Kellie," Tess said. "And good to see you again, Jordan. But now I'm going to get the drink that my date seems to have forgotten."

"I did forget," Holt said, as they made their way toward the bar. "I'm sorry."

"It's okay," she said. "I saw you get waylaid by your mother en route."

"You saw that?"

She nodded. "I can't read lips, but I can interpret body language, and it's obvious she isn't happy about me being here with you."

"About that," he began, pausing when he stepped up to the bar. "Sparkling water, please."

"Lemon? Lime?"

Holt glanced at Tess.

"Lime, thanks."

"About that," Tess prompted, after the bartender presented her with her drink.

"I might have mentioned to her—and my dad—that we got married."

Tess sipped her drink—

"And that we're having a baby."

—then coughed and sputtered.

"I'm sorry," he said, sincerely contrite, as he rubbed her back.

"She must have really pushed your buttons," Tess remarked, when she was able to speak again.

"For what it's worth, my dad was happy to hear the news."

"I wish your mom could be, too."

"He'll bring her around," Holt said.

"Would you be willing to bet an orange chip on that?" Tess asked.

"Maybe not," he admitted. "But I'd bet them all on you and me."

The mistake was in letting her guard down, Tess would acknowledge later. But she was having such a good time with Holt and his brothers and cousins and Meg and Emma—when Emma wasn't off chasing Boone's twin boys—that she forgot to be vigilant. And when she parted ways with her husband (it gave her such a thrill to think of him as such, even if only in her mind) at the edge of the dance floor to make a quick trip to the ladies' room, she wasn't thinking about anything but how much she wanted to be back in his arms again.

"Mrs. Chandler," she said, stopping short when she found herself face-to-face with Holt's mom as she exited.

"Tess," Miranda said coolly.

"It's a wonderful party, isn't it?" she babbled. "Good turnout."

"It seems as if everyone who got an invitation decided to show up, even some who probably should have RSVP'd their regrets."

And the gloves were off, Tess realized.

"I know you look at me and see Abby Leonard's daughter," she said. "But I'm also your son's wife now, and I'd really like it if we could be friends."

Miranda didn't respond to that, asking instead, "Are you planning to make an announcement about your wedding?"

"Not tonight," Tess assured her. "We didn't plan to say anything for at least a few more days, to keep the focus of attention on Raylan and Eleanor's anniversary."

"A smart decision," Holt's mother agreed. "And a lot less messy to undo."

"I'm sorry?"

"You got carried away, let yourself believe you and Holt could make a family with your baby," Miranda's tone fairly dripped with false sympathy. "But you have to know this so-called marriage won't last."

"I'm under no illusions that it will be easy," Tess said. "But I wouldn't have married Holt if I didn't believe we could make it work."

"Or at least believe you'd get a nice settlement in the end."

Tess sucked in a breath.

She shouldn't have been shocked by the accusation. She was accustomed to people talking about her in a less-than-flattering manner. But none of those other people had been the mother of her new husband and grandmother of her unborn child.

"I don't owe you anything," Tess said coolly. "But I'm going to do you a favor, anyway, and not tell your son about this conversation."

Then she turned on her heel and walked away.

Unfortunately, she didn't manage to walk off her anger as Raylan intercepted her before she'd taken three steps, forcing her to tamp down on her fury and put a smile on her face.

"Ah, Tess," he said, taking her hand and tucking it into the crook of his arm. "Just the woman I've been looking for."

"Don't let your wife of sixty-five years hear you say that," she teased.

He chuckled. "You're a sharp girl, you are. And pretty as they come."

"And suddenly I've been demoted from woman to girl," she noted.

"How about dance partner?" he asked. "Any chance you'd be interested in taking a spin around the floor with an old man?"

"Not really. But I'd be happy to dance with you."

"I can see why my grandson's smitten with you," Raylan said, as he began to lead her in a waltz.

"You've got some moves, Mr. Chandler," she remarked, when they'd been dancing for a couple of minutes.

"It's not just my good looks that charmed Eleanor all those years ago," he told her. "But don't you think, after all this time, you could call me Raylan? Or, since I'm old enough to be your grandfather, Gramps even?"

Technically, he was her grandfather by marriage now, though of course he didn't know it yet. "Okay," she relented. "We'll give Gramps a try."

"I'd like that. But now it appears I'm being summoned," he said, as the song drew to an end.

"Looks like it might be time to cut the cake," Tess noted.

"Well, come on, then," he urged. "We don't want to miss that."

"You go on," she said. "I'm going to grab another drink."

Holt caught up with her again at the bar. "I saw you on the dance floor with my grandfather."

"Did you now?"

"He was grinning from ear to ear, waltzing with the prettiest girl at the party."

She tipped her head back against his shoulder. "The prettiest girl at the party, huh?"

"Without a doubt," he said, brushing a kiss against her temple. "You made his day."

"And he made mine," she said.

They stayed standing there together for a long moment, his arm around her, her head tipped back against his shoulder. Then she lifted a hand to stifle a yawn and he glanced at the clock on the wall, surprised to see it was almost midnight.

"Should we elbow our way through the crowd to get some cake?" he asked. "Or are you ready to call it a night?"

"Let's call it a night," she decided.

He pulled the valet ticket out of his pocket. "Your chariot awaits."

Chapter Seventeen

"Your parents seemed okay with the news about our wedding," Holt remarked as they made their way back to the ranch after brunch with Roger and Abby Barrett the following day.

"And that's why I suggested we meet them at Sunrise Grill," Tess said. "Because my mother would never say or do anything to risk causing a scene in public."

He reached across the center console to take her hand. "You think they're unhappy?"

"I wouldn't say unhappy, more…disappointed. Not that I married *you*," she hastened to assure him. "Just about the circumstances of our wedding."

They drove in silence for several more minutes before he said, "Your mom made a cryptic remark that I've been wondering about—"

"Apparently not cryptic enough," Tess muttered.

"—implying you had a crush on me in high school."

"I think it was more of a statement than an implication," she admitted.

"How did I not know that?" he wondered.

"I wasn't anywhere on your radar," she reminded him. "Just a clumsy and nondescript freshman who once dumped her books at your feet."

"I still can't believe I don't remember that," he said.

"I can."

"But maybe it's a good thing I didn't notice you in high

school," he said. "Because I was obviously too self-centered and self-involved to be able to appreciate you back then."

"You didn't notice me because I was flat-chested. Seriously flat-chested," she told him. "I didn't even start to get breasts until my sophomore year, and you'd graduated by then."

He chuckled at that. "And still, that wasn't what I noticed about you the day we met at the hospital."

"What did you notice?"

"How breathtakingly beautiful you are. And then, when I looked into your eyes, I saw sincerity and warmth and compassion."

"You don't have to charm me, cowboy." She lifted their joined hands, drawing his attention to the rings that she wore again on her third finger. "I'm already going home with you."

"I'm not trying to charm you," he denied. "I'm trying to tell you that I developed a bit of a crush on you that day. And then, when I saw you again later at The Bootlegger…something just clicked. It was like 'there she is' and I hadn't even known I was looking for you."

"And when I saw you, I thought, 'please don't let me embarrass myself again like I did in high school.'"

He smiled at that. "So tell me about the girl I didn't know in high school."

"She was the quintessential good girl," Tess admitted. "She followed the rules and did as she was told. She never stepped out of line. She never skipped classes. She never snuck out of the house. She never broke curfew.

"And then, years later, she did the one thing that she was cautioned to *never ever ever* do—she got pregnant before she was married."

"But only a few weeks before," he pointed out.

"That might be my only saving grace," she acknowledged. "It's not that my mother's a puritan. It's just that she's always worried about the potential for gossip and scandal. Because—as

Tallulah Leonard's daughter—her very existence was a scandal."

"So if you knew that your parents would accept the news of your pregnancy more easily if you were married…why did you turn down my first—and second and third—proposal?"

"Because I didn't want you to have to shoulder the burden of my family's baggage."

"Your family's my family now," he pointed out to her. "Which means your baggage is my baggage."

"Lucky you," she said dryly.

"And vice versa."

"You're a Chandler—you can afford to hire people to carry your bags."

"You're a Chandler now, too," he reminded her.

"I guess I am," she acknowledged.

Far more important, as he'd pointed out the day she agreed to marry him, their baby would be a Chandler, with all the rights and privileges that name entailed in Whispering Canyon.

Over the next couple of weeks, Holt became accustomed to sharing his bed with Tess. (Of course, they were married now, so it wasn't *his* bed anymore, it was *their* bed, and he didn't mind that one bit.) But he wasn't accustomed to finding her there in the middle of the day.

Less surprising was that Buddy was with her, curled up by her feet. His so-called best friend had immediately switched sides when Tess moved in, and she didn't go anywhere—except to work—without the dog at her heels. And when she was gone, Buddy's favorite thing to do was wait for her to come home again.

Holt had been reading about pregnancy, wanting to understand the changes that were happening to Tess's body, so he knew that growing a baby was hard work and exhaustion was common in the early months of pregnancy. But growing a baby also took energy, which meant that sustenance was as important as sleep.

"Hey, Sleeping Beauty."

Tess didn't move.

He sat on the edge of the mattress and leaned down to touch his mouth to hers.

A soft sigh whispered from her lips. Her eyelids flickered.

"Holt?" she said sleepily.

"Were you expecting someone else?"

Her eyes flew open and she pushed herself up. "Ohmygod—what time is it?"

"Almost five-thirty."

"I fell asleep."

"I got that impression," he noted.

"It's really five-thirty?"

"Almost," he said again.

She sighed. "I'm a terrible wife."

"Why would you say that?"

"Because I meant to have dinner ready for when you came in."

"It's not your job to cook for me, Tess."

"No," she admitted. "But we agreed that whichever one of us was home first would start dinner."

"I'd say that was a friendly understanding, not an enforceable contract."

"Still. I didn't live up to my end of the deal."

"Once," he noted.

"We've only been married two weeks."

"Two weeks today, in fact," he pointed out. "Which makes this our anniversary. We should go out for dinner to celebrate."

"Nobody celebrates a two-week anniversary," she told him.

"Why not?" he challenged.

"I don't have an answer for that," she admitted.

"Well, tonight we're celebrating," he said. "And if you're

too tired to go into town, we can celebrate with burgers on the grill."

"I've actually been craving pizza," she admitted.

"Pasquale's it is," he decided. "Although they can sometimes have a heavy hand with the garlic."

"I'm okay with garlic now. And coffee," she told him. "The smell of it, I mean. I'm still not drinking it, obviously. Because caffeine isn't good for the baby."

He listened to her, a smile on his face.

"I'm babbling, aren't I?"

"A little bit," he agreed.

"The thought of going into town makes me nervous," she admitted.

"Why is that?"

"Because we haven't made a public appearance since we got married."

"Another reason we should go," he decided. "So people can stop speculating about why I'm keeping my bride hidden away at the ranch."

So they went into town for pizza and ended up sharing a table at Pasquale's with Meg and Emma—and Flynn, too, when he wandered in a short while later.

"I saw your mom at the café this morning," Meg said to Tess, after the server had delivered their drinks and taken their dinner order. "She wants me to try to convince you to let your parents throw a party to celebrate your wedding."

"I already told her we don't need a party."

"But it's something they want to do for you—both of you," she said, glancing at Holt to include him in the conversation. "And because they didn't get to be part of your actual wedding day."

Tess sighed. "No one else can pile on the guilt like my mother."

"Except maybe mine," Meg said.

"Two peas in a pod," her cousin agreed.

"I have no objection to a party," Holt said now.

"I think you got it right the first time around," Flynn chimed in. "Engaged and married on the same day—no muss no fuss."

Meg rolled her eyes. "There was plenty of fuss," she assured him. "Of which you remained blissfully unaware because you weren't required to be part of it."

"And hallelujah for that."

"It's going to be a lucky woman who snags your heart someday," Meg said dryly.

"Not gonna happen," Flynn told her.

She arched a brow. "Because you don't have a heart?"

"Because I already gave it away—to Emma."

The little girl looked up at him and beamed.

"It's a good thing we're having a boy," Holt remarked to Tess. "Because little girls are heartbreakers."

Meg immediately shifted her attention to the expectant parents. "Did the ultrasound tech confirm the gender?"

"No." Tess shook her head. "It's too early to tell."

"But there hasn't been a girl born to a Chandler in five generations," Holt reminded her.

"Our baby could be the first," his wife insisted.

"I wouldn't hold my breath," Meg cautioned.

"I can hold my breath," Emma said, filling her cheeks with air and plugging her nose to prove it.

"But you can't eat pizza while you're holding your breath," Flynn pointed out, as the server appeared at their table with two large pies.

Emma immediately released her breath and slices of pizza were distributed all around.

It was an enjoyable evening with good food and good friends—if Tess ignored the speculative glances and not quite whispers of the diners around them. At first she thought Holt was unaware of the attention focused in their direction, but then he shifted his seat a little closer to hers. And when the empty pizza trays were taken away, he slid an arm across her shoulders and stroked her arm with his fingertips, a casual show of affection for anyone who might be watching—and it seemed to Tess that everyone was watching.

When the check was brought to the table, Flynn picked it up. "My gift to the happy newlyweds," he announced, clearly throwing his support behind his brother and sister-in-law.

Meg pulled out her wallet, intending to pay for her share.

"And to the maid of honor and flower girl," he added.

"You don't have to do that," she protested.

"Put your wallet away and say *thank you*, Megan," he told her.

"Thank you, Megan," she echoed dutifully.

He slid her an unamused glance.

Outside the restaurant, Tess hugged Meg and Emma—and Flynn, too.

"Where's your car?" Flynn asked Meg.

"Em and I walked," she told him.

"Then I'll give you a ride home," he said.

"Thanks, but we don't mind walking."

He scowled. "When someone offers you a ride, you take the ride."

"Not when they don't have a booster seat in their car," she retorted.

"Oh. Right."

"So thanks," she said again. "But we'll walk."

"Then I'll walk with you," Flynn decided.

Meg huffed out a breath. "That's really not necessary."

"What do you say, Em? You want to ride on my shoulders?"

The little girl's head bobbed up and down enthusiastically. "Yes, please."

So Flynn lifted Emma onto his shoulders, leaving Meg with no choice but to fall in step beside him and head toward home.

"Is there something going on there?" Holt asked, when the trio were out of earshot.

"I was just wondering the same thing," Tess admitted. "I honestly don't know, but I promise you, I'll find out."

"In the meantime, I just realized something else."

"What's that?"

"In addition to being our two-week anniversary, tonight was also our first real date."

"Best first date ever," she told him.

"I wholeheartedly agree," he said. "Especially since I haven't spent the last few hours agonizing over whether I should or shouldn't kiss you when I take you home."

"Does that mean you've already decided?" She smiled, flirting a little. "Are you going to kiss me when you take me home, cowboy?"

"I've decided—" he dipped his head toward hers "—that I can't wait until I take you home."

And he kissed her right there on the sidewalk outside Pasquale's, in front of anyone and everyone who might pass by. When he finally lifted his mouth from hers, they were both a little breathless.

"Kiss me like that when you take me back to your cabin and I might be tempted to drag you off to bed," she teased.

"Or maybe I'll drag you off to bed," he countered.

Back at the ranch, there was more kissing, as promised, and then they tumbled onto the bed together. When they were both spent and sated, Holt pulled Tess close and whispered in her ear, "I'm starting to love being married to you."

As she snuggled into his embrace, Tess reminded herself to be grateful for everything she had, which was so much more than she'd ever dreamed. But as she started to drift off to sleep, she couldn't help but wonder if he'd ever say that he loved *her*.

And, more important, if he'd ever mean it.

"I can't believe I have to make an appointment to see you now," Meg grumbled, as they settled into a booth at the hospital cafeteria the following Wednesday.

"Sending a text message and asking if I want to meet for lunch isn't exactly making an appointment," Tess pointed out.

"I guess not," her friend allowed. "But I used to see you all the time and now… I miss you. And Emma misses you."

"I miss you guys, too."

"No, you don't," Meg said dismissively. "You're too busy having sex with your hunky husband to think about anyone else."

Tess felt herself blush. "We don't have sex *all* the time."

"That blush says otherwise. And I'm happy for you—if also a little envious. Because I can't remember the last time I had an orgasm with a man in my bed…or my shower…or on the kitchen table. And watching your face get redder and redder, I can see you have recent memories of all of the above."

Tess stabbed a slice of cucumber with her fork. "I think I'm going to plead the Fifth on that one."

Meg picked the tomato off her BLT sandwich. "And now you've got that little pleat between your brows that usually indicates you're worried about something," she noted.

"I guess I'm just wondering when it's all going to come crashing down around me," she confided.

"What do you think is going to crash down around you?"

"The fairy-tale world I'm living in."

"It might feel like a fairy tale, but it's real," Meg assured her, wiping her fingers on a paper napkin. "I've seen you with your Prince Charming, and he is every bit as head over heels for you as you are for him."

"Still—" she pushed her salad around the bowl, trying to find the right words to confide in her best friend what she didn't dare tell anyone else "—I sometimes wonder if it was a mistake to marry him."

"No," Meg protested. "Why?"

"Because you know that as soon as people find out I'm having his baby, they're going to say that I trapped him."

"What people are you talking about?" her friend demanded.

"Everyone," Tess said. "You saw the glances and heard the whispers at the restaurant—I know you did."

"But why would you care what those people think?"

"Because Whispering Canyon is a fairly small town and some of those people are Holt's friends and neighbors. And his mother."

"Forget his mother," Meg advised. "I saw her at the anniversary party and thought she was an ice sculpture, she was so cold."

Tess choked on a laugh, but her amusement quickly faded. "She accused me of manipulating the situation for financial gain."

Her friend's gaze narrowed. "She said that to you?"

"Something along those lines."

"Forget the ice analogy—she's a stone-cold bitch."

"She's also my mother-in-law. And my baby's grandmother. But most important, she's Holt's mother, and I hate that our marriage has driven a wedge between them."

"She can get rid of that wedge any time she wants to accept that her son has chosen to be with you," Meg said reasonably.

"Anyway, that's enough about me," Tess said. "Tell me how you and Emma are doing."

"I'm afraid to say *good*, because every time I start to think we've turned a corner, she has another nightmare."

"She seemed happy at Pasquale's last night."

"That girl loves her pizza."

"She seems to love Flynn, too," Tess noted.

"They're both members of a mutual admiration society, and it's important for her to have positive male role models in her life."

"And you and Flynn?" she prompted.

Meg shook her head. "There's no me and Flynn."

"I'm only asking because Holt asked me. He thought he picked up…a vibe?"

"No vibe," Meg said firmly.

And though Tess remained unconvinced, she let her friend have the last word.

Tess was uncharacteristically nervous as she lifted her hand to sound a perfunctory knock on the door, then turned the knob and walked in.

"Is that you, Tess?"

"It's me," she confirmed, kicking off her shoes inside the door. Holt removed his boots and followed her.

Tallulah glanced up as her granddaughter entered the kitchen, her easy smile faltering when she saw she wasn't alone.

"You brought company." She brushed her hands down the front of her apron. "You didn't tell me that you were bringing company."

"Because I didn't want you to fuss," Tess said.

"Tallulah Leonard," she said, offering her hand to Holt.

He shook it politely. "Holt Chandler."

She nodded. "I know. I, uh, congratulations. On the wedding."

"Thank you."

"Tess showed me photos. I was glad to see that you made the day special for her."

"She's special to me," Holt said.

Lula slid her hands into the oven mitts on the counter when the timer buzzed.

"What kind of cookies are those, Grams?" Tess asked, eyeing them with interest after the trays had been removed from the oven.

"Brown butter toffee chocolate chip."

"New recipe?" she guessed.

Lula nodded. "Which I wouldn't have tackled today if I'd known you were bringing company, because I don't know if it's any good."

"It's good," Tess said, her words muffled by a mouthful of cookie. "Really good."

"She's always been impatient," Tallulah said to Holt, an obvious note of affection in her voice. "Even as a child, she wanted instant gratification."

Holt raised his eyebrows, a twinkle in his eye that made Tess blush. Thankfully, her grandmother was preoccupied transferring cookies from the trays to the cooling racks.

"Can I get you something to drink?" Lula asked Holt.

"I'll have coffee, if it's convenient."

"It's convenient," she said, setting a mug in place under the spout of her brewer.

"And I'll have a glass of milk with my cookies," Tess said.

"You've already had your cookies."

"I had *one*."

"That you took without asking," her grandmother admonished.

"I did. And I'm sorry. Could I please have a glass of milk and some cookies?"

Lula set a mug of coffee in front of Holt and a plate of cookies in the middle of the table.

"I have to admit, she wasn't at all what I expected," Holt said to Tess, when they were on their way back to West River Ranch.

"What did you expect?"

"I'm not sure—but not a stereotypical grandmother, right down to the cookies fresh out of the oven."

"I don't know if peasant blouses, denim leggings and dangly earrings are stereotypical, but she *is* my grandmother," Tess reminded him.

"She certainly doesn't look like a homewrecker."

"Excuse me?" Tess's back immediately went up. "She never was a homewrecker."

"Come on, Tess. There's no way she didn't know my grandfather was married when she seduced him."

"Why are you so sure that *she* seduced *him*?" she demanded.

He started to respond, closed his mouth again.

"She was twenty years old, cutting hair at her mother's salon, when she met your grandfather. He was twenty-seven, with a wife and two kids."

"I obviously hit a nerve and I'm sorry," he said.

But Tess wasn't appeased by his apology.

"I knew this would happen," she said softly.

"Knew what would happen?"

"That you'd judge her, just like everyone else in this town has always judged her."

"I'm sorry," he said again. "You're right—I judged her like everyone else has always done. And maybe I was wrong—"

"Maybe?" she interjected.

"Maybe," he said again, unwilling to give her any more than that. "Because I grew up hearing one side of the story while you obviously grew up hearing another."

"Actually, I probably grew up hearing the same story you heard. It's only been in recent years that I've started to ask questions and listen to Lula's answers.

"I'm not proud of some of the things she did back then," Tess acknowledged. "But I'm proud of the woman she is now. She worked hard to overcome her addiction—and I know your grandparents helped. They paid for her treatment programs and bought her a house so she had somewhere to live while she was getting back on her feet, but she's the one who did the work."

"My point," he said patiently, "is that there are always two sides to every story and usually the truth is somewhere in the middle, and I apologize for making assumptions. In any case, it's their story, not ours, and we shouldn't let that history affect our relationship."

"But it does," she said sadly. "You sat down beside me at The Bootlegger knowing that I was Tallulah's granddaughter, so when you invited me to come back to your room, it was because you expected me to say *yes*, because I was Tallulah's granddaughter."

"I promise you, Tess, when I invited you back to my room it had nothing to do with your grandmother and everything to do with the fact that you were interesting and funny and smart, and all of those things combined to tempt me more than I'd ever been tempted by another woman—and that's the complete and honest truth."

Chapter Eighteen

"Nothing slows him down for long, does it?" Tess mused, as she watched Raylan bustle off after his therapy was finished.

"Never has," Eleanor confirmed.

"Are you worried that he's overdoing it?"

"Not really," the rancher's wife said. "Because I know the boys won't let him."

Tess had learned that *the boys* referred collectively to Eleanor's sons and grandsons as well as the longtime hands who made West River Ranch their home.

"But you're worried about something," she noted.

Eleanor sighed. "I don't like unanswered questions."

"There still hasn't been any progress on the investigation of the shooting?"

"Not any that I've heard about," Eleanor said. "Which is why Flynn went to California to talk to a couple of girls who were hiking in the area the day of the shooting."

Tess was surprised by this news. "Is Flynn working for the sheriff's office now?"

"No. But he's another one who doesn't like unanswered questions, and when Sawyer told him that the sheriff didn't get their statements before they left town, he offered to follow up personally."

"Hopefully, that follow-up will lead to a breakthrough in the investigation."

"My fingers are crossed," Eleanor said.

"Speaking of unanswered questions," Tess began, grateful for the segue. "Holt and I found something when we were emptying the closet in his office, in preparation for making the room into a nursery."

"Tell me what you found," his grandmother urged.

"I'd rather show you," Tess said, and went to retrieve the letter from her bag.

The rancher's wife seemed startled when she read the name and address on the envelope Tess handed her, but she removed the page from inside and carefully unfolded it.

"Can you read it to me?" she asked. "My eyes are old and the ink is faded."

Tess nodded and began:

"'Dearest Amelia,

"I know I'm going to be home soon and that there's no way for this letter to reach you before I do, but writing makes me feel close to you even when I'm far away.

"I'm admittedly a little uneasy about the upcoming journey. There have been whispers about a possible robbery attempt, though such whispers are commonplace in the business and Mr. Hayworth has assured us that we needn't pay them any attention. No doubt when I'm home with you safe, you'll agree that there was no reason for concern.

"Still, I'm hoping to find another job soon. Not because there's any real danger doing what I do, but because I hate being away from you for such long stretches of time. Especially now that we have a baby on the way. I know it's early days yet, but I want you to know how truly overjoyed I was to hear the news. Having a family with you is my greatest dream come true.

"Your loving husband, Thaddeus.'"

"I imagine, as you're expecting a baby yourself now, this letter really struck a chord with you," Eleanor mused.

"It did," Tess confirmed.

"Is there a date on the letter?"

"September 22, 1857."

"This might have been helpful if we'd found it eighteen months ago along with the other letters," Holt's grandmother mused.

"There were other letters?"

"When we were digging the foundation to renovate what's now your cabin, we found a wooden box filled with letters. More than a dozen, I'd guess. But unlike this one, written by Thaddeus to his wife, the others were all from Amelia to her husband."

"Were they part of your family, then?" Tess guessed, eager to learn more details about the couple and their relationship.

But Eleanor shook her head. "I couldn't find any familial connection."

"Then why was this letter in Holt's cabin?" she wondered.

"The cabin has been added on to and renovated at different times over the years, but the first incarnation of it was basically a single-room shack—the room that you're making into a nursery, in fact—built by Raylan's great-grandfather's older brother, Quentin Chandler."

"I feel like I'm going to need a lot more dots if I'm expected to connect them."

"How much do you know about the infamous stagecoach robbery of 1857?" Eleanor asked her.

"I remember learning about it in school and know it figures into the naming of Whispering Canyon," Tess said. "The so-called whispers that can be heard between the Two Sisters mountains are believed to be the ghosts of the men who were killed when a stagecoach, carrying several chests of gold, was robbed on its way from Oregon to New York."

"That's right," Eleanor confirmed. "The reinsman and all the guards were killed during the robbery. But the tragedy didn't end there as the four men believed responsible all perished within six months of the heist."

"The four men being Cody Blackstone, William Howlett, Roy Sutton and Quentin Chandler," Tess remembered now.

Eleanor nodded.

"So Holt's great-great-great-uncle was involved in the robbery?"

"Allegedly."

"That would explain how the letters ended up buried near the cabin," she realized. "If Thaddeus had them with him when the stagecoach was robbed, they might have been taken along with the gold."

"That was my theory," Eleanor confirmed. "And why, when we found the letters, I wanted to track down the descendants of Thaddeus and Amelia to return them."

"Were you successful?" Tess asked curiously.

"It took a lot of time scouring those online ancestry databases, but yes, I eventually tracked down—I think it was a great-great-great granddaughter of Thaddeus and Amelia—and sent the letters to her about six months ago.

"Come on into the study," Eleanor said. "And I'll show you what I found."

The elderly woman sat in front of the computer and scrolled through her directory.

"This is it," she said, clicking the file to open it. "The child Thaddeus referred to in that letter was born five months after his death. Amelia named him Samuel Thaddeus Dougherty.

"When Samuel married and had a son with his wife, they called him Thaddeus Walker Dougherty—after their respective fathers. Thaddeus Walker Dougherty had three daughters—one of them, Isabella, married a man named Reginald Bradford, and they had a son, Walker, and a daughter, Amelia.

"It's Isabella that I sent the letters to. Her address is right here, if you want to send that one to her, too."

"I think I do," Tess said. "I wouldn't know what to do with it otherwise, and it seems wrong to throw it away."

She printed the page with the address for Tess.

"It's interesting, don't you think, that after so many years, these letters were suddenly unearthed, but the missing gold was never found?" Tess mused.

"Interesting, indeed," Eleanor agreed.

There was no such thing as an ordinary day for a rancher. Depending on the season, the weather, commodity prices and numerous other factors, it might turn out to be a good day or a not-so-good one, because every day had different challenges and rewards. But as far as Holt was concerned, working on the ranch on a not-so-good day was still a lot better than doing anything else.

So far, today was a not-so-good day, and right now he was with Colby and Austin, searching for thirty head of cattle that had somehow gotten separated from the rest of the herd.

"Look at that," Colby said, pointing.

"Some damn fool left the gate open," Holt noted.

"None of us are that foolish—or careless," Austin said.

Holt dismounted to inspect the chain and padlock that ordinarily secured the gate. "It wasn't left open—the chain was cut right through."

"First the fence was cut and now the gate," Austin mused. "I'm starting to think someone is deliberately messing with us."

"But who?" Colby wondered.

"And why?" Holt wanted to know.

"Both good questions," Austin said. "But the answers will have to wait until we've found the missing animals."

"I'd wager we'll find them somewhere on the other side of that gate," Colby said.

"On Dale Bellows's land."

"Soon to be part of West River Ranch."

"But not yet."

It took the better part of the day for them to find the last of the missing cows, including four calves that didn't yet bear the Chandler brand. Thankfully, they didn't encounter any human resistance as they rounded them up and drove them back where they belonged.

"I want a shower and a beer, not necessarily in that order," Austin said, when they finally turned their mounts toward the barn where they would be rubbed down, fed and watered.

"I'd add a hot meal to that list," Colby said.

"We could head into town."

"I'm up for that. You want to join us, Holt?"

He shook his head.

"Of course, he doesn't want to join us," Austin said. "He's gotta get home to the little woman."

"Don't let my wife hear you call her a little woman," Holt warned. "She'll kick your ass."

"See what I mean?"

Colby made the sound of a whip cracking.

Holt let them have their fun, because as tempting as a hot meal and a cold beer sounded, the prospect of Tess's arms around him was even more tempting.

"What's wrong with Buddy?" Jackson asked, setting a bowl of nuts on the table where Holt had gathered with a handful of his cousins for poker a few nights later. "Why's he moping?"

"Because Tess went into town to hang out with Meg and Emma tonight."

"Did she leave because you were hosting poker night?" Colby wondered. "Or did you offer to host poker night because she already had plans?"

"Does it matter?" he asked.

"No," Austin said, as he raked the pile of chips from the middle of the table. "All that matters is that I'll be going home with your money in my pocket."

"His head's definitely not in the game tonight," Colby agreed.

"Probably daydreaming about his new bride," Jackson guessed.

"Shut up and deal," Holt said.

"Well, if a man has to be shackled to a ball and chain, he'd be hard-pressed to find a prettier one than Tess," Greyson noted.

"That's my wife you're talking about," Holt reminded the men around the table.

"No one's disrespecting her," Colby assured him.

"Questioning her judgment perhaps," Austin said. "But not disrespecting her."

"As if you have a right to question anyone else's judgment," Greyson commented to his brother. "You married Karli—who dotted the 'i' at the end of her name with a heart."

Austin shrugged. "I was young and foolishly believed myself in love."

"Holt's still young," Jackson noted.

"And if not foolishly in love—foolish enough to forget the condom," Colby chortled.

Holt hadn't realized his hands were curled into fists until he slammed them on the table. "You're going to want to watch your mouth before I put my fist in it," he warned.

Colby held up his hands, wisely keeping his mouth shut.

"Anyone else want to offer commentary?" Holt challenged.

There were head shakes around the table.

Jackson cleared his throat. "I got a text from Flynn today," he said, in a deliberate attempt to shift the conversation before any punches were thrown.

"Did he give you an update?" Austin asked.

"Only that he'd talked to the witnesses and would be home tomorrow."

Conversation shifted again to more neutral topics as, for the next couple of hours, the men focused on playing cards. And everyone was in good spirits—particularly Austin, the big winner—when they agreed to call it a night.

Colby was the last to leave, offering his hand to Holt on his way out the door. "My sincere apologies," he said. "I swear I never would have cracked any kind of joke about Tess if I'd known you were in love with her."

"I didn't say I was in love with her," Holt pointed out.

"Yeah, you did," his cousin argued. "Even if you didn't use the words."

Holt was scowling as he closed the door behind him.

And Buddy was still moping.

After he gathered up empty beer bottles and dirty dishes, he dropped onto the sofa. His dog gave a plaintive whine.

"Yeah, I miss her, too," he confided, patting the cushion beside him. Buddy jumped up and dropped his chin onto Holt's thigh.

It was odd to think how perfectly she fit into his life—almost as if there'd been a Tess-shaped hole, just waiting to be filled.

"Damn," he muttered, rubbing the soft fur behind Buddy's ears.

The dog lifted his head.

"Colby was right," he confided. "I've gone and fallen in love with my wife."

"What can I do for you?" Billy Garvey asked, barely glancing up from the screen of his phone when Holt walked into his office Monday afternoon.

"I was hoping to get an update on the investigation into my grandfather's shooting."

"If I had an update to give, I'd be giving it to him," the sheriff said.

"So there's nothing new to report?"

"If I had to guess, I'd say that whoever took that shot at your grandfather is long gone."

"I was hoping, seeing as you're the sheriff in this town, that you might actually look for evidence rather than offer guesses."

Garvey looked up from his phone now to glare at his visitor. "I know how to do my job."

"Do you?" he challenged. "Because it looks like you're sitting on your butt playing…*really*? Is that *Candy Crush*?"

"Eff you, Chandler. I'm on a break."

"Well, when your break's over, you might want to look for a youngish, white male with a slender build wearing combat boots."

The sheriff frowned. "I don't know where you're getting your information, but I can assure you I don't need you to tell me how to run my investigation."

"Flynn went to California to interview the witnesses that you let slip through your fingers, because it doesn't seem like you're trying too hard to find out who shot my grandfather."

"I'd think twice before pushing me too hard on this," Garvey warned ominously.

"What's that supposed to mean?"

"Just that further investigation might point in a direction you don't want me to go."

"I want whoever shot my grandfather behind bars," Holt assured him.

"Even if *whoever* turns out to be your bride's grandmother?"

Holt scowled. "You plan on trying to make a case on the basis of threats she allegedly made fifty years ago?"

"Of course not," the sheriff said. "But a call came through the tip line this morning that just might give me what I need."

The only thing Eleanor hated more than a bully was injustice, so there was no way she was willing to sit back and allow a bully to perpetuate an injustice. As soon as Tess got the call informing her that their grandmother had been arrested, Eleanor got in her car and drove into town. Then she marched right past the administration desk of the sheriff's office and into Billy Garvey's private sanctum.

"I heard a rumor, though I'm certain it can't be true, that you arrested Tallulah Leonard."

Billy glanced up from the file he was reviewing, then picked up the receiver of the phone and spoke into it. "Mrs. Chandler's here? Yes, of course, Gina. Please send her in."

Eleanor wasn't amused. "Tallulah Leonard?" she prompted.

He nodded. "It's true."

"You can't actually believe she shot Raylan."

"It doesn't matter what I think, only what I can prove."

"What kind of proof do you think you have?"

"We've got the gun that was used to shoot your husband. An Enfield Pattern 1853 rifle-musket—found in Tallulah Leonard's garden shed."

"What idiotic judge signed off on a warrant for you to search her property?" she demanded.

"We didn't need a warrant," Billy said, sounding more than a little defensive now. "She gave permission for the search."

"Which should have been a pretty big clue that she didn't expect you to find anything there."

"Except that we did," he said smugly.

"Obviously the gun was planted."

"The only thing obvious to me is that I've now got the weapon and a viable suspect with a clear motive."

"Viable suspect," she scoffed. "I doubt the woman—who's eighty years old, by the way—even knows how to load a rifle."

"You don't need to know how to load a rifle to be able to pull the trigger."

"So her fingerprints are on the weapon?" Eleanor challenged.

"No." He shook his head. "There were no fingerprints at all. It was wiped clean."

She stared at the sheriff for a minute, certain there was a piece of the puzzle missing. "How did Tallulah even end up on your radar?"

His gaze skittered away. "An anonymous tip."

"Likely called in by whoever planted the gun in her garden shed," she concluded.

Now he shrugged. "Can't trace an anonymous tip."

"Why are you doing this, Billy? What possible reason do you think Tallulah might have to shoot Raylan?"

"'Hell hath no fury,'" he quoted.

"*I* was the woman scorned," Eleanor pointed out. "Maybe you should be interrogating *me*."

"I considered it," he admitted. "But you have an airtight alibi for the time of the shooting. Of course, an argument might be made that your employee of more than forty years would say whatever you told her to say."

Eleanor's gaze narrowed. "An argument might also be made that you're deliberately stonewalling the investigation."

"The people of this town have trusted me to uphold the law for more than a dozen years and I haven't heard any complaints."

"The people of this town are perhaps a little too content with the status quo," she argued. "Something they might reconsider before you're up for reelection next year."

"Nobody else in Whispering Canyon wants this thankless job," he told her. "Which is why I've always run unopposed."

"Maybe next time, you won't."

"Is that a threat?"

"No, Billy Garvey." Her gaze was as steely as her tone. "It's a promise."

Chapter Nineteen

"They arrested my grandmother." Tess's voice was hollow, her usually sparkling green eyes filled with anguish.

Holt took her in his arms. "I heard."

"This is crazy," she said, her words now muffled against his chest. "There's no way Tallulah was involved."

He rubbed her back, attempting to soothe her obvious distress.

When he remained silent, she tipped her head back to look at him. "Tell me you know this is crazy."

"I know you don't want to hear this, honey, but the rifle was found in her possession."

"No. The rifle was found in the shed in her backyard," she clarified. "Nearly two months after the shooting. After the sheriff supposedly got an anonymous tip. And, coincidentally, only a few days after your brother came back from California with information suggesting the shooter was a young male—a description which does not match my grandmother."

"She did threaten to kill him," Holt pointed out gently.

"Half a century ago. After he took her kids away." Tess laid a protective hand on her belly. "I assure you, if someone took my child, I'd do more than just threaten."

"Take a breath, honey. You're getting all worked up."

"Of course I'm getting worked up! They put my grandmother in handcuffs and took her to jail!"

"I understand the instinct to protect and defend your family,"

Holt said. "But I think you need to ask yourself if you're really one hundred percent certain that she wasn't involved or—"

"Of course she wasn't involved!"

"*Or*," he continued, determined to make his point, "if you don't want to believe she's involved because she's your grandmother."

"Ohmygod." She took a step back, swiping at the tears on her cheeks. "You think she did it."

"I think it would be foolish to disregard the evidence."

Tess took a minute to consider his words, then she nodded. "Apparently I am a fool," she said. "Because I actually thought you'd be there for me."

"I *am* here for you," he assured her.

"But not for my grandmother."

"Tess…"

"Why do you think she's involved in this?" she challenged. "Because she did bad things in the past, she's a bad person who must have done this bad thing, too?"

"I don't think she's a bad person, but the fact is, she has done bad things in the past."

"Yes, she has," Tess agreed. "And she paid for them, over and over again. But it seems that she's not done paying for them yet—and the rest of her family isn't done paying for them, either."

Holt and Tess spent the next few days tiptoeing around one another, so when Holt learned that his uncle wanted to move the cattle, he decided that a little bit of time and space might be just what they needed. Maybe, after a few days apart, they could talk about the situation again like reasonable, rational adults and move forward.

"We're going to be driving the cattle this weekend," he said to Tess, when she came home from a rare late shift at the clinic Thursday night.

"What does that mean?" she asked, because after only a few weeks of marriage, she still had a lot to learn about the seasons and demands of cattle ranching.

"I'll be gone a few days. Heading out around four a.m. tomorrow, most likely back sometime on Monday."

"Okay." She went back to her phone, exchanging text messages with someone. Possibly her mom or dad, who were in Colorado Springs visiting her sister. Or Meg. Maybe even her grandmother.

"Tess," he began.

She looked up, but he didn't know what else to say.

I'm sorry seemed completely inaccurate—and not entirely true. Because while he was sorry they'd argued, he wasn't sorry for what he'd said.

Her phone buzzed and she dropped her gaze to the screen, reading the latest message.

"Emma's had a couple of rough nights lately and Meg's struggling," she confided. "I suggested that a change of scenery might be good for both of them."

"Doesn't seem like it could hurt," he agreed.

"Would it be okay, then, if I invited them to spend some time here while you're gone?"

"Tess, this is your home. You don't need anyone's permission to invite people over."

She nodded as she sent a reply—or maybe an invitation—to her friend. Then she put her phone down and looked at him. "I know we have to talk about things, but I need a bit more time."

"Okay," he said again.

"We'll talk when you get back?"

Now he nodded.

"Four a.m., huh?"

"Yeah. I should probably be heading to bed."

"Okay."

So that was what he did, crawling under the covers alone

and missing Tess like crazy though she was less than a hundred feet away.

Then, only a few minutes later, she came into the room and crawled under the covers on the other side of the bed. He shifted closer to the center, then she did the same, until her back was against his front. He draped his arm over her middle, she tipped her head back against his chest and they slept.

In Western movies, riding the range was portrayed as a romantic venture—wide shots of breathtaking scenery a testament to the cowboy's love of the land. In reality, it was often dusty, sweaty work, but satisfying, too. Holt usually loved driving cattle, as it provided the modern-day cowboy with the rare opportunity to spend all day in the saddle and all night sleeping under the stars.

As he held his position on the flank, he found himself recalling his first cattle drive. He'd been about twelve years old, he guessed, and desperate to be included. Boone and Flynn, being older, had been participating in the drives for a few years already, and there was nothing Holt had hated more than being left behind.

His mom had always planned fun things for them to do together when his dad and brothers were gone, so he wouldn't feel left out. Scavenger hunts, hikes in the woods, game nights and movie marathons. He'd forgotten that. Forgotten the efforts she'd made, the closeness they'd shared when it was just the two of them.

Remembering now, he couldn't help but feel a little sorry that they'd lost that closeness. And frustrated, too, that the woman who'd gone to such efforts to forge a special relationship with her son was unwilling to give his wife a chance.

Thinking of Tess now, he couldn't help but feel uneasy about being away from her. Or maybe he just missed her.

He'd only been gone a handful of hours, but it felt like days. Perhaps because things had been tense between them for days.

But they'd started to bridge the distance last night, which was both a relief and an incentive to get back home again as soon as possible.

"I'm used to seeing cookies on your counter, not casserole dishes," Tess remarked, when she stopped by to see her grandmother Friday afternoon.

"I'm trying to fit them in the freezer," Tallulah said. "And it's like that video game you used to play."

"Tetris?"

Lula shrugged. "If you say so."

"Where did these come from?" she asked, and since her grandmother was otherwise occupied, Tess put on the kettle for tea.

"Nosy neighbors."

"Did someone die?" Tess asked cautiously.

"Ha! That's exactly what I wondered." She shifted and stacked, huffed out a breath and shifted again. "Apparently being hauled off in cuffs is a similar call to the casserole brigade."

"They care about you, Gramma."

"That might be stretching it." She closed the freezer. "This isn't your usual day to visit."

"I know. I just wanted to see you. And…to say I'm sorry."

"What are you apologizing for?" her grandmother asked curiously.

"All the times I wished I wasn't a Leonard."

Lula's smile was wry. "I bet mine outnumber yours."

Tess carried her tea and her grandmother's coffee to the table. "Can I ask you a question?"

"Of course."

"Did you love him?"

"Raylan?" Lula guessed.

She nodded.

"I want to say *yes*, because I'm sure you'd feel better to believe that it was deep feelings that motivated my actions," her grandmother said. "But the truth is, I don't know. Certainly I was infatuated by him. He was so handsome. And charming. With a way of looking at you like you were the only thing he could see.

"It gave me a jolt when you brought your husband by," Lula confided now. "Holt's definitely got the look of his grandfather from back in the day."

"The Chandler men are a handsome lot," Tess agreed.

"I don't know if I loved Raylan," her grandmother said again. "But I was certainly a fool for him."

"What about my grandfather? Or Meg's grandfather?"

"All of that was so long ago... Does it really matter?"

"It matters to me."

Lula sighed. "Okay, then. I'll tell you that they were both decent men, neither of them married or interested in being married to me or a father to any of my kids."

"I can't imagine how scary that must have been for you... going through each of your pregnancies—and childbirth three times—without any support."

"Not something you have to worry about," her grandmother pointed out to her.

Tess sipped her tea. "Holt and I had a...disagreement."

"Obviously I don't know much about marriage, but I don't think a little disagreement should be cause for concern."

"It wasn't a little disagreement," she confided.

"They're all little disagreements unless you make them into something bigger."

Before they were married, Tess had worried that the history between their families would cause problems in her relationship with Holt. And though her name might now be Chandler, the blood that flowed through her veins would always be Leonard.

But maybe Tallulah was right, Tess mused, as she drove away from her grandmother's house. Maybe it was a matter of perspective, and if she wanted to move forward in her marriage with Holt—and she did—she needed to acknowledge that they weren't always going to see eye to eye and accept when they had differences of opinion. (Even when it was patently obvious that his opinion was wrong!)

Deciding to offer a proverbial olive branch, she took a detour to Denninger's Garden Center. A few weeks earlier, she'd mentioned to Holt that it might be nice to have some flowers around the deck—similar to the planters that flanked Raylan and Eleanor's front door. He'd immediately given her free rein to do whatever she wanted, but she hadn't yet decided what that might be.

"This is a surprise," Jordan said, when he found Tess surveying a selection of planters and pots. "I don't think I've ever seen you here before."

"I don't have much of a green thumb," she confided. "I'm good with patients, but not so much with plants."

"Then I'd say you haven't met the right plants."

"Maybe you could make the introductions?"

He grinned. "Tell me what you're looking for and I'll see what I can do."

"Planters," she said. "I want three of them for the back deck."

"Sun or shade?"

"Um…sun."

"Any color preference?"

"No. Just bright and cheery."

She spent another half hour at the garden center. Jordan didn't have anything ready-made that fit her requirements, so she picked the style of planter she wanted and he promised to have the flower-filled containers delivered by the next day.

She had some errands to run herself on Saturday morning. Meg and Emma were coming to the cabin later that day for a slumber party, and Tess was determined to fill their time together with fun activities and games and fuel their bellies with their favorite snacks.

Returning to the cabin just before lunchtime, she was pleased to see a truck with the Denninger's Garden Center logo in the driveway. She parked alongside it, then gathered up her bags and carried them inside, depositing them on the island before making her way to the deck to see what Jordan had put together for her.

There were three square planters evenly spaced across the width of the deck with stunning purple and red flowers. A stake in each of the planters held a tag identifying the plants—Angelonia (purple); Calibrachoa (red); Silver Artemisia (green)—and providing detailed care instructions.

Evidently he'd taken her at her word that she didn't know much about plants, and she was grateful for it.

Thrilled with the colorful additions—and confident Holt would be, too—she returned to the house to put her groceries away.

"Buddy?" she called out, surprised that the dog hadn't been there to greet her when she got home, as he usually was.

Moping, she suspected, as he'd been since Holt said goodbye the day before.

There was no response.

Maybe he wasn't moping, after all. Maybe he'd ventured out to chase rabbits across the fields.

Then Tess heard the toilet flush, and she froze.

She reached into the side pocket of her purse for her phone and unlocked the screen, her thumb poised over the keypad in case she needed to call 911.

She heard the latch of a door closing—or opening—then footsteps in the hall.

"Hello?" she called out, cringing at the shakiness of her voice.

"Is that you, Mrs. Chandler?" A man's voice—but an unfamiliar one.

Then he stepped into view, and she exhaled a shuddery sigh.

"Brad, is it?" she asked, recognizing one of the garden center employees that Jordan had introduced as Brad Walker the day before.

He nodded.

"What are you doing in here?"

"Oh. Um." He looked at her sheepishly. "Yeah, sorry about that. I've been making deliveries all morning and needed to use the facilities. I knocked, but no one answered, and the door was unlocked."

She didn't doubt it was true. There wasn't really any reason to keep the cabin secured out here and while she usually locked the door when she left—a habit developed when she lived in town—it was possible that she'd forgotten.

Still, she felt a little uneasy knowing that this man—this stranger—had walked right into her home.

"Well, the planters look great," she said. "So thanks."

He nodded. "No problem."

Her uneasiness grew when he made no move toward the door.

"Was there something else you needed?" she asked.

"Yeah." He reached behind his back and pulled out a gun. "I need you to come with me."

Someone kicked his boot.

Scowling, Holt shifted his hat away from his face to find Flynn standing over him.

"Go away," he said. "I'm trying to catch some shuteye before my watch tonight."

"You won't be on watch tonight, because we're leaving now."

Holt, recognizing that his brother was in soldier mode—grim, focused, determined—didn't question his directive. He stood up, grabbed the pack he'd been using as a pillow and fell into step beside him.

"We're taking the ATV?" he asked, when Flynn tossed his bag in the back.

"Yeah."

Which meant that wherever they were going, Flynn wanted to get there in a hurry. An uneasy feeling began to gnaw at the pit of his stomach.

"You gonna tell me what's going on?" he asked, as his brother took position behind the wheel.

"I got a call from Meg."

"Emma?" he immediately guessed.

Flynn shook his head, his expression grim.

And Holt's stomach plummeted.

"Tess," he realized.

This time his brother responded with a short nod. "She's missing."

So much for her plans to spend a relaxing weekend with her best friend and Meg's little girl, Tess thought, watching as Brad paced the cabin.

Not Holt's cabin, though. He'd marched her out of there at gunpoint, forced her into her car and told her to drive. Holt often teased that her little Kia wasn't made for life on a ranch, and it certainly proved it, bumping and scraping along a dirt road not worthy of the name.

While she'd been driving, her mind had been racing, trying to figure out an escape plan. She didn't know what Brad's intentions were; she only knew that she needed to get away.

She thought about purposely crashing the car and then making a run for it. And maybe, if she'd only had herself to think about, she might have gathered the courage to do so. But she had to think about her baby.

And so she did what Brad told her, so that he wouldn't be tempted to pull the trigger of the gun he kept trained on her.

He'd directed her to a different cabin, so far off the beaten path she wasn't even certain they were still on West River Ranch. It was essentially a one-room shack, with a table and two chairs and a bare mattress on a metal bed frame. There were two windows, on opposite sides of the cabin, both covered with broken blinds, and doors at the front and back.

The front door was the entrance; the back door led to the toilet. He'd let her use it when they arrived, before he'd tied her to the chair. How many hours had passed since then? She had no idea, as there was no clock on the wall and, with her hands secured behind her back, she couldn't see her watch. Long enough, though, that her shoulders were aching and her legs were starting to feel numb.

"Is there anything to eat? Or drink?"

"Sure. Let me get you a room service menu."

She took that as a *no.*

So far he'd rebuffed her efforts at conversation in favor of text communications with someone who—according to his mutterings—better figure out a way to help him fix this damn mess.

"Maybe I can help," Tess said, trying to sound calm despite the fact she was seriously freaking out. But maybe freaking out was appropriate considering she'd been kidnapped by a man she'd never met before Jordan introduced them at the garden center the previous day. "If you can tell me what you want, maybe I can help you get it."

Brad considered that as he paced back and forth across the length of the cabin. "Maybe you can," he decided. "Maybe I can still get what I came for."

"What's that?" she wondered.

"Just my fair share," he said. "All I ever wanted was my fair share, and I'm not leaving without it."

"Your share of what?" Tess asked cautiously.

"The gold."

She frowned. "What gold?"

"You know what gold. I saw the letter from Thaddeus to Amelia on your dresser."

The thought of him going through her stuff, touching her personal belongings, made Tess feel physically ill. She pushed down the nausea and tried to clear her head. She needed to keep him talking, figure out what was going on and find a way out of this seemingly hopeless situation.

"You mean…are you talking about the gold from the stagecoach robbery of 1857?"

"That's right," he confirmed. "They said it was carrying two hundred thousand dollars in gold. Adjusted for inflation, that works out to about five million, divided five ways makes my share a million."

"But the gold was never recovered," she pointed out to him.

"That's the official story," he agreed.

"What do you think is the unofficial story?"

"Obviously one of the thieves—Blackstone or Lowell or Sutton or Chandler—ended up with all the gold. Considering the size of West River Ranch and the wealth of its owners, the most logical conclusion is that it was Quentin Chandler."

"Wait a minute," Tess said. "You mentioned four names—Blackstone, Lowell, Sutton and Chandler—but you said the money was to be divided five ways."

"Thaddeus Dougherty was supposed to get a cut, too. Instead, they killed him."

She recognized that name from the letter she'd found in Holt's cabin. "You're saying the stagecoach driver was in on the heist?"

He nodded.

"How could you possibly know something like that?" she asked, because she was beginning to worry that he was living in an alternate reality. The gun in his hand already made him dangerous, but dangerous and unstable greatly reduced the odds of Tess talking her way out of this situation.

"Research," he said simply. "I've read every book, article and scrap of paper related to the robbery. And then, about six months ago, out of the blue, a whole bunch of letters dropped in my lap and gave me a new starting point for my search."

And the pieces started to come together for Tess.

"Your name's not really Brad Walker," she realized. "It's… Walker Bradford."

He nodded. "Thaddeus Dougherty was my great-great-great-grandfather."

She gasped as another piece clicked into place. "*You* shot Raylan Chandler."

"I wasn't trying to kill him," her kidnapper said. "I just needed him—and the rest of the family—away from the ranch."

"So that you could break into the house."

"Is it really breaking in if the door's not locked?" he challenged.

"And you framed my grandmother," she realized.

"The old lady's your grandmother?"

She nodded.

"I had no idea," he admitted. "I just dumped the gun where Billy told me to."

"Billy?" Shock jolted through her. He couldn't mean… "As in Billy Garvey—the sheriff?"

He shifted his gaze away. "As in my cousin Billy."

Which wasn't a denial, she noted.

Still, she suspected that any efforts to push further in that direction would prove futile, so instead she asked, "What were you looking for in the Chandlers' house?"

He shrugged. "Anything that might lead me to the gold."

"Tourists and treasure hunters have scoured the caves in the mountains for more than a hundred and fifty years looking for the gold," she told him. "Not a single coin was ever found."

"I'm not leaving without my money. I want my million dollars—and you're going to get it for me."

"I assure you, I don't have a million dollars."

"Maybe you don't," he acknowledged. "But the Chandlers do. And if your husband ever wants to see you alive again, he's going to pay for the privilege."

She should have run when she'd had the chance. As soon as he pulled out the gun, she should have turned on her heel and run. And if it had only been her, she might have taken that chance. But she had to think about her baby. Holt's baby.

Holt.

Her heart squeezed as she recalled their last night together, and her mind railed at the thought it could turn out to be the last night she'd ever spend with him. There was so much that she needed to say to him. So many words that remained unspoken. And the three most important of all: *I love you.*

Chapter Twenty

Holt was a rancher. He knew almost everything there was to know about working the land and breeding cows. And he knew absolutely nothing about what to do when the woman he loved—his wife and the mother of his unborn child—went missing. The situation was a little outside of Flynn's area of expertise, too, but the former soldier's military training kicked in so that he was able to analyze the situation logically and devise a plan.

As they made their way back to the ranch, Flynn shared the limited details he had. Apparently Meg and Emma had arrived at the cabin to find bags of groceries on the counter but no sign of Tess. When text messages and phone calls went unanswered, she contacted the sheriff, who insisted that some melting ice cream wasn't evidence of foul play and it was likely Tess had simply forgotten their plans and decided to go get her nails done or something like that.

Meg had been incensed, because she knew there was no way Tess had forgotten their plans. But Billy Garvey didn't seem concerned about any of it—or even about doing his job, apparently. So that was why she'd called Flynn, and why Flynn had unceremoniously yanked his brother out of slumber.

An hour later, they were at the cabin—where Holt discovered a Denninger's Garden Center vehicle parked in the driveway. Though the sight of the truck certainly raised questions, it didn't trigger his radar. Because Tess and Jordan had gone on one date and both since moved on.

But Flynn, willing to leave no stone unturned, already had his phone in hand to call the number painted on the side of the vehicle. Holt made his way inside where he found Meg staring at the groceries tumbling out of bags onto the counter.

"I wanted to clean up. Put things away. But then I realized this might be a crime scene and I'd be tampering with evidence."

Her gaze was haunted, her tone bleak. Evidently she was every bit as worried about Tess as he was.

"You can clean up, if you want," Holt said. "Or you can take Emma home and—"

"Emma's with my parents. I called them when—" she swallowed "—after I talked to Flynn. They came to pick her up."

"Okay."

Flynn came in through the side door then, Buddy stumbling drunkenly beside him.

"What's wrong with him?" Holt demanded, dropping to his knees to inspect his dog.

"My guess, he was drugged," Flynn said. "I found him in the laundry room, the doggy door blocked from the outside."

"Drugged," Holt echoed, seething.

"Whatever was given to him, he threw it up, or he'd probably still be out cold."

"This wasn't a random, spur-of-the-moment thing," Meg realized. "Whoever took Tess knew about Buddy and came prepared to put him out of commission."

Flynn nodded grimly.

Because there was no longer any doubt in the minds of any of the three people in this room that Tess had been taken.

But by who?

And why?

Holt didn't realize he'd spoken aloud until his brother responded.

"I can't answer either of those questions," he said. "But Jordan Denninger gave me an address for the employee who had that truck out today. It's only a short drive from here."

"Let's get going."

"You need to think this through," Tess said to an obviously agitated Walker. "As of right now, it's possible that nobody's realized I'm missing. If you take me back, you can claim that we just went for a ride. But if you reach out to Holt and demand a ransom, there's no way you'll avoid a kidnapping charge."

"The way I avoid a kidnapping charge is to take the money and run," he argued. "And with a million dollars, I can go where nobody will ever find me."

"Do you really believe that's possible?"

"I have a plan," he insisted.

"And how's that plan been working out so far?"

He glowered at her.

"And what happens if you can't get through to Holt?" she pressed. "He's moving cattle this weekend. I don't even know where exactly he is or what kind of cell coverage might be available."

"You better hope I do get through," Walker said.

His ominous tone made her shiver.

And then, in the distance, she heard…barking?

"What was that?" Walker rose from his chair and made his way to the window to peer between the slats of the blinds.

Tess, tied to her chair, obviously couldn't see anything, but she heard it again.

Buddy.

"I should have skipped the drugs and just put a bullet in the damn dog," Walker muttered.

Tess was incensed. "You drugged my dog?"

"Just put a little Special K in some yummy meatballs for him."

"Why?"

"Dogs are unpredictable," Walker said. "I couldn't take the chance that he might get in the way. But I didn't anticipate that he'd track you."

"He's a dog," Tess pointed out.

My dog, she thought.

And from the sound of it, he was getting closer.

"And how did you know I had a dog?"

"Research," he said again.

"So this plan didn't suddenly come together when I met you at the garden center," she realized.

"No," he agreed. "But delivering the planters presented me with some new opportunities."

Walker winced then as a cacophony of barks came from directly outside the door.

"I might have to shoot him, anyway," he warned. "I can't think with that incessant noise."

"No!" Tess protested. "He'll stop barking if you let him in."

"That's not going to happen," he assured her.

"He's figured out that I'm in here and he's agitated because he can't get to me," she explained. "I promise, if you let him in, I'll keep him quiet."

Walker hesitated.

"Please," Tess said.

"If he tries to attack me, I will shoot him. And then I'll shoot you. Understand?"

Tess nodded.

Her kidnapper finally opened the door and found himself face-to-face with an even bigger threat than the dog—Tess's enraged husband.

Holt didn't see the gun in Walker's hand but, in any event, he didn't give him an opportunity to use it. Surprise had barely registered on the man's face before Holt's fist swung upward, catching him on the bottom of the chin. Walker dropped like a rock.

Holt was almost disappointed the man hadn't fought back, because he'd wanted to pummel the living daylights out of him. But now that the immediate threat was neutralized, he had only one thought: Tess.

Shaking out his fist—because it hurt like a sonofabitch—he stepped over the kidnapper's prone body and into the cabin. Of course, Buddy was already there, having bolted through the door as soon as it opened. His front paws were planted on Tess's knees now so he could lick her face, and she was...laughing.

And crying.

"Down, Buddy."

The dog plopped onto his butt.

"Holt!" Tess cried out his name, fresh tears sliding down her face.

"Tess." He fell to his knees in front of her, running his hands over her face, wiping the moisture from her cheeks. "You're safe now, honey. I'm here."

"Holt," she said again, her voice quiet, shaky.

"I've got you," he promised. But his hands were trembling like crazy as he tried to unfasten the knots that bound her hands and feet.

"Here." Flynn came to the rescue again, offering a knife that he pulled out of his boot.

Holt sliced through the knots.

As soon as she was free of the restraints, Tess fell into his arms. He held her tight. Emotion swelled inside his chest, stealing his breath. He took her face gently in his hands and kissed her, anyway.

"What day is it?" she asked, when he finally lifted his mouth from hers.

"Saturday."

"You weren't supposed to be back until Monday," she remembered.

"And you weren't supposed to get kidnapped," he chided gently.

"But…how did you even know?"

"Meg called Flynn."

"Most people would have called the sheriff."

"She called him first, and when Garvey refused to do anything, absent evidence of foul play, she called Flynn."

"I think he was here earlier. Billy Garvey," she clarified. "I heard Walker outside, talking to somebody. It sounded like Garvey."

"Well, he's definitely here now," Flynn muttered, as the sheriff crossed the threshold into the cabin.

And suddenly, the small space was filled with people. Sheriff's deputies and Flynn and Meg, and everything started to blur together in front of Tess's eyes.

"Tess? Honey?"

She blinked at Holt.

"You're shivering." He rubbed his hands up and down her arms. "Shaking."

Meg stepped forward then, reaching for Tess's wrist to check her pulse.

"Emma?"

"She's with my parents."

Tess winced as she nodded.

"Headache?" Meg asked.

She licked her dry lips. "Little bit."

"Lightheaded? Dizzy?"

"Little bit," she said again.

"When was the last time you had something to eat or drink?"

"This morning. Early."

"Bet you're hungry. Thirsty."

"Thirsty," she agreed.

"She might be dehydrated," Meg said to Holt.

"Ambulance just pulled up," Flynn announced.

"Let's go get you checked out," Holt said, lifting his wife into his arms.

"I don't need an ambulance," Tess protested. "I'm fine."

"You're better than fine," he said, setting her down in the open box of the back of the emergency vehicle, so that her legs dangled over the edge. "You're brave and strong and amazing. But I'm a little freaked out about the fact that you were being held at gunpoint, and it would make me feel a lot better if you went to the hospital to get checked out." He touched his lips to her forehead. "Can you do that for me, Tess? Please?"

She nodded, so grateful that he was here—that he'd come for her—she couldn't refuse him anything.

"Holt?"

He glanced over his shoulder, annoyed at the interruption. "What do you need, Garvey?"

"I've got some questions for you."

"Can't they wait?"

"No, they can't."

Meg stepped up. "I've got this."

"I'll meet you at the hospital as soon as I can," Holt promised Tess. "Okay?"

She shook her head this time. "I don't want to go without you."

But the sheriff was already steering him away and Meg was helping her onto the gurney. And as the driver started to close the doors of the ambulance, Tess saw her husband being put in the back of a police car.

The exam room was crowded with Chandlers, not unlike the day that Raylan had been shot. But this time, they were all here for Tess. Because she was a Chandler now.

Raylan and Eleanor, Clayton and Laura, RJ and Miranda, Wyatt and Kristin, Austin, Colby and Jackson were all there.

Abby and Roger had been notified of recent events and, it turned out, were already on their way back to Whispering Canyon from Colorado. They would be there soon.

Almost everyone was there except Holt. And the only person she wanted was Holt.

Well, Greyson was missing, too. But he'd been sent to the sheriff's office to get his cousin out of jail, with explicit instructions to threaten a lawsuit if the sheriff tried to stonewall Holt's release. And Flynn had stayed behind at the scene to continue his chat with Jordan Denninger and find out as much as he could about Walker Bradford. Boone remained at the ranch with his boys, because no one wanted the twins running around the hospital—and also because Boone preferred to avoid the hospital, after having spent too many hours there when his wife was sick.

But everyone else was there, and when the doctor came in to check on Tess, he glanced around the crowded room and sighed. "I appreciate that you're all concerned about our patient, but what she really needs right now is for you to give me some space to do my job."

Eleanor, taking the doctor's hint, was more blunt. "Everybody out," she said.

And the room quickly emptied.

"Everything looks good to me," the doctor told Tess, after he'd completed a perfunctory exam. "But I'm going to have an ultrasound tech come in to do a quick check, just to be sure your baby's okay, too. Does that sound good?"

She nodded.

"The baby's dad can come in for the scan, if you want."

Tess definitely wanted, but Holt wasn't there. According to Meg, the sheriff had decided that regardless of what Walker had done, he had to charge Holt for his assault on the kidnapper.

But she wasn't going to think about that now, because if she thought about it, she would lose it.

"Tess?"

She opened her eyes to find her mother-in-law standing beside her bed.

"Is it okay if I stay with you until Holt gets here—so you're not alone?" Miranda's voice was surprisingly gentle, almost tentative.

Tess nodded.

Holt's mother settled into the chair beside the bed and, after only a moment's hesitation, reached for Tess's hand.

The unexpected show of support had tears stinging Tess's eyes again, and she clung to Miranda. Gratefully. Desperately.

A few minutes after that, the ultrasound technician came in. Tess had crossed paths with Stasia before, as they worked in the same hospital, and she was eager to reassure the expectant mom.

"The doctor feels confident that everything is A-OK with your baby, but we're going to take a closer look with the ultrasound to be sure. Sound good?"

Tess nodded again, and Stasia got busy prepping her for the scan.

When the image appeared on the screen, Miranda shifted for a closer look, still holding Tess's hand. "It doesn't seem all that long ago that Holt was a baby and now I'm looking at his baby," she said, a note of awe in her voice.

"I just wish he was here to see his baby," Tess murmured.

"He'll be here," his mom promised. "And everything will be okay."

Her unexpected compassion was Tess's undoing, and she couldn't hold back the tears any longer. Holt had come back—he'd saved her. And then the sheriff had taken him away.

And not being with him, not being able to touch him and kiss him and tell him she loved him…

Why had she never told him she loved him?

Why had it seemed more important to hold on to her pride than to let him know he held her heart?

"I need Holt. I need to tell him…"

"Shh," Miranda soothed. "He'll be here soon."

"I know you think I got pregnant on purpose to make Holt marry me," she said.

"I might have been quick to rush to judgment," her mother-in-law acknowledged regretfully.

"And wrong," Tess told her. "To be honest, I wasn't exactly thrilled when I saw the plus sign on the pregnancy test." Her gaze dropped to the subtle curve of her belly. "And for a brief moment, I actually thought about how much easier my life would be if I wasn't pregnant…and who would ever need to know if that status changed?"

Fresh tears slid down Tess's cheeks. She swiped them away impatiently. "It was a very brief moment, and my heart immediately balked at the idea. Because unplanned or not, as soon as I knew I was pregnant, I loved my baby.

"But I assure you, through all of that, it never once crossed my mind that Holt might offer to marry me. To be perfectly honest, I wasn't sure I even planned to tell him about the baby."

"You don't think he would have guessed, when he found out you were pregnant, that it was his child?"

"I'm Tallulah Leonard's granddaughter," Tess reminded her. "I'm sure there are any number of people in town who would assume I didn't know who the father was.

"Anyway," she continued, "I barely knew Holt then—and I definitely didn't have any designs on marrying him. But your son can be incredibly persuasive when he wants something, and he wanted our baby to have a family."

"He loves you," Miranda acknowledged now.

"He's stepped up," Tess said cautiously. "And he seems to be looking forward to being a father."

"He loves you," her mother-in-law said again. "And it fills my heart to know that you love him back."

"You're going to make me cry again," Tess warned.

"If you do, they'll have to pump another bag of fluids into you."

She managed to smile then.

"Now I'm going to tell you something that only a handful of people know," Miranda said. "Because I want you to understand why I reacted the way I did when I learned that Holt married you."

"Okay."

Her mother-in-law blew out a breath. "It's not easy, even after so many years, to say it out loud," she admitted. "But when RJ and I were engaged, I stopped taking my birth control pills so that I would get pregnant, so that he would stop vacillating and finally agree to set a date for our wedding.

"We'd been together since high school and talking about our future together before graduation. Then he came back from his first year at college and decided we should take a break. I thought he'd met someone while he was away at school, but it was actually when he came home and was reunited with a girl he'd known for years that he suddenly developed feelings for her.

"They were together only a few months…but I was devastated. I tried to date other boys, but I knew my heart would always belong to RJ.

"When they broke up, he came back to me. Said he'd made a mistake and realized he still loved me. I told him he was going to have to prove it, so he bought a ring and asked me to marry him.

"But he wasn't in any hurry to set a date for our wedding, and I couldn't shake the feeling that he was still waiting to see if someone better came along. So I stopped taking my pills. I didn't talk to RJ beforehand or even tell him about my decision. And, not surprisingly, I got pregnant."

Miranda closed her eyes for a moment before she continued.

"I'm not proud of my actions," she confided. "I was young and foolish and immediately regretted what I'd done. And when I told him I was going to have a baby, I was braced for questions and accusations." Now she smiled, just a little. "But RJ surprised me in the very best way. He said, 'well, then, I guess we better get married sooner rather than later.'

"We didn't tell either of our parents that I was pregnant—though they had to suspect something when we were suddenly anxious to move our plans forward. I was so excited about the wedding. Thrilled that I was finally going to be Mrs. Raylan Chandler Junior.

"I didn't think too much about the baby I carried—probably because I felt guilty about its conception. And I reasoned that I'd have plenty of time to focus on impending motherhood later, but right then, my priority was the wedding.

"And then, nine days before the wedding, I lost the baby."

Tess's eyes filled with tears and her free hand instinctively moved to cradle her baby bump.

"I'm sorry," Miranda immediately apologized. "I seem to have picked the worst possible time to tell you this story."

"It's okay," Tess said. "I've just got so many hormones running rampant in my body right now..." She dabbed at her eyes with a tissue. "Please. Go on."

"I was devastated," Holt's mom confided now. "Not just because I'd lost the baby but, selfishly, because I was certain I'd also lost the chance to ever be RJ's wife. Certain he'd call off the wedding.

"But he only told me that we'd just have to wait a little longer to start our family. Because he loved me and was as eager as I was to start our life together. So we got married as planned and, eighteen months after our wedding, Boone was born. Flynn came along two years later, and then Holt followed another two years after that.

"We've been married almost thirty-six years now," Miranda said. "And we've hit our share of bumps in the road during those years, but we've navigated them together. And I know you and Holt hit a bump before all this happened, but I'm confident you'll get back on track."

Tess was still absorbing her mother-in-law's revelations—and marveling over her unexpected support—when a knock sounded on the door.

Another rush of emotion filled her heart when she glanced up to see her mom there. "You're supposed to be in Colorado Springs with Sage for another week."

"Your sister kicked us out when she heard about Gramma Lula," Abby said. "Told us to come back here to take care of her, so we were already en route when Holt called. Your dad will be up in a minute, after he parks the car."

Miranda rose to her feet then and stepped back to make room for Tess's mom.

Abby moved in and hugged her daughter tight, holding her for a long moment and still letting go too soon. Perhaps it was impending motherhood that made her appreciate her mother even more, Tess mused, or maybe it was not knowing if she'd ever see her loved ones again that made her determined to let them know they were loved.

"I'll just go wait…in the waiting room," Miranda said.

Before she could pass, Abby touched a hand to the other woman's arm, making her pause. "Thank you."

A look of understanding passed between them—an acknowledgment that they were no longer rivals for the affections of the same man but mothers brought together by their love of their respective children.

Tess's mom and dad were positioned on either side of her bed, holding vigil while their daughter slept, when Holt finally arrived at the hospital. As he stepped into the room, Roger rose to his feet and silently offered his hand. Then Abby kissed his cheek, and they both slipped out, leaving him alone with his wife.

Holt took the seat his mother-in-law had vacated and spent several long minutes just staring at Tess. She looked so pale in the hospital bed, her face nearly as white as the blanket tucked around her. One of her hands rested on top of the covers, on top of the subtle curve of her belly. An IV was taped to the back of her other hand and a plastic hospital bracelet was looped around her wrist.

Meg had sent text updates when he was in lockup, and he'd

read them eagerly when he was released—with no charges filed—and his belongings returned to him.

Dr confirmed that she was slightly dehydrated so giving fluids

No cause for concern

No cause for concern except that she'd been kidnapped and held captive at gunpoint. Anything could have happened.

He could have lost her.

And the thought of his life without Tess…

No, he refused to contemplate it.

Her eyes opened then, as if she sensed his distress—or at least his presence.

"Hey," she said softly.

"Hey." He leaned forward to kiss her forehead. "How are you feeling?"

"A lot better now that you're here."

"I would have been here sooner, but…"

"I know," she told him. "I saw the sheriff putting you in the back of his car."

"I'm so sorry, Tess."

"Why are you sorry?"

"I should have been there," he said. "I never should have left you alone."

"None of this was your fault, Holt."

"But if I'd been there—"

She lifted her hand to press her fingers to his lips, silencing his words. "I'm fine."

He took her hand, cradling it gently between his palms, and shook his head. "I'm not," he realized, and dropped his forehead to the edge of the mattress, so that his wife wouldn't see that he was falling to pieces. So she maybe wouldn't notice that silent sobs were racking his body and hot tears were coursing down his cheeks.

She lifted her hand—the one not trapped between his—and gently stroked his hair, soothing him as if he was a child instead of a grown man bawling like one. It took some time for him to get his emotions under control, to dare look up at her—and see that she was crying, too.

He grabbed a handful of tissues from the box beside her bed and dried his eyes before gently wiping her tears away.

"I love you, Tess."

She pressed her lips together to still their quivering as fresh tears filled her eyes.

"You don't believe me," he realized, when she failed to respond to his long overdue declaration. "And maybe I can't blame you for that. It certainly took me long enough to acknowledge the depth of my own feelings."

"Or maybe the fear you felt for our baby, when you learned I'd been kidnapped, amplified all your emotions, making you think your feelings for me are deeper than they really are," she said cautiously.

"My fear was definitely amplified," he agreed. "But my love for you—it was already there, Tess. I'm starting to think it was always there—or at least the seed of it—from the first day I saw you at the hospital."

"And now we're back at the hospital," she noted.

"I love you," he said again. "And I'm going to love you wherever we are—whether it's the hospital or West River Ranch or having dinner with our friends at Pasquale's or shopping for groceries at the Market Pantry—for as long as we both shall live."

She gave a little sniffle then, and he knew that she wasn't only listening to his words but also, finally, starting to believe them.

"You make a pretty good argument, cowboy."

"It's okay if you're not entirely convinced," he told her. "Because I'm happy to spend every day of the rest of my life showing you how much I love you."

"And I'll show you right back," she promised. "Because I love you, too."

"There's nothing I want more than a life and a family with you. And when I found out you were gone… I can't even think about it, because when I do…when I think about how differently things might have gone…"

"Don't think about it," Tess said. "I'm fine. Better than fine. And… I may even have bonded with your mom."

That surprised a laugh out of him. "No kidding?"

"I think seeing our baby—her grandson—on the ultrasound helped her focus on what really matters."

"Grandson?" He was thrilled by the reveal. He'd joked for weeks about Chandlers having boys, but the knowledge that in a few months he would become a father to a son—with the woman he loved—shifted something in him.

Tess nodded. "Definitely a boy."

"We'll try for a girl next time," he promised.

She laughed softly. "You're jumping the gun again, cowboy. How about we hold off making plans for a second baby until after we've had the first one?"

"All right," he agreed.

"In the meantime, maybe you could track down a doctor and see about getting me sprung from here? I really want to go home with my husband."

He didn't know if she was aware of it or not, but it was the first time she'd referred to their cabin as home and hearing her do so now filled his heart. "Your wish is my command."

Epilogue

Six months later

At the conclusion of trial, after seeing the total sum of evidence presented to the jury tasked with deciding his fate, Walker Bradford changed his plea to guilty on all charges. And though the sentencing was put over to a future date, there was no question that Tess's kidnapper would be going to jail for a very long time.

The Chandlers left the courtroom en masse, breathing a collective sigh of relief and eager to put this unfortunate chapter in the history books.

"It's over now," Raylan said, expressing what they were all feeling.

"Finally," Eleanor said.

She'd suffered with horrible guilt since Tess's kidnapping, convinced she'd set Walker's nefarious plan in motion when she sent the bundle of letters to his mother.

It turned out that the young man had always been a history buff—and a little bit obsessed with the stagecoach robbery of 1857 as a result of stories (possibly true) that had been passed down through his family.

When he lost his job as a research assistant in the history department at Princeton—having been caught using school resources for personal projects—he'd eventually fallen into the dark web where his fantasies about seeking revenge for his great-great-great-grandfather's untimely death and retrieving his rightful fortune were fueled by anonymous online supporters.

The package of letters—"new evidence"—strengthened his determination to find the missing gold. It also put the Chandler family on his radar. It didn't take much time or effort for him to discover that West River Ranch was an impressive spread or that the value of the land and the animals raised on it was substantial, leading him to the conclusion that Quentin had financed the operation with the gold from the robbery after stiffing his partners of their shares.

It wasn't true, of course. Or at least, there was no evidence that it was true. And in the end, Walker Bradford turned out to be just another man who'd lost his way in pursuit of an ill-gotten fortune.

Further investigation also revealed that he hadn't acted entirely alone. Upon his arrival in Whispering Canyon, he'd connected with a distant cousin on his father's side and, without sharing too many details of his plan, promised the cousin a share of his fortune if he could run interference as required. That cousin was Billy Garvey.

"Anyone want to grab pizza before we head back to the ranch?" Greyson asked, as the family began to disperse.

The response was almost unanimous enthusiasm, and Holt was surprised to note that the one person who hadn't chimed in was his wife.

"You're not in the mood for pizza?" he asked her.

Tess had been complaining of lower back pain for the past couple of days, and he noticed that she was rubbing her back now. Of course, the wooden benches in the public gallery weren't comfortable for anyone, never mind a woman in the final weeks of pregnancy.

"You know how much I love pizza," she said. "But we should probably head to the hospital instead. I think… I'm in labor."

* * *

Once again, the waiting room was full of Chandlers, though the Barretts were also well represented. Meg and Emma were there, too—and even Tallulah Leonard. Holt knew everyone was eager for a glimpse of the new baby, but he wanted a few quiet minutes with his amazing wife and their perfect son before he let them in.

"Are you braced for the chaos?" he asked.

Tess smiled, because even after ten hours of intense labor, she felt pretty good. And grateful to her husband, who hadn't left her side for a single minute of those ten hours.

"I love the chaos," she assured him.

"I love *you*," he said. "And I'm already head over heels for Blake Leonard Chandler, too."

Their son's middle name had been his idea—another way to not only acknowledge but also embrace the connection between their families.

Tess tipped her head back against her husband's shoulder now, happier than she'd ever imagined she could be. "Today was a really good day," she mused.

"The second best day of my life," Holt told her.

Surprised, she asked, "What was the first?"

"Our wedding day." He'd answered without hesitation, but now he reconsidered. "Or maybe that was the second and the first was the day we met in the ER—and again later at The Bootlegger."

She lifted a brow. "You're saying the day your grandfather was shot was the best day of your life?"

"I didn't say it was the best day of *his* life," he clarified. "But it was the best day of mine, because meeting you was the first link in a chain of events that changed my life for the better, including the discovery that we were going to have a baby and then marrying you and now, finally, holding my wife while she holds our baby in her arms."

Tess's smile widened. "You really are a romantic, Holt Chandler."

"Shh. Our secret," he reminded her.

"Our secret," she agreed, drawing his mouth to hers for a kiss.

* * * * *

Don't miss Flynn's story,
the next installment in Brenda Harlen's new miniseries
The Cowboys of Whispering Canyon
Coming soon!

Harlequin® Reader Service

Enjoyed your book?

Try the perfect subscription for Romance readers and get more great books like this delivered right to your door.

See why over 10+ million readers have tried Harlequin Reader Service.

Start with a Free Welcome Collection with free books and a gift—valued over $20.

Choose any series in print or ebook.
See website for details and order today:

TryReaderService.com/subscriptions

RSBPA2409